D1604432

LAYER by LAYER
NEW YORK TIMES BESTSELLING AUTHOR
KAYLEE RYAN

LAYER BY LAYER

Cover Design: Lori Jackson Design
Cover Photography: Alfred Liebl
Cover Model: Mike Chabot
Editing: Hot Tree Editing
Proofreading: Deaton Author Services
Paperback Formatting: Integrity Formatting

THE BEST THING about traveling first class is that you get to board first. Well, that's not the only good thing about it, but today, that's my favorite part. I've been in San Francisco for a week, and I'm exhausted and ready to go home. Unfortunately, there were no direct flights, which means this is the second plane I've had to board today. Hence the early boarding. Shoving my carry-on overhead, I take my seat near the window, stretch out my legs, and close my eyes. This plane can't take off fast enough for my liking. The company jet was undergoing maintenance. Just routine but essential for safety. I'm not opposed to purchasing another so this doesn't happen again. I can hear my brothers now as they laugh and call me spoiled.

They're not wrong.

As CEO of Riggins Enterprises, I have a fully packed schedule, and delays for things such as commercial flights can't be tolerated. Besides, my brothers are just as spoiled as I am. They just don't have the pressure on them, the future of the company on their shoulders. Owen, who is two years younger than me, is the only one who comes close as CFO. The financials are in his hands. Our younger three brothers all play a role in the company as well, but the stress, the worry, that's all on me.

I feel someone take the seat next to me, but I keep my eyes closed and block out whoever it might be. I just want this plane in the air and landing in Nashville as soon as possible. The hustle and bustle of the other passengers boarding fills my ears, and while it's annoying, that means we are one step closer to taking off.

Several minutes later, I hear a female voice ask, "Can I get you something to drink?"

"N-No, thank you," a soft feminine voice replies. The voice is angelic and intriguing enough to get me to open my eyes and turn to look at my seatmate. Green eyes, wide with visible fear, capture mine. "I'm sorry if I woke you."

"You didn't." I keep my reply short. I'm not sure if she's a chatty Kathy, but I don't need that on this flight. I just want to sleep through it and get home.

"I'm nervous," she says, holding her hand out in front of her. My eyes watch as a slight tremble appears.

"First time?" I find myself asking. Why I'm not sure. I'm not a man who takes on casual conversation. No, I'm usually in my office or at home on my computer working. There is always so much to do. Running a multi-billion-dollar company doesn't leave much time for casual anything.

Sadly.

I allow my eyes time to rake over her. She's gorgeous. Not in that "she could be a supermodel" way. No, she's naturally beautiful. From my first impression, I'd say she's one of those women who has no idea that she turns heads wherever she goes.

"No." Her reply is shaky. "Just not a fan of flying or heights for that matter."

I nod, acknowledging her statement and close my eyes again. Surely, we should be taking off soon. It will be late by the time we land. I won't be going into the office; however, I know I'll have a hundred new emails to deal with, and I want to get started on reviewing the construction contracts that this trip was for.

We're building a new facility in San Francisco, and this trip was to interview construction companies. I need to follow up with references and get the contract started, so we can proceed with the build.

"Do you fly a lot?" she asks. The tremble in her voice seems to be getting worse.

"Often enough. My job requires it," I reply, but I'm not sure she actually heard me. Glancing down at the arm of the seat, I see her fingers gripping it so tight, her knuckles are white. The plane hasn't moved. "What about you? Traveling for work?" I'm not sure why I'm engaging her in conversation. Something about her fear pulls at me, and if a little idle chitchat can soothe her fear, then I can handle that. Besides, I have a feeling she's going to keep talking whether my eyes are closed or not.

"N-No. I actually got fired from my job."

"Oh, yeah?" I ask like I'm interested when I'm anything but.

"It was a mix of me telling them to take the job and shove it and being fired." She turns those wide green eyes toward me. Her chest rises and falls, a tell-tale sign of her anxiety.

"Which was it?"

"I quit, but it was made clear that my refusal to do what was asked would result in my termination." Slowly, she exhales, trying to gather her wits.

"Insubordination." I've dealt with a few of those myself. Disrespect in the workplace isn't tolerable.

"S-Something like that." She leans back against her seat and turns her body toward me. "I hate this," she says quietly.

"What's your name?" I ask to keep her talking—anything to keep her mind off what's about to happen.

"Sa—" She doesn't get to finish before the flight attendant comes over the speaker, telling us to fasten our seat belts. "Oh, God," the blonde beauty whimpers. Her leg begins to bounce up and down as she fumbles with her seat belt.

This is hard to watch. She's terrified. Reaching over, I grab her belt and make sure she's buckled in. "Just breathe," I whisper.

"Sir, you need to fasten your seat belt," the flight attendant scolds me.

Fighting the urge to roll my eyes, I quickly strap in. "Hey." My neighbor turns to look at me, her green eyes misty from tears, from fear. I don't know what to do. I don't know how to calm her down. She bites down on her bottom lip, her teeth sinking in deep.

"I really hate this."

"Why didn't you drive?"

"I start a new job next week and needed the extra time to get settled in my new apartment."

The plane begins to taxi down the runway, and if I thought her breathing was accelerated before, I was wrong. Her chest is rapidly rising and falling with each strangled breath. At a loss about what to do, I reach out and cradle her cheek in the palm of my hand. Her skin is warm and clammy from fear. "Look at me." My voice is soft as I try to comfort her. "Just watch me," I tell her again as she rests her head against the seat. I go to move my hand, but she places hers on top of mine. Maybe she needs the connection. It's a small price to pay to help her stay calm. I've never seen someone with this kind of fear. I just need to get her through the takeoff, and once we level out, she'll be fine.

"Talk to me," she whispers. "Please."

Fuck. I don't make small talk. That's not who I am. *Think, Riggins, think.* "Is this your first time going to Nashville?" I ask her.

"Yes. I've heard it's a fun city to live in."

"A new job, huh?"

"Yes. I hate starting over, but this job was the best option," she says, and her breathing is starting to slow. "To be honest, I wanted to be as far away from Seattle as I could get."

"Sounds like a story."

"One I won't bore you with."

"So, new job, new city. Do you have any friends or relatives in Nashville?" I ask, wanting to keep her talking. She's starting to calm.

"My best friend, Hadley, and her fiancé moved there about a year ago."

The plane begins to take off, and she sucks in a breath. I can see her panic coming back in spades. "Hey, hey, look at me." I tuck a loose strand of hair behind her ear. "Keep your eyes on me. That's it," I praise her. "What's your name?"

"S-Sawyer."

"Nice to meet you, Sawyer. I'm Royce."

"Sexy name for a sexy guy," she says. Her eyes widen like she can't believe those words left her mouth.

I give her what I'm told is my panty-melting grin. "You think I'm sexy?"

Those bright green eyes roll back in her head, but there is a small tilt to her lips, and she's not freaking out. The plane levels out, and I find that I don't want to pull away from her. That's not me. That's not the guy I am—not anymore—so I force myself to drop my hand to my lap. I keep my head turned and my eyes on her.

"Hey." She smiles. "Thank you for that."

"You all right?"

"Yeah. I'm just… really afraid of heights. Planes specifically."

"Is there a reason?" I ask, and realize that I'm interested in her reply. I want to know the root of the fear I just witnessed.

"You mean other than flying through the air at Mach speed in a tin can?"

A chuckle escapes me before I can stop it. "Come on now, it's safer than driving. Look at all the car accidents each year versus the number of plane crashes."

"Can we not?" she whispers.

"Why are you whispering?"

"You're not supposed to talk like that." She gives me a disapproving look.

"Like what?"

"You know what you just said."

"That there are more car accidents than plane accidents."

"That!" She reaches out and places her hand over my mouth. Her scent wraps around me, and her skin is the softest I've ever felt. "The plane gods might hear you and think it's a good idea."

Carefully, I wrap my hand around her small wrist. The contrast to her smooth, delicate skin against mine covered in ink is apparent. "There are no plane gods, and this plane isn't going down. I fly all the time. You have nothing to worry about."

Her eyes show me she's not buying what I'm selling. "Are you saying you're going to protect me, Royce?" she asks.

Is it me or is her voice suddenly huskier? Sexier? "I won't let anything happen to you." The words are meant to be teasing, but something shifts inside me. For the first time in a long time, I feel… something. I just can't describe what it is.

"Have you always lived in Nashville?"

"Yes. Well, except while in college. I went to Ohio State. When I graduated, I came home and then took over the family business soon after."

"What do you do for fun?"

I pause as I think about her question. It's been way too long since I've done something just for the fun of it. "I work a lot."

"Surely you take time for you?"

I notice that her breathing is almost back to normal, and she looks like she's relaxing. I'm not a fan of all the small talk, but I don't mind it with her. Besides, it's keeping her from a panic attack. It's for the greater good of her and everyone on board that I keep her calm. "Music. That's one of the best parts of living in Nashville. I used to go out and listen to live bands a lot in college, and I used to be somewhat of a movie buff. I also spend a lot of time at my family's lake with my brothers."

"Am I being punked?" She tilts her head up and then looks over her shoulder.

"What are you doing?"

"Did Hadley put you up to this?"

"Hadley? Your best friend? I don't even know a Hadley. Are you feeling okay?"

I'm watching her intently, and that's how I see it. The way her face transforms with the most beautiful smile I've ever seen. The fear from earlier washes away as happiness takes over. Her smile pulls the breath from my lungs as I look at her. "That's my thing. Music and movies. That's why I started looking for new jobs in Nashville. Well, that and I missed my best friend, but the music scene is on point. Had has sent me some videos when she and her fiancé, Derek, have been out, and I've never been so jealous."

"Nashville is a good time," I say, nodding. "As long as you're a country music fan?"

"I'm a fan," she assures me. "Especially the older stuff, you know like Johnny Cash and Waylon Jennings. I grew up listening to those guys with my grandpa." Her eyes soften. "I miss him."

"What about your parents?" I find myself asking. "Siblings?"

"No siblings and my parents are gone too. They passed away in a car accident about three years ago. They were coming home from a weekend getaway from Vegas. They were two miles from home. Hit head-on by a drunk driver."

"I'm sorry." I don't tell her that my theory of being safer in the air is even more justified. I don't want to hurt her like that. Besides, something tells me that she knows all too well the dangers of both. Fear is a real thing.

She nods just the slightest bit and gives me a watery smile. "What about you? Parents? Siblings?"

"Yes. My parents have been married for thirty-four years, and I have four younger brothers."

"Four?" Her eyes widen. "Your poor mother."

"Hey, we weren't that bad." She gives me a look that tells me we both know I'm full of shit, and I'm surprised when a laugh escapes my lips. "Fine, we were that bad, but it was a good time growing up. My parents made time for us, and we always had someone to play with or a lookout when we were getting into trouble."

"Five rowdy boys. Your mother is a saint."

"That she is." I smile at her, and she returns it easily. Her eyes no longer hold fear, but laughter, and for some odd reason, I want to puff my chest out because I did that. I eased her fears. It's been way too long since I've felt… anything, and here she is a beautiful stranger, pulling out of me what I thought was locked away a long time ago. This day couldn't get any weirder.

"I'm sorry about earlier. Thank you for helping me. I'm embarrassed you saw me like that."

With a mind of its own, my hand reaches out and cradles her cheek for the second time. Her skin is soft and warm against the palm of my hand. "We all have fears, Sawyer."

"Oh, yeah?" she murmurs. "I bet you're not afraid of anything."

I'm afraid of many things. Not once have I ever been compelled to speak them aloud, other than to my brothers. Until now. "I have fears," I say before I can think better of it.

"You?" Her voice is soft. "I can't imagine that you'd be afraid of anything."

"Lots of things." I search my mind for something that I'm willing to share. "When I was nine, my two younger brothers and I were playing on our grandparents' farm. The middle brother decided it would be cool to toss his stuffed monkey that he took everywhere into the trunk of an old car. He was five at the time, and my other brother, who was with us, was seven. Anyway, as the older brother, it was my job to rescue the damn monkey. I climbed into the trunk to retrieve it. The weather was starting to get bad, and I was irritated. I knew that Grandma would be mad if we stayed out in the storm. So, I was in the trunk, my hands wrapped around the monkey, when suddenly it shut me in. I'll spare you the details, but the car was old, the trunk was huge, and it had been sitting out in that field longer than I had been alive. There were bugs, and it felt as though I was in there for hours."

"You're afraid of the dark?"

"Confined spaces."

"Like this plane?"

"No. I can see other people. The area is large enough that I don't feel enclosed. But yeah, I don't particularly care for any situation where I feel trapped." I drop my hand from her cheek because it's too intimate. I'm two seconds away from leaning in and pressing my lips to hers. That's not me. I don't kiss strangers on planes, but Sawyer, if given the chance, she could be the exception to my every rule.

The remainder of the flight is spent giving her my full attention. I'm no longer tired, and instead of wishing the flight would land, I want more time with her. All too soon, we've landed, and we're exiting the plane. "You need a ride?" I find myself offering.

"Thank you, but no. My new employer sent a car for me. Or they are supposed to."

"Nice." I nod even though she can't see me. Like a puppy, I follow her to baggage claim. I only have my one carry-on, but it's more time with her.

"That's me." She points to a large black suitcase. When it gets near us, I grab it from the belt. "A true gentleman." She smiles up at me. Her green eyes hold nothing but ease, no lingering fear from the flight.

"You seem to have that effect on me," I say, reaching out to tuck her hair behind her ear. It wasn't in her face, but it gave me an excuse to touch her. "I'd like to see you again." The words sound foreign, but I mean them. "I could show you around the city."

A slight blush coats her cheeks. "I'd like that."

"Hand me your phone." She pulls it from her pocket, unlocks the screen, and hands it over. Quickly I program Royce Plane Guy as my contact name and enter my number. "It was nice meeting you, Sawyer."

"You too, Royce." She glances over, and there is a man in a suit holding up a sign that says, Sawyer Gibson. "That's me." She points over her shoulder.

"Good luck with your new job. I can't wait to hear all about it."

"Thank you." She smiles and steps closer. She falters before taking another step and pressing her lips to my cheek. "Thank you for saving me." With that, she turns, a bag in each hand, and walks away.

I watch her until I can no longer see her. I want to insist she let me drive her wherever she needs to go. Pulling my phone out of my pocket to call her and do just that, I realize I don't have her number. Like an idiot, I didn't text myself from her phone. I don't have a choice but to wait for her call. I'm not a patient man, but for Sawyer, I'll have to be.

MY HEELS CLICK against the tile floor, echoing throughout the quiet lobby. I keep my head held high and try not to fidget. Today is my first day on the job, and to say that I'm nervous is an understatement. Stopping at the reception desk, I wait until I have the woman's attention. "Sawyer Gibson for Gail Hines," I say with a surprisingly steady voice.

"Of course, Ms. Gibson. Gail is expecting you. Take the elevator to the tenth floor. She should be at the desk, just around the corner as soon as you exit."

"Thank you." I give her a polite smile and turn for the elevator. It's completely made of glass and offers a view of the city. Royce would appreciate that fact, not liking enclosed places and all. Shaking out of my thoughts, I board the elevator. Once inside, I watch as the numbers climb. I can't seem to make myself turn around and look at the city from above. My fear of heights won't let me. Instead, my eyes are glued to the numbers until I reach the tenth floor, which also happens to be the very top floor of the building. The top floor where I'll be working as the administrative assistant to the CEO. It's not a far leap from my old job, but I'm still nervous. When the door slides open on the tenth floor, I exit, and round the corner to find Gail waiting for me at a reception desk.

"Sawyer, good morning." Gail stands from the chair behind the desk and walks around to greet me. She extends her hand, and I place mine in hers in greeting. This is our first face-to-face meeting. My interviews were done via video chat, which I'm thankful for. No way would I have wanted to have to fly here twice. *Flying.* My mind immediately goes to Royce. I've been doing that a lot the last three days. What are the chances that I'd meet a kind, handsome stranger on the plane? I haven't called him yet, but I plan to tonight. I spent the weekend getting settled into my new apartment, thanks to the help of Hadley and her fiancé, Derek. Hadley tried to get me to call yesterday, but that makes me seem desperate, right? There's a three-day rule for a reason. At least that's what I tell myself. Part of me feels like the moment was too magical to be real.

"Good morning."

"This is where you'll be working." She motions to the huge workspace/reception desk. "The drawers and cabinets lock. I think Samantha, that's who you're replacing, placed her personal items—her purse and what not—in this bottom drawer." She points to a drawer to the left of the computer under the desk.

"That's perfect. Thank you," I say politely.

"So, as we spoke in your interview, Samantha is no longer with us. We knew she was leaving, but not as soon as she did. We thought we had time to replace her and let her train the replacement, but that baby of hers decided to try and come early, so she's on bed rest."

"Oh, no. That's awful. I hope that they're both okay." It's the polite thing to say, and I really do hope they are all right.

"She's doing great. Her fiancé is driving her crazy, but you'd just have to meet Jase to understand," she says with a wide smile. "Anyway, she's going to be working with you virtually. She insisted since she's just sitting around, that letting her train you remotely would keep her sane." Gail smiles fondly. It's obvious how much she liked Samantha.

I smile at her and nod. I'm nervous as hell. My previous job was as an administrative assistant at a law firm. I spent my day answering phones, scheduling meetings, and fetching coffee and snacks for meetings. The firm was one of the largest in Seattle, and yet they seem small compared to this building that houses Riggins Enterprises. Riggins has locations all over the United States. This is a big jump for my career. It's also good for my bank account as it's a significant pay raise, and I can let the worry of kicking my old boss in the balls and quitting my job fall to the wayside. He deserved it. Trust me on this one.

"As we discussed, your position will be mainly to support the CEO. However, the other four executives have their offices on this floor as well, and you will also provide support to each of them. They are not nearly as needy as the CEO as he runs the entire operation. Oh, and they're brothers." Gail grins.

"That's going to be confusing calling them all Mr. Riggins," I say with a nervous laugh.

"Oh." Gail waves her hand in the air. "They all go by their first names. It's a laidback yet professional environment. They all say that Mr. Riggins is their father, Stanley, not them. He started this company all on his own." She waves again. "That's a story for another day. I have a printout here that has a picture of each of them with their names so you can keep them straight. Samantha actually created it and sent it over. I believe her exact words were, "It's hard as hell to keep those Riggins boys straight."

"So, I work for all five of them, but the CEO is the one who needs the most support?" I ask to clarify, taking the folder that I assume has the images of each brother that she's trying to hand me.

"That's correct. Your title is Executive Administrative Assistant, and your overall job is to provide support to the executives, which also happens to be all five Riggins brothers."

"Got it." I think, but I'm not going to tell her that. As long as I can learn each brother's face and their roles here, I should be fine. I'm not against a little homework to give me an edge in the position.

She smiles. "It sounds more intimidating than it is. Trust me. They're all big teddy bears. As I said, the CEO is the one who needs the most support, and he's the one most upset about Samantha leaving us."

"Oh." I'm not sure what to say to that.

"Jase is his best friend."

I stare at her blankly. I don't know who Jase is.

"Jase is Samantha's fiancé. Royce is not impressed that his best friend hit on his assistant and got her pregnant, and now he's replacing her after five years. Once he took over, it took him a while to find an assistant that he meshed with. Royce isn't one to like change. He likes routine and hates surprises."

Royce.

I've gone twenty-six years never knowing anyone with that name. I move to Nashville, and suddenly there are two in a matter of days. What are the odds? Wait... Royce said he had four brothers. No. It can't be. Can it? I realize that Gail is watching me, waiting for a reply. "Good to know," I say with a smile, making her laugh. I'm glad she's unaware of my internal freak-out. Could Royce, my Royce from the plane, be my new boss?

"We are a large corporation, but family-owned and operated. Riggins Enterprises doesn't have the feel of a large organization. Sure, we occupy this entire building, as this is the main headquarters for all of the locations." She chuckles when she sees the look on my face.

This totally feels like a large corporation to me, and I'm still freaking out about the possibility that my savior is the same Royce. My boss.

"Trust me. Once you meet the boys, and yes, I call them boys—I changed their diapers, and I've earned the right." Her smile is genuine. "When you meet them and get to know them, you'll see what I'm talking about. Even Royce loosens up when he's with his brothers. Those five—" She shakes her head. "You just have to see for yourself. You're going to feel like you've been here for years in no time. None of that funny business you had to deal with at your previous employer."

I nod. I'm impressed with her memory of my situation with my previous employer. Then again, I'm sure it's not every day that the candidate you hire tells you that she kneed her old boss in the junk before telling him he could shove the job up his ass. In case you're wondering, that candidate is me. Just so we're clear.

The elevator dings, alerting us to an arrival on the floor. I stand still and watch as a man in a white dress shirt comes around the corner. My knees go weak at the sight of him. I watch him closely as each step brings him closer to where I'm standing behind the desk with Gail.

"Good morning, Royce," she says, her voice chipper.

Royce.

My Royce.

"Gail." He nods, then turns his gaze on me. Something flashes in his eyes that I can't name. "What are you doing here?" His voice is deep and sexy, sending tingles down my spine.

I open my mouth to speak, but nothing comes out. He looks the same, but he's… harder than my Royce.

"If you'll take a breath, I'll introduce you," Gail chastises. "Royce Riggins, this is Sawyer Gibson. She's Sam's replacement."

Royce stares at me with those brown eyes that seem to twinkle under the fluorescent lights. It's awkward, and I realize he's probably waiting on me.

"Sawyer Gibson," I offer my name even though he already knows it, knows me. I hold out my hand for him anyway. "It's a pleasure to meet you." I will my hand not to shake and chastise myself for not wiping my sweaty palm on my skirt before offering it to him.

My hand stays suspended in the air for about four heartbeats, and yes, I count before he extends his long arm and takes my hand. My eyes drop to our hands and take in the tattoos that cover his. The same hands that cradled my cheek and talked me down from a panic attack. The same hands I've imagined touching every inch of my body since the moment I walked away from him at the airport.

Those hands.

His stare is intense and intimidating. It's not at all what I was expecting from him. What happened to that kind and endearing man? He wants me to think he's this stiff responsible CEO, but I know another side of him. The side that, along with the tattoos on his hands, tell me another story. They tell me that he might be serious, but there is a wild side, a free artistic side to him as well. To me, it makes him less intimidating, and I can feel my shoulders begin to ease. My smile grows at the thought. I'm sure he would not be impressed with that admission. Considering today is my first day, I think I'll keep that little nugget of knowledge to myself. He can't be mad at me for not telling him because I didn't know.

My eyes move back up to his to find him watching me intently. There is a look on his face that I can't describe, nor do I get the chance to when Gail speaks up.

"Your nine o'clock canceled. I'm waiting for confirmation on the rescheduled date."

Royce blinks and looks down at our hands that are still joined and pulls his out of mine. I already miss the warmth of his skin wrapped around mine. "Why didn't she handle that?" he asks.

"She is standing right there, and she also has a name," Gail says sternly. "Sawyer has been here maybe fifteen minutes. It's not her job to handle it. Not yet. It will be. I'm going to be working up here with her, and Sam is going to be training her remotely."

"Can she do that?" he asks, raking his hand over his hair. It's dark brown, almost black, and cut short. He has a few days of beard growth, and the overall look is causing me to think thoughts about my new boss that I should not be thinking.

"Of course she can. Conrad set her up to work remotely. She has full access to everything she needs. She has her company phone and laptop with her, and I have all the faith in the world that she will do just fine guiding Sawyer in her new role." Gail gives him a look that dares him to argue with her.

"Fine." One single reply before he glances at me, and stalks off down the hall.

"Um, should I worry that he doesn't seem happy that I'm here?" I ask Gail. I leave out the part that we've already met, and over the last two days, I'd convinced myself that he could be my soul mate. My romantic heart twinges at the loss of our potential happily ever after.

"Nonsense. He needs an assistant, and you were by far the most qualified candidate. Now, let's get started. I had Conrad, who is one of the brothers," she taps on the folder she handed me earlier, "set up all of your usernames and passwords. Normally, that would be something we would let the IT department handle. However, I pulled in a favor from the CIO." She winks. "You will be supporting him as well. Otherwise, we could have been waiting a while until everything was signed off on." She takes a seat and motions for me to take the chair she was sitting in when I arrived. "You ready to get started?"

"As ready as I'll ever be." I take the offered chair, put my purse and phone, which I already made sure was on vibrate, into the drawer to the lower left, and pull out my pen and notebook. "Let's do this," I say, grinning. I'm not going to let Royce's broody behavior keep me from doing my job. Nothing happened. We were two strangers on a plane who enjoyed each other's company—end of story. We're adults, and we can act as such. At least I know I can. The jury is still out on Royce.

"That's what I like to hear. You know, maybe we should start with a tour of the floor. Maybe get an introduction to the others if they're not busy." Gail stands from the chair she just sat in and motions for me to follow her.

"This is Royce's office." She points to the office that's closest to my workspace. "He's the oldest, and as you know, the CEO of Riggins Enterprises," she explains.

"Gail?" a deep gruff voice asks.

"It's me," she says, sticking her head through the open office doorway. "I was just giving Sawyer a tour. Do you need something?" Gail asks.

"No. Just heard voices."

She chuckles. "Nothing gets by this one. I'm going to show her the rest of the floor, maybe meet the others and we'll be back at her desk if you need us."

"Thank you," he replies politely. It's not at all the reply I was expecting from him, but I'm glad to see he still has manners. Apparently, just not when it comes to me. Then again, maybe it's because it's Gail. There seems to be a strong connection there, not just with Royce, but from what she's told me with all five of the brothers, and their parents. Gail is chatty, so I've learned a lot in a short amount of time.

We take a few steps down the hall and stop at another door. The name on the wall reads Owen Riggins, CFO.

"This is Owen's office. He's the second oldest. He's our CFO, the Chief Financial Officer." She points at the nameplate and smiles. "His door is often shut as he locks himself away with his numbers and spreadsheets. He's very good at what he does, and rivals his older brother in the serious department."

"Their positions are important. I can only imagine the pressure of running this entire operation, and being in charge of the financials would be a lot of stress." I had it all on my shoulders at the law firm, and I was always riddled with anxiety. Then again, that probably had more to do with my skeevy boss than it did me performing the jobs assigned to me.

"You're right, but all work and no fun leads to a life of regrets. These boys need to loosen up a bit." She shakes her head as if she's disappointed and continues our tour. We turn the corner, and she stops at the next door. "Knock, knock," she says, walking on into the office without invitation.

"Gail, what can I do for you this fine morning?" a deep, sexy, flirty voice asks.

"Always the charmer," she comments, and I can hear the playfulness in her voice. "I want to introduce you to our new executive administrative assistant. This is Sawyer. She's taking over for Sam." Gail motions for me to step into the room. I've just been hovering in the doorway.

The man, who has a strong resemblance to Royce, stands and walks around his desk, offering me his hand. "Grant Riggins, middle brother, and most charming. It's nice to meet you."

I'm immediately at ease. "Sawyer Gibson, likewise," I say, keeping it professional.

"Grant is our COO, Chief Operating Officer. The director of each Riggins branch reports directly to him."

Grant leans back on his desk, crossing his legs at the ankle and his arms over his chest. If he's trying to be intimidating, he's failing miserably from the smile that lights up his face and those sexy eyes. "How are you liking it so far?" he asks me.

"It's my first day."

"And?" he prompts, grinning.

The view is nice, and your brother and I had a moment. "So far, so good. Gail has been amazing and getting me acclimated."

"Good." He nods. "I'm not near as needy as my brother, but we will work together from time to time. However, that goes both ways. If I can ever do anything for you…" His eyes sweep over my body, head to toe before his eyes collide with mine once more. "I'm your guy."

"All right, Casanova, the tour must go on. You"—Gail points at him—"behave." His deep throaty chuckle follows us out of his office and down the hall to the next. "This side of the hallway houses three conference rooms." Gail motions to the right as we continue down the hall.

"This is Conrad's office. He's the CIO, the Chief Information Officer. He oversees all aspects of IT. He's the one who set up all of your log-ins and passwords. He's on the phone, so we'll catch him later today. Conrad is the second to the youngest brother," she explains as she peeks her head through the doorway and waves.

A few more steps and we reach the end of the hall. "This is Marshall's office. He's the youngest of the five and is our CMO. As Chief Marketing Officer, he handles marketing for all of our locations. He's out meeting with a new vendor for marketing materials this morning. We'll catch up with him later as well."

"You know all of their schedules?" I ask her.

"Yes. But not because it's my job. Only because I'm the one who's been filling in for Sam. You will have access to each of their calendars, and they will often request for you to schedule or reschedule meetings for them. That's the majority of the work you will do for everyone except for Royce. He's constantly meeting with potential franchise owners and current owners as well. He will lean on you heavily." She must see the apprehension in my eyes. "Don't worry. It's not near as overwhelming as it sounds. I'm always a phone call away, and so is Sam. In fact, I've set up a meeting with the three of us tomorrow. We're having a virtual lunch since she's on bed rest."

"Tomorrow, lunch with Sam. Got it." I nod, taking a mental note.

"It's already on your calendar." Gail grins.

"I have a calendar?"

She chuckles. "Definitely. Come on. Let's go get you settled in."

The next four hours fly by. I've already taken a few pages worth of notes and learned to operate the phone system. Thankfully, since it's just me and the five brothers on this floor, there are only three lines that are inbound lines, with an additional six lines that are outgoing. Surely I can handle that.

"Are you about ready for a break?" Gail asks, standing and stretching. "Lunch is on us today. It should be here any minute. I ordered it yesterday." As if her words summoned the delivery, the elevator pings, and the whooshing sound of the doors sliding open fill the silence of the floor.

"I have a delivery for Gail Hines," a young woman says.

"That's me." Gail stands and signs the credit card slip and takes the three large bags from her. "This way." She motions for me to follow her as she leads us down the hall to one of three conference rooms on this floor. This is the largest if I remember correctly from my earlier tour.

"That's a lot of food for just the two of us," I comment as she sets the bags on the large conference room table.

"That it is. It's a good thing the boys are joining us."

It's hilarious that she refers to them as boys. From what I've seen, there isn't anything boyish about them. The Riggins brothers are hot as hell. Speaking of the Riggins brothers, I hear a rumble of deep voices that grow louder as they get closer to the conference room. I busy myself pulling the boxed lunches from the bags. I'm nervous about being face-to-face with Royce again.

"They're all the same. Just set them around the table and the boys will follow."

Doing as she asks, I begin to place a box in front of each chair. My heart races as I think about me in a room with Royce and his hot-as-hell brothers. I'm not sure my lady bits can handle all that hotness in one room.

I should have googled them before today. Then I would have had time to process the fact that my bosses are all drop-dead gorgeous. All five of them. I had no idea what I was getting myself into. That would have also helped me with Royce. I would have recognized him, surely. Hindsight is twenty-twenty, right? There was so much to do in Seattle. Gail wanted me to start right away, and since I didn't need to give notice, I packed up my things, broke the lease on my apartment, which cost me an arm and a leg, shipped my belongings, and got on a plane, all in a matter of days.

"Have a seat." Gail pats the spot at the long conference table next to the one she now occupies.

Grateful to be sitting next to her, needing her as an ally, I take the seat beside hers, and we begin to unpack our boxed lunches. "This looks great. Thank you," I tell her. I'm starving, but I'm not sure I'll be able to eat, knowing that I'll have five sets of sexy eyes on me in no time. Speaking of those five sets of eyes, their deep voices are growing closer by the second.

"I swear those boys are a rambunctious bunch when they're all together." Gail chuckles. "Always have been. Their momma, Lena, she's a saint of a woman raising those five." There is nothing but fondness in her tone. It tells me that she's not only been with the company for years but the family. I can tell they are more than just an employer to her.

I don't have time to comment before the first one steps into the room, followed by the other four. I stop what I'm doing and stare at each of them as they take seats around the table. My palms are suddenly sweaty, and my chest is rising a little faster as my breathing accelerates. I was nervous for today, starting a new job. Not once in any of my scenarios did I imagine myself sitting across from Royce and his brothers. All five of the sexy, suit-clad, gorgeous men. It's more than I bargained for.

Turning, I look to Gail. "Thank you for lunch," I say politely. I know I've already thanked her, but I need to focus on something other than the panel of men who are sitting across from me.

"Of course, we're going to feed you lunch on your first day. Anytime you order for these guys"—Gail points across the table—"add something for yourself as well."

"Oh, that's not necessary," I tell her.

She waves me off and turns her attention to the men in the room. "Your formal introduction. This is Sawyer Gibson. She's taking over for Samantha. I sent you all an email this morning, briefing you that Sam has agreed to train her remotely. Something I'm sure you are all grateful for." I can hear the smile in her voice.

The guys all mumble their agreement that they were aware of my existence and the fact that Sam will be training me. Royce stares at me for a few seconds longer than the others before busying himself with his lunch. Oh, how I wish I would have done a little research. Maybe then, I wouldn't be so intimidated by the line of Adonis-looking men staring at me. I would have known who he was on the plane, and I would have known that there were four others just like him.

"Now, let's go down the line, shall we?" She looks at me, and I nod my agreement. "Royce, Owen, Conrad, Grant, and Marshall." She points out each one as she says their names.

The pictures in the folder that she gave me don't do justice to the real thing. How am I going to work with all five of them every day, all day long? I wipe my sweaty palms on my skirt. I don't know if it's nerves or the fact that five very attractive men are watching me intently.

"So, Sawyer, what's your background?" one of them asks me. I have no idea which one he is. The only name, and face I remember is Royce. I chance a look at him, and he's watching me, waiting for my reply. I think it's Grant. Damn, I wish I would have been more prepared.

"I worked at a law firm in Seattle as an administrative assistant."

"What did you do there?" another asks. I think this one is Owen, but I can't be sure.

"Everything," I say with a small nervous laugh. "Answered the phone, scheduled meetings and appointments for ten attorneys. Prepared meeting rooms, filed depositions, coordinated hearings with the courthouse, got lunch, coffee, snacks. You name it, I did it."

"I'm surprised you left with that kind of responsibility. I'm Conrad, by the way." He winks. My confusion as to who is who must be apparent. "Don't worry. You'll learn all of us eventually."

"Sorry," I say sheepishly. "Gail gave me a cheat sheet, but we've been so busy today, I didn't have time to study it." I give him what I hope is a confident smile. "As far as the job, there were... issues. Things I didn't agree with, and I felt it was time that I leave the company."

"So you weren't prepared for your first day?" This comes from Royce. "What kind of issues?" he adds.

Sexy, brooding, and 100 percent the alpha CEO I'm sure he's known for. Good to know, I think, as I take mental notes about each brother. He's nothing like my Royce from the plane. "I knew that Riggins Enterprises was family-owned and operated, but I did not know to what extent. I felt it was important to learn the company and the owners firsthand, not read and fall into what very well could be false from the internet." I keep my shoulders straight and maintain eye contact.

"Our company website would have been a good place to start," he counters.

I nod. "You're right. I did skim over the website, but your pictures are not there."

"They are."

"No, I'm sorry, but they're not," I counter. I've been steamrolled enough by men in power. I won't do it here. No matter how bad I want or need this job.

"She's right," Conrad chimes in. "We agreed it was time to update the pictures of each of us. The last one was when Marshall still looked like a baby right out of college." He smirks at his brother. I make another mental note that Marshall is the youngest.

"Fu—" Marshall starts. "Forget you," he quickly corrects, making Conrad throw his head back in laughter.

I ignore both of them and keep my eyes locked on Royce. I raise an eyebrow waiting for him to say I was right. He doesn't.

"What issues?" he asks.

I watch as he leans back in his black leather chair and crosses his arms over his chest. His brown eyes stare at me intently, waiting for an answer. This time I do break eye contact to glance over at Gail. She gives me a nod and a comforting smile that tells me I should be honest with him. "I hate to talk ill of my previous employer."

"As your current employer, I demand it," Royce counters.

I nod, take a deep breath, and slowly exhale. "I was tired of my boss making passes at me. I was tired of the sexual comments that would fly from his mouth daily. I was tired of feeling objectified as a woman." I watch as Royce's jaw tightens, just the slightest bit. He otherwise seems unaffected by my confession.

"How long did you work there?" Marshall asks.

"Four years."

"Enough interrogation," Gail speaks up. "Let's just enjoy the rest of our lunch. Sawyer and I have lots of work to get through this afternoon." That's an excuse, and we all know it. I pull my focus from Royce to the boxed lunch in front of me and begin to eat. I don't make eye contact with any of them as they start to talk amongst themselves. I just hope I didn't screw up and lose my job.

Gail and I make small talk about the programs I've used in the past, and the job duties that I held at the Sanders, Bower & Green

Agency. This is all stuff that we discussed in my interview, but as we talk, she correlates each task to something similar here at Riggins that I will be responsible for. It helps weld my past experiences into my new position. It also helps me relax and let the conversation with Royce settle in the back of my mind.

I'm thankful for both.

Royce is the first to stand. "I have to get back to work." He nods at Gail. "Thank you for lunch," he tells her, tossing his trash, and walking out of the room. He doesn't even spare a glance at me.

One by one, each of them agrees, and thank both Gail and me for lunch, and disappear down the hall.

"I'm sorry," I say as soon as it's just Gail and me. "I didn't mean to talk that way to him. I'll be sure to apologize." I let my emotions get the best of me. I have to let the Royce I thought I knew go. Besides, none of these guys are my slime ball of an ex-boss. At least not that I know of. I was out of line.

"You'll do no such thing. Royce was being an ass. He knows it, we all know it. He needs someone who's going to stand up to him. That's why he and Sam got along so well. She didn't take his snide comments to heart, and she gave it back to him. He needs someone strong-willed and trustworthy. I believe we've found that in you. Just don't go falling in love and getting knocked up by any of his friends." She laughs. "He's been even more of a grumpy bear ever since. As soon as the two of you get into a routine, it will all work itself out."

I'm not sure I believe her, but I nod and clean up my trash, tossing it into the now full trash can on our way back to my desk. The afternoon passes by in a blur of information. It's a lot to learn, but I'm up for the challenge. On the drive home, I think about how I acted and vow that tomorrow, no matter what happens, I'm not going to let Royce or any of the Riggins brothers get under my skin.

I'm a professional. I can do this.

I think.

I'M EXHAUSTED. I barely slept a wink last night, and for the first time in years, it wasn't because I was too buried in my work to bother to go to bed. No, this time, it was the blonde beauty that has done nothing but consume my thoughts since the moment I met her. The same blonde beauty that is my new assistant. I spent hours running every scenario over in my mind. Did she know who I was on the plane? Was she faking her fear? I quickly determine that no way could she have done that. I'd felt the panic coming off her in waves. It was real. No matter how I spun it in my mind, I still came to the same conclusion. Sawyer didn't know who I was. Fate is a motherfucker like that. Send me a woman who enthralls me, and then surprise, she's your new assistant.

Fuck my life.

Stepping into the elevator, I hit the button that will take me to the top floor. I watch as the numbers climb, thinking about everything on my schedule and everything that's not but still needs to get done today. I'm already feeling Sam's absence and

Sawyer's presence. To say that I was flabbergasted when I walked off the elevator and saw her with Gail is an understatement.

In my mind, Sawyer was going to be mine. After years of not being interested, she lit a spark inside me. I waited all weekend for her call, the one that never came. I was surly to her yesterday, unintentionally. However, at work, I can't be the sweet guy who helped her overcome a panic attack. I have to be a leader. Not to mention, I was already in a sour mood because she never called.

Fucking Jase. I blame him for this. He had to relentlessly pursue Sam, and eventually knock her up. He's lucky that she's in love with him, and he with her, or I'd have to make his life hell. Who am I kidding? I'll do that anyway. That's what best friends are for, right? Besides, he did this. He put Sawyer in my path, on the plane, in the seat next to me. He made me push a few bricks from my sturdily constructed walls and open up to her. This is all on Jase.

That's my story, and I'm sticking to it.

The elevator doors slide open, and I step off. I make my way around the corner and freeze. There in front of me is an ass shaking in the air. Not just any ass, no, this one is spectacular. Round and tight, an ass that makes a man want to fall to his knees and worship. Before I can speak a word, the owner of the ass stands and turns to face me.

"Oh, Mr. Riggins, I mean, Royce, good morning." A red-faced, flustered Sawyer stumbles over her words as she greets me.

"Sawyer." I acknowledge her and stare down at the floor to a potted plant. "What are you doing?"

"The plant was dying. I took it down to repot it." She points at the corner of the desk where the plant used to be. "I noticed it was too big for the pot, but now I can't seem to lift it back up there." She bends over again, giving me another grand view of her fine ass.

"You came in early to repot a plant?" I ask, needing clarification.

"Yes. I'm always early, and I noticed that this thing needed some love, or it was going to die."

"So, you what? Lugged up a new bigger pot and potting soil?" Again, I need to make sure I understand the situation I just walked in on. She's a little thing to be lugging all that around. I don't like the thought of her struggling, but I push it down.

"Yes, well, not exactly. Harvey at the door helped me. He had a dolly, which made it so much easier," she explains, and then leans over the pot and tries to lift it.

"Move." My voice is deep, and the one-word command is taken as such as she huffs and stands, stepping out of the way. With ease, I bend down and lift the potted plant. "Where do you want it?" I ask her.

"There, on the corner where it was." She motions toward the corner of her desk.

"Isn't this thing too big to be sitting there?"

"Am I allowed to move it?" she asks.

"Now you ask permission?" I shake my head.

"Well, I think it would look nice there, by the seating." She points to the small row of chairs where guests wait to meet with one of my brothers or me.

"Are you sure that's where you want it?"

"Isn't that… heavy?" she asks. Her eyes rake over me as if she sees under my clothes. My body heats and my cock twitches. Just days ago, I wanted nothing more than those green eyes to devour me. And those soft hands, I wanted them everywhere. I still do.

"No." I carry the potted plant with ease to where she pointed next to the guest seating.

"Perfect. Thank you, Royce."

Is it just me or does my name seductively roll off her tongue? Did I forget to mention that in addition to a great ass, my new assistant is the most beautiful woman I've ever laid my eyes on? It sounds like a good problem to have, right? Beautiful woman at my beck and call. It's not. Trust me.

My dick needs to stay far away from her. I can't and won't mix business with pleasure. Any intentions that I had for us are now squashed. She's my employee, and I won't cross that line. The future of Riggins Enterprises rests on my shoulders. Sure, my brothers are here with me, but I'm the CEO. Ultimately, it all lies with me. I need to stay focused, and lusting after the sexy Sawyer is not the way to do that. I don't have it in me to give more than that. To anyone. Not anymore. Sure, I let myself get lost in the moment, the connection we shared on the plane, but the flight landed, and she walked away.

That's that.

Now here she is, and I have to try like hell to forget those moments. Wallowing in those memories won't do either of us a bit of good.

"Good morning," Gail says cheerily. "Oh, what is all of this?" she asks, looking at the mini garden center Sawyer has turned the reception area into.

"The plant, I noticed it was too big for the pot." Sawyer points to the plant and its new home. "So I came in early to repot it."

"And you helped?" Gail asks me with raised eyebrows.

"No. I didn't help." It takes everything I have not to growl the reply.

"He did." Sawyer is quick to add. "He moved it for me."

"Well...." Gail beams, and I inwardly groan. I don't need her romanticizing the act of kindness. Besides, if my new assistant threw out her back, I'd be even more fucked than I already am. It was for the greater good of the business that I offered my assistance.

"Get this cleaned up," I say, narrowing my gaze on Sawyer before turning and stalking toward my office. I don't stick around to see what I'm sure is pain from my brashness flash in her eyes.

My morning consists of a conference call from hell. We have a new location in Idaho, and the manager doesn't know his ass from a hole in the ground. At least not anymore. When we hired him, he checked off all the boxes, his references were tight, and he impressed all of us. Now, however, he's slacking on the job, missing deadlines, and doesn't appear to be the same guy we hired over a year ago. I made it clear that if he doesn't pull his head out of his ass, he'll be looking for a new job. Then I spent an hour typing up the conversation to send to Gail for his personnel file. Needless to say, that's not my favorite part of the job.

My favorite is seeing the company thrive. A company that my father built with one truck, just he and my mother. We've grown by leaps and bounds over the last twenty years, and eight of that I've been at the helm. I love watching the family legacy live on. I was young, merely twenty-four years old when Dad decided to retire. He said he wanted more time with Mom while they were both still healthy enough to travel and live life to its fullest. Marshall, the youngest, was sixteen, but that didn't stop my parents from enjoying life. They didn't start to travel until Marshall was a freshman in college.

As the oldest of five brothers, it was always I who would take the reins. Not that my brothers minded. They all have their own niche, so to speak, and they each bring that to the table to help make this company what it is today. All five of us love this company and what it stands for. They make my job easy. I know I have my four best friends, my blood, who have my back. I don't have to worry about some money-hungry CFO or marketing guru who thinks they know what's best for Riggins Enterprises. We are Riggins Enterprises. It's in our blood.

"Knock, knock," Sawyer says, sticking her head in the door. "Sorry to interrupt. Your one o'clock canceled. I told them we'd have to see where we could fit them back into the schedule in the next month or so," she says, stepping into the room.

"How did you know to do that?" I ask. I hate when there is a last-minute meeting cancelation that's been on the books for months. If there are extenuating circumstances, I look past it. However, my time is just as valuable as theirs, and if they cancel, they have to wait. That's my rule.

"Sam." Sawyer smiles, and I swear it lights up the already bright room. "She said if they didn't have a good reason to push them off. Was that okay?" she asks, suddenly unsure.

"What was the reason?"

"They needed more time."

I nod. "Thank you, Sawyer."

"You're welcome. Can I get you anything?"

"No. Thank you," I say, rubbing at my temples. She nods and slips out the door. I'm glad Sam is training her; that's one less stress I need to worry about. Turning to my laptop, I pull up a contract I've been working on and begin to read through it.

Riggins Enterprises also buys up smaller companies who are struggling, and often times, we've even invested in them to help them thrive. Our motivation is not to eliminate the competition, but to make money. Sometimes investing makes sense, and other times, it's more beneficial for both parties for them to sell. The contract I'm working on now is for a sale. Grant is taking the lead on this one, but as CEO, it's my job to review and approve the contract before he closes the deal.

My headache throbs and I'm glad that my meeting was canceled. Pulling open my desk drawer, I search for a bottle of headache medicine and come up empty. That's when I remember that I asked Sam to order me some more. "Damn you, Jase," I mutter. Placing my elbows on my desk, I bury my face in my hands. I guess it's time to go in search of the first aid cabinet and see what I can find.

"Sorry." I hear a soft whisper. Looking through my fingers, I see Sawyer, stepping into my office. With a groan, I drop my hands to my desk and watch her as she strides toward me. She places a bottle of water and a small pack of Tylenol on my desk. "You looked like you could use these."

"Order me a bottle," I say, tearing open the packet, tossing back the pills and downing the entire bottle of water. "Thank you, Sawyer," I say once I'm done. I'm not a complete asshole. "Did Sam tell you to do that?" I ask.

"No, but you were giving me the 'I have a headache that would kill Clint Eastwood' signal, so I took a chance I was right."

I can't help but chuckle. "Kill Clint Eastwood, huh?" I ask, the humor evident, even with my pounding head. Memories of our talk of old movies and older country music filter through my pounding head. It just makes the headache worse when I think about our connection and how we will never be able to pursue it.

"Yep. You've seen his movies, right? The man is unstoppable." With that, she gives me a smile that I feel everywhere like a caress against my skin, turns on her black heels, and disappears out of my office.

Grabbing my phone, I fire off a text. If I'm going to be tortured by my sexy new assistant, Jase should be as well. After all, I'm in this mess because of him.

Me: I'm still pissed at you.

His reply is immediate. It's a picture of Sam sitting with her feet propped up on a pillow as she relaxes on the couch. She has a book in one hand and the other resting on her baby bump.

Jase: One day, you'll understand.

He knows damn well that's never going to happen. There was a time in my life I wanted the white picket fence, a wife, a family of my own. I learned the hard way that finding a partner you can trust, one you can lean on who is solid, is rare, and I stopped looking. This company, my brothers, my parents, hell, even Jase and Sam, and their little one on the way, they're the only family I'll ever have.

"TO YOUR FIRST week on the job." My best friend, Hadley, raises her glass in the air. I clink mine with hers, and we drink. "Tell me all about it."

"It's good. I really like it. It's a lot of responsibility, but the support is there, which is something I'm not used to."

"You said you're admin to five people?"

I nod, taking another long pull from my margarita. "Yeah, five brothers."

"Oh, tell me more." She wags her eyebrows.

"They're all… gorgeous," I admit.

"Now we're talking." She holds her hand up in the air for a high-five, and I slap my palm against hers.

"There's more."

"Do tell." She wiggles in her seat and flashes me a grin.

"You remember the guy on the plane, the one who calmed me

down?" She nods. "Well, he's the CEO. He's my new boss."

"Shut the front door." She leans her elbows on the table, getting closer. "Sexy plane guy is your new boss?" she clarifies.

I nod and take another drink. I need it after the tension-filled week I've had.

"What did he say?"

"Nothing. It's as if he's not the same guy. He's broody and short-answered. I've yet to see the man who calmed me down."

"Maybe that's just him at work. You should talk to him about it."

"Nope. Not happening. I'm there to do my job, and I'm going to do it to the best of my ability, and that's it. Done."

"The mature thing to do would be to discuss it with him." She takes a long pull from her drink. "And if I were you, I'd be reading the handbook, you know, just in case." She wags her damn eyebrows again, causing me to roll my eyes.

"Seriously, Had, it's like I'm walking onto a *GQ* photoshoot every damn day. I had no idea what I was getting myself into," I admit.

"Hey, at least it's not Phil's slimy ass crack you're looking at." She shudders at the thought.

"Facts!" I raise my glass to her. Phil was my sleazeball boss who got my knee in his balls. He's in his late fifties, with a protruding belly and a porn 'stache. "My view of the Riggins brothers is definitely an upgrade."

"I need names," Hadley says, grabbing her phone from the table and swiping at the screen.

"What would Derek think?" I tease her. Derek is her longtime boyfriend turned fiancé, and Hadley can do no wrong in his eyes. He knows she's not going anywhere.

"There's no harm in taking a look. Besides, I need to see what I'm dealing with here."

"What do you mean? What're you dealing with? I'm the one working with them."

"Exactly. I'm the best friend, and I see that gleam in your eye. I need to see the man who has caught your attention." She points at me accusingly.

"They all have," I admit. "They're all gorgeous. The Riggins genes are strong and on point," I say, draining the rest of my margarita.

"Even their last name is sexy," Hadley says, her fingers flying across the screen of her phone. "Holy shit," she breathes. Tearing her eyes from her phone, she looks across the small high-top table we were lucky to snag. "You work with all of them?" she asks, turning her phone so that I can see the screen.

There, in all their sexy glory, are the Riggins brothers. Conrad loaded the new images yesterday. "That's them." I nod, lifting my glass to my lips, remembering that it's empty.

"I'll go grab us a couple more. You hold our table." Hadley slips off her chair, exchanges her phone for her small clutch, and makes her way toward the bar. Unable to resist, I reach for her phone, type in her password, and take a look at my bosses.

I've learned a lot about the brothers this week. Gail is rather chatty and offered up information freely. I know that Conrad and I are the same age. That Marshall is, of course, the baby. Grant is a people person, while Owen keeps to himself, and in Gail's words, Royce carries the weight of the world on his shoulders. I've witnessed how hard the five of them work, and the dedication that each of them holds to the family business.

"Sawyer?"

I turn to look over my shoulder to find a smiling Marshall. "Hey." He leans in for a hug. I don't hesitate to return it, which surprises me. I'm not exactly in the habit of hugging my boss. Especially the slimeball Phil.

"Fancy meeting you here," he says, stepping back. "Are you alone?" he asks, looking at the seat that Hadley just left.

"No. I'm here with my best friend, Hadley," I say as the woman herself slides back into her seat and pushes a fresh margarita across the table to me. "Marshall, this is Hadley. Hadley, this is Marshall, one of my bosses."

"No," he groans, rolling his eyes playfully. "Not one of your bosses." He switches his beer to his other hand and offers it to her. "Marshall Riggins, a friend of Sawyer's." He winks.

"Nice to meet you, Marshall. Join us?" Hadley offers.

"Yeah, let me call Conrad and tell him where to find us." He pulls his phone out of his pocket and taps the screen. "Yo, where are you?" he asks. Placing his beer on the table, he covers his other ear to hear better. "I found Sawyer. Yes, that Sawyer. We're at the high-tops near the bar." He ends the call, slides his phone back in his pocket, and grabs his beer from the table. "He's on his way."

"Hello, ladies," Conrad's smooth voice greets us. He doesn't wait for an invitation, sliding into the chair across from Marshall. "Sawyer, who's your friend?" he asks, eyeing Hadley.

"This is my engaged, very-much-in-love-with-her-fiancé, best friend, Hadley. Had, this is Conrad, another one of my bosses."

"Just Conrad, lose the boss. We save that title for our older brother Royce." He grins, offering Hadley his hand.

"So, is it just the two of you tonight?" I ask them. I don't know if I could handle all five of them at once. Who am I kidding? I don't know if I could handle Royce being here. The other four, a piece of cake.

"Yeah. Grant left this morning to go to Idaho to check on things there, Owen probably has his nose buried in a spreadsheet, and Royce I'm sure is either at the office or in his home office. He never stops," Marshall says.

"I thought Grant was leaving on Monday?" I ask. I'm suddenly panicked that I messed up the schedule.

"He was, but shit hit the fan there last night. The guy in charge has gone AWOL, and we need to get things in order. He caught a flight out earlier. We dropped him off on our way here," Conrad explains.

"Well, I'm glad you could join us. We're celebrating Sawyer's first week at her new job. It only seems fitting that the two of you join us for a toast." Hadley smiles at each of them.

"Oh, we're celebrating, but we need shots." Marshall is out of his chair and headed toward the bar before any of us can object.

"How was your first week?" Conrad asks.

"Good." I nod and offer him a smile. "Gail and Sam have both been great."

"That's right." He nods. "I forgot that Sam was training you from home."

"She is, and it's been so helpful," I tell him.

"All right," Marshall says, setting a shot in front of each of us. He lifts his in the air and waits for us to join in. "To Sawyer. Welcome to the Riggins family. May your journey be long and prosperous." He smirks and tosses back the shot.

From across the table, Hadley giggles and throws back her shot. Conrad does the same, and I realize all eyes are on me. Bringing the glass to my lips, I down it, and smile at them. "That's so good. Doesn't even taste like alcohol."

"Nope, but trust me, it's in there. You ladies want to dance?" Marshall stands and grabs Hadley's hand, pulling her to her feet. She gives him zero resistance as she follows him out to the dance floor.

"Am I going to have to save his ass for that later?" Conrad asks, motioning his head toward his brother and my best friend.

"No. Derek and Had are tight. He knows she's not going anywhere, and vice versa. They've been together for years."

"Good. What about you? Anyone I need to worry about wanting to kick my ass if we join them?"

"Nope. Just me." *Definitely not your brother.*

"You plan on kicking my ass?" he asks with a smile tilting his lips.

"Depends, you think you can keep up?" I take a couple of large drinks of margarita until it's gone, and stand. "Show me what you've got, Riggins." I'm probably playing with fire, drinking and dancing with my new bosses, but the guys are nice and friendly. As long as it stays that way, there shouldn't be an issue.

"Oh, it's on." Conrad finishes off his beer, leaving the empty on the table, and places his hand on the small of my back, leading me to the dance floor. Once we're in the crowd, close to Marshall and Hadley, he places his hands on my hips, and we begin to move. Over the course of a couple of songs, I somehow end up with Marshall, and Hadley with Conrad. The guys are a blast to be around, and I soon forget that they're technically my bosses.

"I need a drink," I say over the loud music. Hadley nods, and we motion to the guys that we're headed to the bar. They nod in agreement and follow us, helping us move our way through the crowd.

"Two margaritas, two bottles." Conrad points to the beer of the guy next to him. "And four shots, something fruity for the ladies," he tells the bartender, sliding his black Amex across the bar.

We down our shots, and take our drinks with us back out on the dance floor. We repeat this same process more times than I can count. Finally, the bartender announces last call, and we realize we're all too drunk to drive.

"I'm calling D-Derek." Hadley grins.

"Fuck," Marshall mutters. "Grant is usually who we call. He's more laidback than the others." He looks over at Conrad. "Owen or Royce?"

"Owen," they say in unison.

I feel my shoulders relax that they didn't choose Royce. I tune them out and try to focus on Hadley and her conversation with Derek. He's picked us up before, but it's been a long time, a very, very long time since we've let loose like this. And I did it with my bosses!

"Am I getting fired?" I blurt the question.

"No. Why would you even ask that?" Conrad asks.

"You're," I drunkenly wave my hand in the air toward them, "you're my bosses, and I'm drunk."

"You're not on the clock, Sawyer. Besides, it's a free country. You can drink if you want. You're of legal age. You've done nothing wrong," Conrad assures me.

I nod and notice that with that simple act, my head feels heavier and fuzzier than before. I'm piss-ass drunk, and I know tomorrow I'm going to be nursing the hangover from hell.

"Derek is about five minutes out," Hadley says. She links her arm through mine, and together we start making our way through the thinning crowd to the exit.

"We'll wait with you. Owen's almost here," Marshall says, stepping up beside me.

The four of us head out of the club, and the cool breeze of the night air does wonders for my heated skin. My hair and clothes are wet from sweat from all the dancing and close bodies. I know I'm a hot mess without even looking in the mirror.

A sleek black sports car that looks like sex—yes, cars can look like sex. At least they do in my current drunken state—pulls up next to us.

"That car is hot as fuck," Hadley says from beside me. It's like she can read my thoughts. That's why we're best friends.

"I'll tell Owen you said so." Conrad chuckles.

"Th-That's Owen?" I ask.

"Yep. I'm going to go tell him to wait for a few. We're going to wait until her man gets here." Conrad gives my elbow a gentle squeeze before he saunters over to Owen's waiting sex on wheels. He's walking straight and doesn't seem the least bit drunk.

"How is he not swaying?" I ask the night air.

"We're men, and we can drink more than you. You two are tiny things. However, we also know when it's too much to drive. We're not about that," Marshall explains.

The way that he says it almost sounds as if he's repeating a small piece of a lecture he's heard many times in his life. I can't imagine the hell the five brothers put their parents through growing up.

"There's my man." Hadley cheers as Derek pulls up in his SUV.

With her arm still linked with mine, we make our way to the SUV. She climbs into the front, and I open the back door but stop before climbing inside. I turn to look at Conrad and Marshall. I wave at them, and then my eyes seek out Owen. The windows are tinted, but from the glow of the street light, I can make out the figure of his body sitting behind the wheel. I wave to him too. I'm sure he's watching me, wondering what kind of a mess they got themselves into hiring me. So much for good impressions. I need water, a shower, and sleep. In that order. I manage to climb into the back seat of the SUV and rest my head against the window. Through my drunken haze, I make a mental note to check the handbook to see if any rules were broken.

Derek takes me to my place and helps me inside. Hadley is already passed out in the front seat. "Thank you. Take care of her," I tell him.

"Always. You good?"

"Yep," I say, and even I can hear the slow sluggish tone of my voice. "Night, D."

"Night. Lock up."

I do as he says, knowing he won't leave until I do. Kicking off my shoes, I don't bother with lights as I make my way down the hall to my bedroom. Flopping down on my bed face-first, all I can seem to think about is, what is Royce going to say?

FOR AS LONG as I can remember, my mom insisted on Sunday dinners. It started when we were just kids, and Dad was working all the time to expand the company. She didn't want us to lose out on family time, so she deemed Sundays family days. We loved it. Both Mom and Dad were home, and we got all of their attention, which was a difficult task for them—I'm sure with five boys running around the house. When I went off to college, I would come home as much as I could, as did my brothers who followed after me. Now that we're all graduated and living on our own, my mother still insists on Sunday dinners. If they're not traveling, there will be dinner every Sunday.

That's why I'm pulling into the driveway of the house I grew up in. Dinner is served at five every Sunday. There is always way more food than the seven of us can eat. I asked Mom once why she made so much. She said that one day she hoped that each of us would find a nice woman to bring home, and she wanted us to have the reassurance that there would always be room at the table and plenty of food for each of them.

Mom's a romantic. She and Dad met in high school, and here they are now, married thirty-four years, and still going strong. Not all of us are that lucky. To find the one person in the world who will give you unconditional love—and trust. I learned the hard way that trust is extremely hard to find. In fact, if your last name isn't Riggins, I don't trust you. Well, outside of Jase, my best friend. I give him shit for falling in love with my assistant, but the fact of the matter is, they are both deliriously happy. I want that for them. It's just not for all of us.

Walking into the house, it's not as loud and boisterous as it usually is. I'm the last to arrive from the looks of the vehicles in the driveway. Grant's out of town, but he alone doesn't make up for the quiet of the house. I make my way toward the living room, following the sound of the television to find three of my brothers and my dad.

"What's up?" I ask.

Dad chuckles. "Seems your brothers don't know their limits."

I look over at Conrad and Marshall, and although they look a little haggard, they seem fine. My eyes then land on Owen. "You drank?" I ask him. Not that he doesn't drink; he's just not one for going out to clubs. He's more of a social drinker or having a beer at night once he's home. Owen is by far the most serious of the five of us.

"No, but they woke my ass up at two this morning to come and get them."

I nod. Grant is usually the lucky brother who gets the calls in the middle of the night, but he's out of town. It makes sense they would call Owen and not me. As the oldest brother and the CEO of Riggins Enterprises, they know the ride home would have been a lecture. Owen, on the other hand, I'm sure picked them up and dropped them off without a word.

Their actions directly affect the view of the company. It's not fair, but it is the way things are. Our company has money, more than my kids' kids would ever be able to spend, and with that come the vultures—the media or some random person at the club looking to get a quick payday from a grainy image snapped from their cell phones. The CEO in me understands the implications. The brother in me understands wanting to go out and let loose for a night.

It's been years since I've done that. In fact, not once have I had more than a drink or two since I took over the reins at Riggins Enterprises. The entire company rests upon my shoulders. I take that seriously.

I know what you're thinking, that I'm the serious one, not Owen. That's true in a sense, but Owen, he keeps to himself. He's private about his dating life. Hell, I'm not even sure he has one. Whereas I don't hide it, or the fact that it's one and done. Always. Those trysts may be few and far between, but they all know I have them. I tried the yellow brick road that led me to forever, and it was a dead end. Lesson learned. It's no longer about the marathon when it comes to the women in my life, but the sprint. It's always short-lived, and women know before it even starts that nothing will come of it.

I just don't have it in me.

Not anymore.

"You haven't heard the best part. Ask them who they were with," Owen says. His expression's unreadable behind his thick beard, but the glint in his eyes tells me he's enjoying this little game of verbal torture on our younger brothers.

"Who were you with?"

"A girl we met. Her name is Hadley." Conrad is quick to answer.

Why does that name sound familiar? I glance over at Owen, and the slightest shake of his head tells me there's more. "Who else?"

"Her best friend," Marshall adds.

Another look at Owen and I know they're still not telling me everything. "Does this best friend have a name?" They share a look before Conrad opens his mouth and knocks me on my ass.

"Sawyer."

Sawyer? "Wait. *My* Sawyer?" I ask them. My voice is raised, and instead of flinching, my two younger brothers grin like I just told them we won the fucking lottery. I'm kicking myself in the ass for my blunder. Thankfully, I've kept that I already knew her to myself.

"Is she yours, Royce? Is there something you're not telling us?" Marshall asks.

"Sawyer from the office. *My* assistant?" I clarify. She's not mine, something my dick has taken offense to in the last week.

"Yep," Conrad says, popping the *p* and wearing a shit-eating smirk on his face.

"You were out drinking with my new assistant?"

"Not technically. We ran into her and her friend. We had a shot to celebrate her first week at the office, and then hit the dance floor," Marshall explains. "And she's not just yours." He gives me a pointed look that we both know is fucked up. She is mine.

"Rinse and repeat," Conrad adds.

"How did she get home?" I look over at Owen, and he holds his hands in the air. "I didn't take her. She was climbing into the back seat of an SUV when I saw her."

"You let them drive?" I seethe.

"No. Chill, Royce. We didn't let them drive. Hadley's fiancé picked them up." Conrad watches me closely. I don't like it, and I don't like the way my stomach feels as though it's tied up in knots. And while I'm at it, I'm going to add that I don't like that they got time with her and I didn't. She's off-limits to all of us, but this past week didn't keep me from fantasizing about her.

"Sawyer is off-limits." I make sure to look at each one of my brothers in the eye. I make a mental note to tell Grant the same.

"Hmm," Marshall says, tapping his chin. "Dad, is there a rule in the handbook about dating employees?"

"Nope." Dad grins.

Traitor.

"It's in the works." I'm already mentally preparing the email to Gail for first thing tomorrow morning.

"Well, you see, big brother, it's not written in stone, not yet, and we did nothing wrong. What harm is there in buying a coworker a shot to celebrate her new job?" Conrad asks.

"Or spinning her and her cute—despite being engaged—friend around the dance floor?" Marshall adds.

"You were at a club. There is no spinning on the dance floor. More like grinding," I say as I clench my jaw.

"That too." Marshall grins.

"Motherfucker," I mumble as Mom walks into the room.

"Royce Riggins! You watch your mouth. It's time to eat," she announces as she turns on her heel and heads back to the kitchen.

Like the teenage boys we'll always be when we get together, we race to the dining room to take our seats. The same places we sat in growing up. No one ever assigned us seats; it just sort of happened one day, and then the next, until it became routine. The dining room table is huge and could seat many more than just the seven of us. In fact, it can seat sixteen in total. It makes it nice for big holiday dinners for family gatherings.

"What were you boys going on about?" Mom asks once all of our plates are full, and we've begun to eat.

It doesn't matter how old we are; we will always be boys in her eyes. "Your offspring thought it would be fun to take my new assistant out and get her drunk last night." I give Marshall and Conrad a pointed look.

"That's not what happened. Royce has his panties in a wad." Marshall rolls his eyes.

"Sawyer?" Mom asks. "Gail has said such nice things about her."

I heave a heavy sigh before taking another big bite of my mother's homemade mashed potatoes. I should have known that Gail would fill my mother in on my new assistant. I can only imagine what she's told her.

"She's great," Conrad tells her. "She was at the club last night with her best friend, Hadley, and we bought them a few rounds, danced a little. Nothing over the top."

"Yeah, her friend is engaged," Marshall explains. "It was just a fun night out."

"And you're upset?" Mom asks. There is a gleam in her eye that tells me exactly what I was afraid of. She thinks I'm jealous. She's not wrong, but she's not right either.

"Yes. She works for us. They shouldn't be drinking and dancing with her." My excuse sounds lame even to me.

"Why on earth not? It sounds like it was a nice friendly evening."

"Mom, there is nothing friendly about dancing at a club. Trust me on this one."

"Oh, you mean twerking, and what not? I'm sure your brothers enjoyed that."

Marshall and Conrad crack up laughing, and even Dad is struggling to hide his grin behind his glass of sweet tea. "There was no twerking. Although, Sawyer did this thing where she bends over and touches the floor."

"Hot!" Marshall declares. "So hot."

"Boys." Mom laughs. "It upsets your brother when you talk about his new pretty assistant that way."

"How do you know she's pretty?" I ask without thinking.

"Gail, and well, now you." Her grin tells me it was a trap that she expertly placed, and I fell into blindly. I'm thirty-two years old. You would think that I would be smarter than that by now. Mom's got game. Of course, raising the five of us boys, she had to have.

"Can we all just agree that it's bad form? Think about how that makes the company look? When the owners are getting the employees drunk. Dad, back me up here."

"Royce is right, and your actions do affect the company. However, you are of legal age, and I assume that she is as well?" He gives them a pointed look, and they reply with a nod. "I see nothing wrong with dancing and a few drinks."

"Owen? Some backup?" I ask my brother, who's closest to me in age.

"I don't see what's wrong with it. She was smiling and laughing. Both girls were. It looked like they were having a good time."

"Conspiracy," I mumble under my breath. Dad's deep chuckle pulls my attention, and I don't miss the wink he tosses my mom's way.

I decide to let it go. The battle has already been lost, and I don't want to spend the rest of the meal arguing with them. Besides, even I know that I'm reaching. I would never admit that. No, that means I'm admitting defeat, and that can't happen. I'd never live it down. Instead, I turn the conversation to work. It's what I know, and it's who I am. Mom just smiles and shakes her head as the Riggins men, yes, *men,* regardless of what she likes to call us, talk about the shop in Idaho that Grant is visiting and the issues we've been having.

I'm in the conversation, offering my thoughts and commenting where appropriate, but the entire time in the back of my mind, all I can see is Sawyer and my two younger brothers. I'm sure the scene in my head is much worse than the real-life event. That doesn't stop me from glaring at them both as they talk to our parents and Owen. They know better.

"Royce." Mom waves her hand in front of my face. I shake out of my thoughts to look at her and realize it's just the two of us.

"Where did everyone go?"

"I was about to ask you the same thing." She gives me a pointed look.

"Just going over my day tomorrow in my mind."

"Uh-huh." She shakes her head. "There is nothing wrong with what your brothers did."

"She's our employee."

"Gail was our employee and my best friend," she reminds me.

"That's different."

"How?" She's giving me that mom look, the one that says we

both know she's right and she's trying to hide her glee and look stern at the same time.

"It just is."

"You like her."

"No. I mean, yes, I have to on some level to work so closely with her."

"No, you like her more than just your assistant."

"Mom," I sigh. "I know you want me to settle down, but that ship has sailed. After Jennifer, I'll never go down that road again. I have the company, you and Dad, those knuckleheads you tell me are my brothers. That's enough for me." I'm not against love and happily ever after. In fact, I once thought that I had it all. Then I found out it was all a lie. I've had my fill for a lifetime.

"Oh, Royce." Mom stands and makes her way to where I'm sitting. She wraps her arms around me in a hug, and suddenly, I'm a ten-year-old boy all over again. I might have given up on the romance of my life, but I have my family, and my mother's hugs, they're still one of a kind.

I'M MORE NERVOUS about going to work today than I was my first day. Was that really just a week ago? I managed to start a new job, get drunk with my bosses, and I'm sure I'm either getting fired, or getting my ass chewed today. It was stupid, and I knew better. I have no one to blame but myself. Sure, Hadley was encouraging, but if I stood my ground, she would have gotten the hint. I barely put up a fight.

The kicker to all of this? I had a good time. Conrad and Marshall are fun to be around. They're flirts, and other than dancing, kept their hands to themselves. It was nice not to have to fend off advances, to just cut loose and have a good time. Maybe after Royce fires me, we can still be friends?

"Good morning, Sawyer," Gail greets me.

"Good morning." I give her a bright smile, and hope like hell she doesn't see the nerves.

"What's wrong?"

Shit. Might as well face the music. "I think I made a mistake."

"You think?"

"I know I did?" It's more of a question. I'm still not sure if I did or not.

"Well, whatever it is, I'm sure we can fix it. There is nothing that we can't trace your steps and put it back."

I nod. "That's good to know, but I didn't make it here." I wring my hands together in my lap.

Gail walks around the desk and takes the extra chair she's been occupying while training me. "Sawyer, what's going on? Are you in some kind of trouble?" She places her hand over mine that are still twisting and knotting together. The act is motherly, and the pang of loneliness and missing my own mother hits me so hard it takes my breath.

I stop the movement of my hands and slowly exhale before taking a deep breath and look into her eyes. "I'm okay, but I have a feeling I'm getting fired today."

Her eyes widen, but that's the only tell that I've surprised her. "Tell me what's going on."

So, I do. I tell her about how Hadley and I were having a girls' night and ran into Conrad and Marshall. I tell her about the drinking and the dancing—all of it. I don't leave anything out. I've never been one to shy away from my truth or my responsibilities. This is on me. I made a choice, and I need to take the consequences.

"And?" Gail asks.

"And, I know I was wrong."

"Why was it wrong? You weren't on company time or even company property." She's looking at me like she truly doesn't understand.

"Isn't there some kind of rule or something? Employees shall not drink and dance with bosses?" I ask.

"Not currently, but we're going to fix that," a deep voice says from behind me. Slowly, I turn to see Royce standing there, and his hard stare is laser-focused on me. "Gail, can I see you in my office?" he asks. He moves his gaze to her.

"Sure. Sawyer, grab your tablet," she instructs as she stands.

"Just you," Royce says, stalking off to his office.

"I'll just be a minute." Gail pats my shoulder.

I watch her as she disappears into Royce's office. Panic starts to rise, and I hate that my poor decisions are going to cause me to lose my job. "You made it a week, Sawyer," I say under my breath.

"Talking to yourself now?" Conrad asks with a friendly smile. My expression must say it all. The smile drops from his face, and he's suddenly serious. "Sawyer, what's wrong?"

"N-Nothing." I try for a reassuring smile, and I fail miserably.

"What's going on?" Marshall asks, stepping up to my desk.

"She's upset."

"What's up, Sawyer?" Marshall asks.

Great. This is what I don't need. I don't need Conrad and Marshall defending me and making things worse. I don't know what's going on in his office, or what he's saying, and even though I deserve whatever it is, I still hate it. "Royce is pissed," I whisper, like cussing at work is going to get me fired. It's not my mouth that's going to do it but my poor decisions. I immediately clamp my hand over my mouth. Not just because I cussed at the office, but because I didn't want to tell them.

"Fuck that." Conrad storms off toward Royce's office. He doesn't knock. He just turns the handle and walks on in.

"Come on." Marshall holds his hand out for me.

"W-What? Where are we going?"

"In there." He motions toward Royce's office with his head.

"No. Nope." I shake my head vigorously. "I'm not going in there."

"Yes, you are." Walking around my desk, he grabs my hand and gives a gentle tug to get me to climb to my feet.

"Marshall, this isn't a good idea. He's pissed. He heard me telling Gail and said he was going to make a rule about employees and bosses socializing." That's not exactly what he said, but I read between the lines. He's going to make sure that it never happens again.

"He's being a grumpy dick," he says, pulling me from behind my desk. My heels click against the tile floor, and the closer we get to Royce's office, the more nervous I become. My knees are literally shaking. I hate confrontation. That's why I put up with Phil's harassment for so long.

"Come on, man, you're being a dick," Conrad says as we enter the room.

"Told you," Marshall says, not bothering to keep his voice down.

Everyone stops talking and turns to look at us. I can feel the stare of everyone in the room, but my eyes are locked on Royce. "Mr. Riggins," I start, and Marshall snorts from his place beside me. I elbow him and try again. "Mr. Riggins—" I start, and this time it's Royce who stops me. Not his words, but his glare as he takes in my hand that's still clasped in Marshall's. I try to pull away, but his hold is firm. When I look up, Marshall is grinning from ear to ear.

"Out. Everyone but Sawyer leaves the room. Now!"

"Not gonna happen," Conrad says, crossing his arms over his chest. "We're not going to let you badger her when she did nothing wrong."

"I thought we already talked about this?" Marshall asks.

Again, I try to pull my hand free, but he's not budging. "It's okay," I assure them.

"Come on, let's give them a moment to talk." Gail links her arm through Conrad's. "Sawyer, I'll be right outside when you're done." She's training me, so where else would she be? That's my first thought, but then I register that she just winked at me. She's telling me that she's on my side and that there's nothing to worry about. At least I hope that's what it means.

"You good?" Marshall asks me.

"Yes." I try to give him a reassuring smile. He nods, gives my hand a gentle squeeze before finally releasing me and following the others out the door. The audible click of the door closing has me reaching for the back of the chair for support. I thought my knees were weak before, and it's nothing compared to this—standing before him on my own. His gaze is intense as he watches me.

"Sit."

I want to object, but my knocking knees tell me I should do as he says. Slowly, I step around the chair and take a seat. Carefully, I cross my legs, tilted to the side, mindful not to give him a show, and fold my hands together, placing them in my lap. Finally, I look up, meeting his gaze.

"Sawyer." Royce's deep voice washes over me. His brown eyes are intense as they watch me. The same eyes that brought me through the storm of my panic attack now regard me much differently.

"Mr. Riggins."

He sighs. "Mr. Riggins is my father. Just Royce."

I nod. "Royce."

"Is there something going on with you and my brother?"

"No, sir." I'm quick to shut that line of thinking down.

"Any of them?" He raises his eyebrows.

"No, sir." I look him in the eye and will him to believe me. I don't want to lose this job.

"You and Marshall looked awful cozy." There is a steel harshness to his voice.

What on earth is he talking about? "I'm sorry? I don't know what you mean by that?"

"He didn't want to let you go."

"What? When?"

I watch as he closes his eyes and mumbles under his breath. Slowly, they open. "He was holding your hand. Just now. Here. In *my* office."

Oh, that. "He's just looking out for me. Look." I sit up straighter in my chair. "I'm sorry. It wasn't planned. I was out with my best friend, and Conrad and Marshall were there. They bought us drinks, and we ended up hanging out. It was nothing more than that. I promise you it will never happen again." He stays silent, so I keep rambling. "I didn't mean to break any rules. I would never."

"You didn't break any rules, Sawyer."

My shoulders relax. "Then… why am I here? Am I in trouble for something else?"

"No. However, you are aware that I lost one assistant that I worked well with to my best friend. I'd like very much not to lose another."

Is it just me, or did his voice soften? "I enjoy my job. I have no plans to leave."

"Sam didn't either until she did."

"I promise you, sir. There will never be an intimate relationship with me and any of your brothers." It's a bold statement, one I know that I have to stand behind if I want to keep my job at Riggins Enterprises.

"You're mine, Sawyer." My eyes widen, and he clears his throat. "My assistant. You support them, but ultimately, you're mine." His eyes flare when he says it, and I can't help but wonder what it would be like to be his. I adjust my seating, my thighs rubbing together. Now is *not* the time to get turned on by my new boss.

"Yes, sir."

"Royce."

"Yes, Royce."

"That'll be all, Sawyer." He dismisses me. I stand on shaking legs and exit his office, shutting the door softly behind me.

"Well?" Marshall asks.

"He didn't yell at me." His eyes widen in disbelief.

"What did he say?" Conrad asks. "We can go talk to him."

"No." I raise my hand to stop his movements. "He said I didn't break any rules." *He said I was his.* I decide to keep that to myself.

"Good. Now, you boys get back to work. Sawyer and I have some training to do." Gail shoos them to their office and pats my chair for me to sit. Just like that, my job is still secure, and my panties are ruined. It's wrong to think about Royce in any other way but professionally. I know that, but all I can think about is him telling me that I'm his, and the heat that flared in his eyes when he said it.

Sure, it was probably anger, but this is my fantasy, and I want to believe his words had a double meaning. A girl can dream. This is another side of him I've never seen before. Another layer of Royce Riggins.

DROPPING MY PEN to my desk, I lean back in my chair, covering my face with my hands. My dick is hard and pressing painfully against the zipper of my dress pants, but I refuse to adjust it. It's my punishment for lusting after my new assistant. It doesn't help that her eyes widened, and she licked those full luscious lips when I told her she was mine. I don't even think she realized that she did it. When she squirmed in her chair, rubbing what I imagine are smooth, creamy thighs together, I went from half-mast to full-on steel. I've never been more thankful for the barrier my desk provided, or the coverage.

It's been over a week since the smoke show that is my new assistant appeared in my life. Coincidently, that's the same amount of time that my concentration has been complete shit. Of course, I didn't know that she was my assistant the day I met her. No, that day on the plane, she was a beautiful woman battling her fears. I was just the lucky bastard who got seated next to her and got to help her through it. When she walked away from me that day, I hoped that I would see her again. I had no idea it would be in this capacity. I didn't know that those green eyes and her soft skin would taunt me day in and day out.

I have contracts to read through and a mountain of other paperwork that keeps piling up. Instead of being the beast that I am, or that I usually am, all I can think about is her. *Sawyer.* She's here when I arrive and checks in with me before she leaves for the day. Anytime I start to forget her sexy ass is sitting just outside my door, her sweet voice filters into the room, and poof. Concentration is gone.

When Marshall and Conrad told me they were out with her, I can't explain the anger that made me feel. I don't understand it. All last night and this morning, on the way here, I told myself it was because I didn't want to lose another assistant. Not that it would be a huge inconvenience since she's only been here for a week. She's barely trained, but something deep inside me wants her to stay. My plan was to make her fearful of losing her job. I wanted her to think long and hard before agreeing to a night out with my brothers again. Then she walked in here, holding Marshall's hand, and the only thing I could think about was to get him away from her and to get her closer to me.

I'm losing my fucking mind.

I need to get over whatever this is. I have a billion-dollar company to run. I don't have time to fantasize about bending the beautiful Sawyer over my desk. I groan out loud at the mental image that gives me. My dick twitches in my pants.

This. Has. Got. To. Stop.

The intercom on my desk buzzes, and her voice fills the void in my office. "Royce," she says softly.

"Yes."

"I have Grant on line one for you."

"Thank you, Sawyer." Grabbing the receiver, I place it next to my ear. "How's it going?"

"It's not as bad as we thought. Tony, he's a mess, but Scott, he's got his shit together. He's the one that's keeping this branch running."

"What do you suggest?"

"We demote Tony. My guess is that he'll quit, but that's his choice. We have enough evidence to fire him altogether, but this is cleaner. He's just not cut out to run the day-to-day. Scott, on the other hand, he's got what it takes. I've spent the morning with him, and he was able to rattle off numbers, ship schedules, you name it, Scott is in the know."

"I agree. What do you need from me?"

"Nothing. I'll take care of it. Gail is having her team in HR work up the documents and emailing them to me. It will be done before the end of the day."

"Good. When are you heading back?"

"I think I'll take another day. See what Tony decides to do and then help Scott if he needs it. I don't think he will, but I want him to know that the support is there if something comes up."

"Thank you." I relax back in my chair. "Something I can mark off the list."

"From the sound of things, you've got your hands full on the home front." I can hear the smile in my voice.

"I swear you all are like a bunch of gossiping women."

"I'll tell Owen you said so." He laughs.

"Owen?"

"Yep. I just talked to him about a salary increase for Scott, and he filled me in on everything I've missed. A lot can happen in just a few days."

"It was nothing."

"Oh, it was nothing, huh? Then why did you get all fired up? Over nothing?"

"Is that all? I've got work to do." His reply is to laugh, so I hang up on him. Not my finest or most mature moment, but my brothers know how to press my buttons.

Pushing all thoughts of my sexy assistant out of my mind, I pick up the contract for the new operation in Tulsa and start reading through the suggested changes. Each location is unique to its specific demographic. For the most part, the contracts are the same, but I still read through not wanting to miss an addition that could come back and bite me or Riggins Enterprises in the ass.

"Knock, knock," Sawyer says, appearing in my doorway a couple of hours later. "Sorry to interrupt. Your lunch meeting was canceled, so I went ahead and ordered you something." She sets a bag from a small deli across the street on my desk. "I didn't know what you liked. I had to guess."

"Where's Gail?"

"She had to run down to the HR department. Something about making sure Conrad had what he needed."

"You could have asked me."

"I peeked in, and you were so engrossed in what you were doing I didn't want to interrupt." With that, she smiles. It's a soft smile that barely tilts her lips, but it's genuine. She turns on her black heels, the same heels that do wonders for her legs and ass, and walks out of my office.

I stare at the bag from the deli, and my stomach growls. My eyes scan my computer, looking for the time, and I see it's half-past one. Thirty minutes after my meeting was supposed to start. I never lose track of time like that. Reaching into the bag, I pull out a turkey on wheat, if the sharpie written description on the wrapper is any indication, plus a bag of plain potato chips, and a bottle of Lipton Sweet Tea.

I dig in, devouring every bite as if it's been months since I've eaten. That gives me pause as I think back to this morning, and I didn't eat. All I could focus on was getting to the office to talk to Gail, to initiate a policy. One that I was deftly talked out of. Gail was right. I can't keep her from living her life outside of these walls. I can't keep her from hanging out with my brothers or anyone else. It's not my choice. What I can do is discourage it, which I did strongly. My only hope is that it's enough.

I'm just shoving the last bite of my sandwich into my mouth when Sawyer appears at my door. "I forgot to grab you something for dessert." She holds up a Snickers bar. "Vending machine for the win." She grins and steps into my office. I watch her every move. The way the skirt she's wearing forms to her hips, the way her blouse stretches over her ample breasts. The way her green eyes seem to always sparkle, lighting up the room.

She reaches my desk and hands the candy bar out to me.

"Thank you."

She nods. "I don't know if you eat sugar. I mean, you look really fit, so if you don't want it, I won't be offended." Her cheeks are a light shade of pink, telling of her embarrassment.

"I don't usually indulge, but I do make exceptions."

"Good to know." She takes a step back, ready to go back to her desk, but my words stop her.

"Have a seat," I find myself saying. Suddenly, I need more time with her. She does as I ask. Crossing those legs, causing her skirt to pull tight over her thighs. "You didn't break the rules." She nods. I watch as her throat bobs when she swallows. I can't help but wonder what her skin tastes like. Is it as soft as it looks?

Focus, Riggins. "With that being said, your actions, as well as those of my brothers and every employee of this organization, is a representation of this company."

"I agree with you. To some extent," she adds. "When I'm here, I am a representative of this company. My having drinks and dancing with friends, that doesn't look bad on the company or me. We didn't break the law, and nothing we did was inappropriate." She wrings her hands together in her lap. I can tell she's nervous, but her back is straight, and her shoulders are pushed back. Her green eyes are looking at me, straight on. She's standing behind what she feels is right. The boss in me is irritated. The man in me thinks it's sexy as fuck. Not that she needed to be any sexier in my eyes.

She's right. We both know it. Hell, everyone knows it. I still don't like it. "It's strongly discouraged that you not duplicate what you did on Saturday night." I'm trying to be a hardass, but I just can't seem to be when it comes to her. Not to mention that I'm spewing bullshit.

"I'll take your suggestion into consideration. Is that all, Mr. Riggins?"

I'm not one of those men who are into kink. I like sex, but I'm not really into the controlling aspect. I like for both parties to be involved. However, her calling me sir gives me all kinds of fantasies, and again, I'm relieved my desk is hiding my dick that seems to be in a constant state of arousal when it comes to my new assistant.

"Royce. Mr. Riggins is my father."

"Is that all, Royce?" she asks as she stands.

"That's all."

She nods and makes her way to the door.

"Sawyer." She stops to look at me. "Thank you for lunch and dessert." I hold up the candy bar.

"You're welcome." Her face is void of emotion as she exits my office.

Setting the Snickers on my desk, I dive back into work. I take a break on the contract I was reviewing and go straight to my emails that seem to never end. Those emails turn into half a dozen phone calls that need to be made, and before I know it, Sawyer is sticking her head into my office.

"Anything you need before I head home?"

You. "No." My reply is gruff even to my own ears. "I'll see you tomorrow," I say, my voice softer this time. I can't keep snapping at her because she's gorgeous. She waves and turns to leave.

My cell phone rings, pulling me out of my thoughts. A quick glance at the screen tells me it's Jase. I debate on answering, but he'll just keep calling back if I don't. "Some of us have to actually work for a living," I say in greeting.

"I heard that about you. Wanna know what else I heard?" he asks with amusement, and I already know what's coming.

My fucking brothers and their big mouths. "That you owe me an apology?"

"Rumor has it that you've got a new assistant."

"That's not news. You knocked up my other one, remember?"

He chuckles. "Oh, I remember," he replies, and I can practically hear his smirk through the phone. "I also heard that you're enamored with her?"

"Enamored? Who in the hell are you, and who have you been talking to?"

"My wife."

"She's not your wife yet," I remind him.

"She's carrying my baby, and it's my rock that's on her finger. She's my wife."

"Your fiancée hasn't even met her."

"No, but Gail has."

Son of a bitch. "You know that's not me. Not anymore."

"What I know is that it only takes one woman, the right woman," he adds, "to change your life."

"That's not a street I plan walking down anytime soon."

"Come on, man, you can't let her control your future. She's not worth it."

"Did you need something?" I ask, ignoring his words.

"Yes. Sam wants you to come over for dinner. Friday night."

"What time?" I might be irritated that she left, but they are two of my favorite people.

"Seven."

"What can I bring?"

"Just your sunny disposition." He sniggers.

"Fuck you," I say with zero heat, which has him laughing even louder.

"Friday. Seven. Don't be late," he says, his laughter is the last thing I hear before he ends the call.

Not able to wrap my head around work, I save the document I'm working on and close down my computer. I need food, a cold beer, and my bed. In that order.

I'M NERVOUS. I don't know what I was thinking when I accepted this invitation. I even ran it past Gail, needing to make sure I wasn't breaking any kind of unwritten rules. I'm paranoid, and she told me so. Sam technically no longer works for Riggins Enterprises, and even if she did, there is nothing wrong with dinner.

That's why I'm standing on the front porch of what I'm sure is the largest house I've ever or will ever step foot in. My hand that holds the bottle of wine is sweating, and I'm afraid I might drop it. I can do this. I can have dinner with a stranger and her husband. Besides, we've talked on the phone so much the last two weeks that I feel as though I already know her. Shoulders back, head held high, I push the doorbell.

I hear footsteps, and then the large wooden door opens, and a very attractive man is standing there. Not just any man. Jase Andrews. I open my mouth to speak, but no words come. I like sports, and I grew up watching football with my dad. Jase

Andrews was the best quarterback the professional league has seen in a long time. That is, according to my father. He retired about a couple of years ago. The league hasn't been the same. If Dad were here, I'm sure he would agree with me. Sadness washes over me. I miss them.

"Hey," Sam says, appearing next to him. I recognize her from our video chats. "Come on in." They each step back to allow me to enter. Not that they need to. The front door is massive, and we could all three easily walk through it at the same time. "This is Jase." She smiles up at him.

"Future husband," he says, offering me his hand. I quickly rub mine against my thigh before shaking his. "And this one isn't supposed to be on her feet." I watch as he bends and scoops her up in his arms. "This way," he calls out, not bothering to look back to see if I'm following them.

I push the door closed and follow their voices to a huge living room. Sam is settled on a couch that looks more like a long bed, surrounded by pillows, and next to a small table with her laptop and phone.

"Have a seat," she says, pointing to the various seating options around the room. I choose the small loveseat. "I'm so glad to finally meet you in person."

"This doesn't feel like our first in-person meeting at all." It doesn't. Sam and I have been talking multiple times a day, and she has been incredible with her training. She's made sure that I have all the little things that the guys prefer to make my job and theirs much easier. So far, the only one I've yet to really crack is Royce. He's hot and cold with me at times, and I don't understand it. The other four are friendly and pleasant all the time. Sure, they've had bad days and their irritation shows, but never at me. Royce, on the other hand, I don't know if it's me, the job, or something else entirely that has him being short and broody.

"I know. I feel like I've known you forever."

"Do you ladies need anything?" Jase asks, stepping back into the room.

"Sawyer? Would you like something to drink?" Sam offers.

"No, thank you. Do you need help with anything?" I ask her before my eyes dart to Jase.

"Nope. I ordered Italian from Sam's favorite restaurant. It's in the oven warming now."

"What are we waiting on?" she asks him.

"Oh, I wanted to give you ladies a few minutes to chat. I'm going to go set the table." He bends over the back of the couch, pressing his lips to hers, and saunters off to I assume the kitchen.

"How are things going?" Sam asks.

"Great. At least I think great." I chuckle. "Conrad, Marshall, Grant, and Owen are a breeze. They barely need me for anything. I send them daily reminders for their schedule for the next five days each morning like you suggested, and they've all thanked me for it."

"And Royce?" she asks.

"He's not as easy. One minute he's nice and friendly. The next, he's all growly CEO. Is it just me, or is that him?"

She smiles. "That's Royce. He's a complicated man, but I promise it will get easier. Don't let him intimidate you."

"I told you about how he was short with me about hanging out with the others, right? I pretty much told him he couldn't tell me what to do. I was so afraid that I was going to get fired. Gail told me not to let him walk all over me. He didn't seem to be mad that I stood up to him, more… dismissive, I guess."

"Hmm," she says.

"Hmm? What do you mean, hmm?" I watch her closely to see if her facial expression can tell me what she's thinking.

The doorbell rings, taking our conversation off course. "Jase!" Sam calls out. "Babe, there's someone at the door."

"I'll get it," he says, appearing in the doorway.

"Are you expecting someone?" she asks him.

"Yeah. I told Royce to stop by for dinner." Jase grins at his wife like his idea was the best in the history of ideas. Too bad I don't agree with him.

My shoulders tense, and my stomach flips. This was not part of the plan. To have dinner with my boss. The one who scolded me earlier this week for this type of thing. This isn't good. Not good at all. "Maybe I should go." I start to stand, and Sam holds up her hand to stop me.

"You will do no such thing. You are a guest in my home. I invited you to be here. We're friends. I don't give a rat's ass what Royce Riggins has to say about it." Her tone of voice is what I imagine her mom voice will be like. I give her a subtle nod, and she turns to look over the back at the couch at her husband. Jase smirks at her. I have to admit it would be hard for me to be mad at him with him looking at me like that either. "You." She points her finger at him. "I'll deal with you later."

"Love you, baby." He leans over the back of the couch and kisses her forehead. The doorbell chimes again, and he walks away to answer it.

"I'm so sorry, Sawyer. I'll handle Royce and my husband. You were invited here. Don't let him make this into a big deal."

I don't have time to reply before Royce and Jase are walking into the room. He's looking at Sam, which gives me time to look at him. I've only ever seen him in a suit. Even on the plane, he had on dress pants and a dress shirt. So to see this side of him, his tattoos on display, I can only come to one conclusion. Royce Riggins is by far the sexiest man I've ever laid eyes on.

And he's my boss.

He's in a pair of well-worn denim jeans, and there are rips at the knees. His T-shirt is black and tight-fitting, and the ink that adorns his arms is on full display. I've only ever seen the evidence on his hands, and this… this is so much hotter. He looks nothing like CEO Royce or even plane Royce. I cross and uncross my legs to ward off the feelings seeing him does to me. I can't be attracted to my boss. I love my new job. Sure, there has been a small amount of drama, but the actual job, I love it. I don't want to lose it. I need to get over this feeling of… lust. That's what it is. It's been too long since there was a man in my life. I need to change that. Losing this job is not happening.

"And you know Sawyer, right?" Jase asks.

I'm not looking at him, but I can hear the smirk in his voice. My eyes are trained on Royce's face as he turns and gets his first look at me, sitting on the loveseat staring at him. I want to fidget with my hands, but I hold his stare and offer him a smile. "Good to see you, Royce."

"Sawyer," he replies, his voice gruff.

"Well, dinner's ready," Jase says cheerily. "Baby, you need me to carry you?" he asks Sam.

"No. Sawyer can help me." Her irritation is evident.

"Sam—" he starts, but the look she gives him shuts him up. "All right, come on, ladies. I'll just grab everything from the kitchen. I'll meet you in the dining room."

"I'll help," Royce mumbles as he ambles along behind him.

"Sawyer, I'm so sorry. I didn't know Jase was inviting him. I promise you."

I nod, swallowing hard. "It's fine."

"It's not fine. I don't know what he's up to, but I'm going to find out."

"I should probably go," I say again, side-eyeing the door, ready to run.

"No. You're staying. You are a guest in my home. We've had this planned all week. If anyone is leaving, it's Royce. Now, give me a hand, would ya?" She holds her hand out, and carefully, I help her stand from the couch.

"How are you feeling?"

"Good. No more contractions, but I can feel my ass getting larger by the second. It's hard for me to just sit around."

I chuckle. "I doubt that, but I understand. Sitting all day has got to be hard. It will all be worth it though, right?"

"Yes." Her eyes light up. "Helping you has been a lifesaver for me. It gives me something to focus on. Not that I'm going to need to help you for much longer. You're a quick study," she says as we enter the dining room.

"What are you studying?" Jase asks.

"Royce," I blurt. Embarrassment washes over me. What is it about this guy that has me putting my foot in my mouth? "I mean Riggins Enterprises. Sam was talking about our training sessions," I quickly explain.

"She's pretty much a sponge," Sam chimes in. "Anything I tell her, she retains, and she's not going to need me much longer."

"You seem sad about that," Jase comments.

What would it be like to be with a man so in tune with my emotions?

"I am. I've enjoyed getting to know her, and the training helps the long days pass by." She turns her gaze from her husband to me. "It's a good thing we're friends. Otherwise, I'd never get to talk to you once you're done."

"I'll keep in touch," I assure her. Other than Hadley, I don't have any close friends. I worked sixty hours a week for no extra pay right out of college. That didn't leave much time for going out and socializing. The more I think about it, the more I can't believe I put up with that position for as long as I did. I guess everything happens for a reason, and it led me here. Having dinner in Jase freaking Andrews' house, becoming close friends with his fiancée, and rubbing elbows with the Riggins brothers… how is this my life?

"I appreciate you helping out," Royce speaks up.

"Now, maybe you can quit giving Jase such a hard time." Sam gives him a pointed look.

"Nope." Royce grabs the bottle of salad dressing and smothers his salad. "That's what he gets for stealing you from me."

"She's mine. She's always been mine," Jase says.

"She was mine first." Royce grins.

"Riggins," Jase growls, causing Royce to bust out in laughter. It's a deep throaty sound that I feel deep in my gut. It's a sound I've never heard from him, but one I would be happy to hear every single day.

"Enough, you two." Sam rolls her eyes, but the smile on her

lips tells me she's enjoying the show as much as I am. Well, maybe not as much as I am. I'm sure she's not rubbing her thighs together at the sound of her former-boss's laughter. That's just me.

"Thank you for having me," I tell Sam.

"I need girl time. My best friend, Carrie, moved to San Francisco over a year ago. I've missed this."

"I'm similar," I say, accepting the basket of breadsticks from her. "I have my best friend, Hadley, but she's really it. I worked so much after graduating from college, and there weren't really many opportunities to go out and be social. When I wasn't at work, I was doing things around the house or sleeping." I chuckle. "I live such a wild life."

"We need to have a girls' night. You can invite Hadley," Sam says, her eyes wide with excitement. "I'll call Jase's sister, Logan, and invite her and a few of her friends too. It'll be fun."

"No girls' night for you," Jase chimes in. "Bed rest, remember?"

She turns and sticks her tongue out at him. "Fine," she says, turning back to me. "Girls' night in, but it could still be fun. What do you say?"

"Sure. Just let me know when, and I'll call Hadley and set something up."

"Next weekend. Here. We'll have snacks and wine. Just because I can't drink doesn't mean the two of you can't. I can live through you."

"Sounds good to me. I'll call Hadley. I'm sure she's in." I busy myself eating my salad, lasagna, and breadstick. The food is delicious, and I keep the small talk going with Sam so I can avoid Royce. I feel his eyes on me, but then again, maybe that's just my imagination. I'm not brave enough to look. No matter how bad I want to. I need to just get through this dinner, thank them for having me, and slip out the door.

SHE'S AVOIDING ME. I know because I keep glancing over at her. No matter how hard I try not to, my eyes betray me and wander to her. To Sawyer. It pisses me off, and that's an issue. It shouldn't matter that she's not looking my way. I'm even more pissed at the fact that I care. I shouldn't care.

"Royce."

Turning my head to the sound of my voice, I see Sam is staring at me expectantly. "I asked how things were going in Idaho? Grant's back, I hear."

"Good. We had to do some staffing changes, but we're on the right track."

Sam nods. "We all knew that Tony was limited after the first few months. We just hoped we were wrong."

"Yeah, Scott's taking over for him, and Grant feels good about it," I reply.

"No work talk," Jase grumbles.

"Like you don't ever talk shop," Sam sasses.

"Babe, you've been cooped up in this house for weeks. You have company, and all you want to talk about is work?"

Sam grins mischievously. "Fine." She turns to look at Sawyer. "How are you doing with all that hotness around you every day?" she asks, smirking.

"Nope. Not going there, Samantha." Jase stands and starts clearing the table. "I'm not going to listen to you talk about the Riggins brothers like pieces of meat."

"Hello." I wave my hand in the air. "Riggins brother sitting right here."

"Don't you start too." Sam gives me a stern look. It's one I've seen on her many times over the years as my assistant. Usually, it's when I'm being an ass. This time I have Jase to thank. We're friends and men, so by proximity or the process of elimination, I'm grouped in with him.

"Just saying." I smirk at her, knowing that it will piss her off.

"Sawyer, grab your wine. We're on the move." I watch as Sam stands, as does Sawyer. I notice she stays back, making sure Sam doesn't need help before she follows along behind her. I also notice her ass in those jeans. Damn. I thought those skirts she wears at the office were sexy. The leggings she was wearing on the flight were hot as fuck. However, there is nothing comparable to Sawyer Gibson in a pair of tight-fitting jeans.

"Here." Jase tosses me a napkin.

"What's that for?"

"The drool. Right there." He taps the corner of his mouth.

"Fuck off." I toss the napkin back at him. "You knew she would be here."

"Yep." He grins, clearly proud of himself.

"And Sam?"

"Oh, Sam invited her."

"I get that, Einstein. Sam didn't invite me over for dinner, did she?"

"Nope." Another grin. This one makes his eyes crinkle in the corners.

"Dick move, Andrews."

"Nah, I had to see it. Between Sam singing her praises and the intel I got from your brothers this week, I had to see it for myself."

"See what?" I pretend that I have no clue what he's talking about. We both know that I'm lying.

"Avoidance. Nice." He nods.

"There is nothing to avoid. She's my new assistant because you knocked up my old one." I raise my eyebrows, daring him to argue. We both know he can't.

"Damn right, I did. That's my future wife you're talking about."

"Are you done? Don't you have dishes to do?"

"Don't go changing the subject on me, Riggins. What gives?" He crosses his arms over his chest. He might be retired from football, but he's still in game day shape.

"It looks bad on the company."

"You're full of shit." He studies me for several long minutes, and I try not to squirm. "Just admit it. You like her."

"Sure, she's nice enough." And yes, I've imagined myself between her thighs.

"What's it going to take to bring you back to the land of the living? Not all women are like Je—" he starts, but I stop him.

"Don't even say her name."

"Come on, and it's been what? Four years?"

"We are not talking about this. I should get going."

He coughs into his elbow, and I can easily make out the word pussy. He's quick to judge, but he's never walked a mile in my shoes. Having your wife cheat on you in your bed with another woman, it fucks with your head. Especially since they're now married and parents to a little girl they adopted. I try not to think about her. Instead, I block out anything that has to do with relationships and go on my merry way. I lived it, it's over, and

I've moved on. I'm not the same man I was back then. Her betrayal changed me.

"You and I both know you're not going anywhere but to the living room to see your girl."

"She's not mine."

"No? Cool. I'll fix her up with one of the guys from the team. Josh needs to find a good woman and settle down."

"You're not fucking fixing her up with Josh," I say through gritted teeth.

"That's what I thought. Come on, lover boy." He tosses the dishtowel on the counter and makes his way toward the living room. I follow along behind him, just like he knew that I would. I should leave. I'm sure this is awkward for her, especially after the fit I through earlier this week about her meeting Conrad and Marshall at the club. This is the same scenario, but this time it's me, and even though I know I should leave, I don't. I can't. Something inside me wants to soak up as much of her time and attention as I can.

Jase takes a seat on the couch next to Sam, while I take the chair. I'm sitting directly across from Sawyer. She's talking to Sam and making it her job to not look over at me. I watch as she finishes her glass of wine, and Jase quickly stands to refill it, bringing Sam a tall glass of milk when he does. The women keep talking about baby names, and a lot of other things that I tune out. It's Friday night, and I'm sitting here staring at my new assistant like the stalker that she's turning me into, and I realize there is nowhere else I'd rather be. I get to watch her freely as Jase and I sit back and pretend to be following the conversation.

"Don't you two have something else to do?" Sam asks, looking at Jase, then turning her head to look at me. "Go down and play some pool or something."

"You up for a game?" Jase asks.

"You mean, am I willing to kick your ass in a game of pool? Sure." I stand and watch as he kisses Sam on the forehead before walking toward the basement steps. I have a strong urge to do the same with Sawyer, but she's not mine. So, instead, I follow Jase down to the basement.

For the first time in my life, I'm jealous of my best friend. I've never been jealous of his fame that came from not only his talent but his career. Hell, I wasn't even jealous when he and Sam finally stopped dancing around one another and quickly fell in love. I wasn't jealous when he told me they were having a baby, but right here tonight, I'm green with envy. All because of her. *Sawyer.* Jase and I met in college. While he was hitting the gym or going to practice, me and a few of our other buddies were hanging out at a local pizza joint working on our pool game. Jase hates that I'm better than him. At least I used to be. It's been a while since I've played. I need to pull my head out of my ass and stop thinking about my assistant, who is just upstairs, or I might lose my winning streak.

"I'm gonna head out," I say, placing my pool stick on the rack a couple of hours later.

"It's like that, is it?" Jase laughs.

"What? Beating your ass three games in a row isn't enough?" He mumbles something under his breath I can't make out. That's fine, though. I don't need to know what he's saying to know he's irritated that he only won one of the four games we played. I might have even let him win that one, but I'm not telling him that.

"I need to check on Sam anyway." Turning off the lights, we head back upstairs to find the women right where we left them. Sam is smiling, holding her belly while Sawyer is standing, acting something out. "Looks like we got here just in time for a good one," Jase says, going straight to the couch and taking a seat next to Sam.

I should head home, but the smile that's lighting up Sawyer's face, the carefree look in her eyes, has me taking my spot in the chair across from her. I open my mouth to ask her what she's doing, but Sam beats me to it.

"You're killing me, Sawyer," she says, wiping her eyes.

"What did we miss?" Jase asks.

"She was just reenacting how she kicked her last boss in the balls."

My eyes widen. This is news to me. I'm irritated she didn't tell us, or if she did, Gail kept it from me, and I'm pissed off because she was in a position where she felt like kneeing the jackass in the balls was her only option. "Sawyer—" I start, and she turns to face me.

"Don't worry, Mr. Riggins, I mean, Mr. Royce, sir, your balls are safe from me." There is a slight slur to her voice, and I can't help but wonder how many glasses of wine she's had. Not to mention the fact that my balls are tight and aching for her.

"He deserved it," Sam chimes in. She's completely sober, but she's acting as though she's also had one too many.

"Babe? You been drinking?" Jase raises a brow in question, but there is a smirk tilting his lips that tells me he's just giving her a hard time.

"Jase Andrews, I should kick your ass. You know better than that." She rubs her belly affectionately.

I watch as Jase reaches over and places his hands on hers. "I'm sorry, baby, and I've only seen you like this when you've been drinking. You ladies look like you've been hitting the happy juice."

I don't comment on the fact that they only dated for a hot minute before he knocked her up. I have a feeling my opinions aren't wanted.

"That's because she's great. I miss having a girlfriend around. It's been too long, and Sawyer reminds me so much of Carrie."

"I might have had a couple of these." Sawyer raises her wineglass in the air before placing it to her lips and draining the remainder.

"I think you've had enough." My voice is gruff even to my own ears.

"Oh, the boss says I can't have anymore." She giggles, setting her glass on the table.

"Really, Samantha? Why did you let her drink that much?"

"Hey, don't blame me. You're the one that's got her worried she's going to get fired for being here. She can stay here."

"I'll take her home." I stand and hold my hand out for her. "Time to go."

"Oh, I'm not supposed to do that." She points at my outstretched hand. "Mr. Riggins says I'm his, and I'm not allowed to do this. His brother held my hand, and he was mad."

"Really?" Jase grins. "Tell us more, Sawyer," he says.

"Mr. Rig—" she starts but stops suddenly when I step around the table and slide my arm around her waist.

"Time to go."

Her body leans into mine, and I feel my world tilt on its axis, but I've not had a drop of alcohol. She stares up at me, her eyes glassy. "You smell good."

Damn this woman. "Come on, let's get you home."

"I miss this, Royce."

"What are you talking about?" I ask her. We have yet to take a single step toward the door that gets us out of here. My best friends are enjoying this moment too much for my liking.

"Plane Royce. The gentleman who helped me over my fear. He's nicer than broody CEO Royce."

"Babe, you want some popcorn?" Jase asks.

I don't pull my eyes from Sawyer, but I flip Jase the bird. His cackle tells me he got the message. "I'm the same man, Sawyer."

"Nope. Not the same." Reaching up, she rests her hand against my cheek. "I missed you."

Something inside me shifts, and I want nothing more than to kiss the hell out of her. Right here. Right now. Consequences and audience be damned.

"Sawyer, call me," Sam says, interrupting the moment.

"Girls' night," Sawyer replies.

"I'll be back to get her car tomorrow," I tell them.

"Drive safe," Sam says.

"You kids be good. Don't do anything I wouldn't do," Jase calls out.

With one arm around Sawyer and my hand on the door, I ignore him while making a mental note to buy their baby a set of drums and every other toy I can find that makes all kinds of noise. Payback's a bitch.

I manage to get us in my car, but I have no idea where she lives. "Sawyer, can you tell me where you live?"

"Nope. I'm new here." She's wasted and cute as hell, and I can't help but chuckle at her. Now that it's just the two of us, I couldn't care less if we drive around all night.

"I'll be right back." Climbing out of my car, I go to hers and don't see a purse or anything that might have her license in it. Jogging to the front door, I knock, and Jase answers. "Did Sawyer bring a purse or anything with her license? I have no idea where she lives."

"Nope," he says, popping the *p*. "Didn't see anything."

"Can you ask Sam?"

"She's already in bed."

"It's been maybe five minutes."

"She's growing my baby and gets tired easily."

I don't argue with him because what do I know about pregnant women? "Fine. I'll be back in the morning for her car."

"No rush. It's fine where it is. Drive safe," he says as he shuts the door in my face.

Jogging back to my car, I slide back behind the wheel and glance over at Sawyer. She's sound asleep. I weigh my options. I could call Conrad and have him log into the HR files to get her address. Then I would have to explain why and how I ended up with Sawyer. Not on my top list of things to do tonight. The only other option is to take her to my place. When my brothers hear about this, they are never going to let me live it down.

Glancing over at sleeping beauty, I know what I'm going to do.

My place it is.

I FEEL A flutter against my cheek and a hushed whisper telling me to wake up. My eyes slowly blink open to find Royce turned sideways in his seat, his head resting against the headrest, watching me. "There she is," he says softly as his hand pushes my hair out of my eyes.

"Where am I?"

"We're sitting in my driveway."

"Why?"

"Because you were passed out, and I didn't know where you lived."

"You could have woken me up."

"I tried, but you were out of it. You slept the entire way here."

"How long was that?"

"About twenty minutes."

"What are we doing now?" My mouth is dry, and I can hear

the slow slur to my words with my own ears.

"I was going to carry you inside."

"That's breaking the rules."

"Yeah," he agrees. His eyes stare intently into mine. "Do you want me to take you home?"

"Are you going to fire me?" What I really want to ask is if I get to sleep in his bed with him. Luckily my drunken tongue kept that question to myself.

"No, Sawyer," he replies. I love the way my name sounds on his lips, especially when he's all sweet, and his voice is low and husky.

"I can call a cab." I move to sit up. My head pounds, but I ignore it. "Where's my purse?"

"You didn't have one. I didn't see it in your car, and Jase said you didn't come with one."

"I did. It was sitting next to me on the floor in the living room."

"Of course it was," he sighs. "Are you sober enough to tell me where you live?"

"I-I don't know. I don't really know the city all that well."

"Give me your address, and we'll make it happen."

"You don't have to. I can call a cab."

"Sawyer, it's late. No way am I letting you take a cab home by yourself with you in this current condition."

"I'll pay you for gas," I say because I feel bad. I don't know how I keep getting myself in these messes. I'm going to lose this job, and then where will that leave me? In a new city, jobless and homeless once my meager savings runs out.

"You're not paying me for gas." He grabs his phone from the cupholder. "Address."

"Before we do that, I... um, I have to pee." He just grins and shakes his head. I watch as he opens his door and climbs out of the car. I watch his every step as he reaches my door and pulls it open. "Sorry," I say sheepishly and climb out.

"There is nothing for you to apologize for." With his hand on the small of my back, he leads me to the front door, and inside his house. "This way," he says softly.

This Royce, the sweet guy I met on the plane, I've missed him. "Thank you," I say when we stop outside the bathroom door. He reaches in and turns the light on for me.

"I'll wait right here." I don't wait for a reply from him before stepping into the room and closing the door. It's weird that he's out there listening, so I turn on the cold water and proceed to empty my bladder. Switching the water from cold to warm, I wash my hands and take a look at my reflection in the mirror. My eyes are glassy, but I look like me—just Sawyer. I had once hoped that the sexy man on the plane could be more to me, but fate had other plans.

"Sawyer, you okay?" Royce calls through the door.

Time to face the music, or my boss. I don't know what's gotten into me lately, but this is not who I am. I don't go getting drunk at dinner parties and end up in my boss's bathroom in his house. "Yes," I say, pulling open the door. "Thank you."

"You ready to go?"

"Yes." I nod. "Thank you, Royce."

He nods, places his hand on the small of my back, and guides me back out to his car. I want to tell him that we can stay here. That I'll curl up next to him in his bed and let his tatted arms wrap around me. That's what I want to say, but I know that I can't. He's already warned me that my behavior looks bad on the company. Besides, I'm the girl who kneed her ex-boss in the balls for coming onto me. I don't need a sexual harassment case against me. No, what I need is to get my shit together and not lose this job.

"Thank you," I say politely when he opens my door for me. He doesn't reply, just waits for me to climb back into his car and buckle in before shutting the door. The drive to my place is quiet. None of the banter like the day we met. Then again, things have changed between us. We're no longer two strangers sitting next to each other on a flight. He's my sexy new boss who I can't stop thinking about.

At least I'm consistent.

Even though I feel sluggish, I'm wide awake, so when Royce reaches for the dash and the low croon of Johnny Cash flows through the speakers, I smile, remembering our conversation about music on the plane.

"Good choice," I tell him, pointing to the radio. At least I think I am; there are two of them, so I'm not sure.

"I thought you might approve." He glances over at me, his lips tilting in a grin, and I wish I could kiss them. I wish I could feel the press of them against my own.

"This it?" he asks, pulling into the parking lot for my apartment building.

"Yes, drive around back. It's the second building." My voice is soft as I reach for the door handle, saying, "Thank you, Royce."

"I'll walk you."

"That's not necessary."

"I'll walk you up," he insists.

I don't have it in me to argue with him, and even if I did have the energy, I wouldn't want to. We spent four hours together on a plane, and somehow it feels like a piece of me is missing. I see him every day, but he's not the same person. I'm realizing his layers run deep. I want to peel back each one and observe and memorize everything about him. I wish I could say it's the wine that's making me talk this way, but it's not. It sounds crazy even to me, but that's the only way I know how to describe it.

Maybe I should look for a new job.

"You're not getting fired."

Shit. I said that out loud. "I'm sorry. I shouldn't have drunk that much. I was nervous, and it was there, and… it was wrong, and I'm sorry that you had to take care of me."

We stop outside my apartment door, and I turn to face him. He leans in close, and I move until my back hits the door. "Taking care of you isn't that bad." His eyes glance at my lips and then back to my eyes. "There are worse things in life, Sawyer."

"You like routine."

He nods. "I do." He leans in, and I lick my lips, certain he's going to kiss me. "Sleep well, Sawyer. Lock up behind me," he says softly in my ear before his lips press against my cheek. He steps away from me, and I already miss the heat of his body next to mine.

"Thank you for tonight."

He nods.

Turning, I reach for the door handle and realize I don't have my keys. "Shit."

"What's wrong?"

"My keys."

"Fuck," he mutters under his breath. "I should have thought about that. Well, it looks like we're headed back to my place."

"I can just call Hadley. She has a spare."

"Sawyer, it's late. I have a spare room you can crash in. When we wake up, I'll take you to get your car."

"I'm so sorry," I say, burying my face in my hands. "I keep messing up, and I don't know what's wrong with me. This isn't who I am. But when I get around you… it's like I lose all common sense."

"I already know you think I'm sexy." He winks.

I gape at him. "You remember that?"

"Sawyer." He pauses to make sure he has my attention. "I remember everything when it comes to you." He reaches out and offers me his hand. "Let's go."

Tired of fighting this pull he has over me, I place my hand in his and allow him to lead me back to his car.

"Wow, not at all what I was expecting," I say as he leads me into his house.

"What were you expecting?" he asks, tossing his keys on the kitchen island.

"I don't know. More of a bachelor pad, I guess."

"I'm thirty-two."

"And that means what exactly?"

"Just because I'm not married doesn't mean that I live like I did in college, in a party pad."

"No, I didn't mean that. I guess I just didn't expect it to be this clean and… homey."

"Do I look like a man who lives in filth?" he asks. There's humor in his voice.

"I should just stop while I'm ahead. It's the wine talking." Likely excuse, but I'm going with it.

"Uh-huh," he replies playfully. "Here." He hands me a bottle of water. "Drink this and take these." He holds out the other hand with two Tylenol. "I know how those headaches that could kill Clint Eastwood can be." He winks.

"Playful Royce," I say before tossing the tablets in my mouth and downing half of the bottle of water.

"Owen is the serious one."

"I don't know. I think you give him a run for his money."

"You seem to think you know my brothers and me awful well."

"I do." I nod. "I'm a quick study." I give him an overzealous grin, and he shakes his head in amusement.

"This I've gotta hear. Come on. Let's go sit down." He holds his hand out for me, and I take it without hesitation. It feels intimate to be here with him like this. I know that's not what this is, but I like being here in his space—having his attention. Well, playful and sweet Royce can give me all the attention. Broody CEO Royce can stay at the office.

He lets go of my hand and points to one end of the couch while he settles on the other. "So, tell me about my brothers and me."

"Easy. Marshall and Conrad are the lively ones of the bunch. Being the youngest, they're still sowing their wild oats, so to speak. Grant, he's a mix of the four of you. He's still in that 'I'm young and cool' stage, while he's getting older and wiser like you and Owen. He knows that there's more to life than partying all the time, but when Conrad and Marshall call him for a ride, he knows where they are because he was there not long ago himself."

"And Owen?"

"He's a thinker that one. He's not one to make a rash decision, and when he does make a decision, it's absolute."

He nods. "Four for four."

"And you." I pretend to be thinking when I already know what I'm going to say. "You have so many layers. You have the weight of the world on your shoulders, and that makes you broody. But when you let yourself relax, you become sweet and playful. Both of which I adore," I say, the wine taking over my mouth, apparently.

"You're not wrong about the weight, but it's not the world, just Riggins Enterprises."

"The guy on the plane, he's with me right now, and I've missed him." Might as well go ahead and toss it all out there.

"I'm the same man."

I shake my head and point at him. "Layers. So many layers."

"You were… refreshing." He gives me a grin. "You didn't know me for my money, or the business, I don't get that often. In fact, it's been way too long since that's happened."

"That's why you were nice to me?"

"No. Not at first. I felt bad for you. I wasn't sure what to do, but I knew I couldn't have you freaking out next to me."

"Thank you for that. You helped me so much." He nods. "And tonight. It looks like I need to add savior to the list."

"Just yours," he says softly.

"Royce." His name from my lips is just as soft. His eyes bore into mine, and I wish I knew what he was thinking. Does he want to kiss me? Is he annoyed that he had to save me again? Annoyed that his employee is in his home, in his personal space?

"Your eyes… they're mesmerizing." He leans in to get a closer look. I find myself leaning in as well. "Beautiful," he murmurs. Reaching out, his hand sweeps my bangs away from my eyes.

Any buzz I had is gone, replaced by the thickness of attraction layering between us. "Th-Thank you." I manage to force the words. My mouth is dry, and my panties are wet. He moves to frame my cheek in the palm of his hand. I lean into his warmth, wishing I could feel it, feel him everywhere.

"I should get you some clothes," he says, his voice raspy and thick.

Does he feel this? He has to, right? "Yeah." I nod. "Clothes." Should I take mine off here? "That would be nice. Thank you," I say instead.

"Follow me." He stands from his place on the couch and holds his hand out for me.

Not only does the warmth of his hand envelope mine, but his thumb… he's driving me crazy as he traces it over mine. Is he trying to drive me wild for him?

"This is my room," he explains huskily. Without letting go of my hand, he leads me to his dresser, where he pulls out a pair of sweats and a T-shirt.

Glancing down at our hands, his are covered in ink, and mine clear of design, there is such a contrast between the two, but I don't hate it. In fact, I'd be okay if he never let go. I don't know what's gotten into me. Has to be the wine. No more drinking for me for a while.

"Sawyer." My eyes snap to his. "You okay?"

I nod. "Thank you for the clothes." I reach the hand that's not locked with his out toward him.

"You tired?" he asks.

"Not anymore."

"Watch a movie with me?"

I nod. "Where can I change?"

"Here." He's quick to say. "You can change here. I'll show you to the room you're going to be sleeping in later."

"Thank you."

He gives my hand a soft squeeze. "I'll be in the living room."

He's reluctant to let go, and so am I. He finally releases my hand and disappears into the hallway, leaving me alone in his bedroom.

I glance at the huge bed with longing. I'm sure it's comfortable. The thing is massive, with its dark gray and black comforter. It looks enticing. What would it feel like to fall asleep with those inked arms wrapped around me and to wake up the same way? Realizing I'm just standing in the middle of his room fantasizing about his bed, and the two of us in it, I strip out of my jeans and blouse and slip into his sweats and T-shirt. I want to take my bra off, but I decide it's best to keep it on for now. Just a few more hours, and I can set the girls free.

Folding my discarded clothes, I place them neatly in the chair in the corner of the room. When I open the bedroom door, I'm startled to find Royce standing there, back against the wall, strong tattooed arms crossed over his chest.

Without a word, he uncrosses his arms and holds his hand out for me. Together, hand in hand, we make our way back to the living room. He sits on the couch and pulls me down next to him. Neither one of us says a word as he hits Play on the remote. Clint Eastwood fills the screen and I smile. With his hand still linked with mine, we watch the movie in silence. The warmth of his body pressed next to mine is arousing and soothing at the same time. Soothing wins out as I rest my head on his shoulder. Royce wrapping his arm around me is the last thing I remember.

IT'S JUST AFTER 3:00 a.m. I should be sound asleep by now, but I can't seem to pull myself away from her. I should be a gentleman and carry her to the guest room so she can get a good night's rest. Instead, I'm holding her on my couch. The movie ended long ago. The TV is now off, and only the glow from the moon shining in through the patio door lights the room. Not that it matters. I have her memorized. The moment we stepped off that plane, I had already committed Sawyer to memory. The beautiful woman with a fear of heights who managed to pull me under her spell in a matter of hours.

With each passing day, my concentration wanes, and my attraction to her grows. Two weeks feels like two years. I don't know why I can't shake my obsession with her. And she works for me, yet here I am holding her like she's mine. Here in the darkness of my living room, there are no eyes to judge me, to tell me that I'm close to falling off the ledge. No, here in the darkness, with her scent surrounding me, her soft skin under my palm, I don't care about any of that.

I know I should, but I don't.

She sees me. Not just the boss or the CEO, but me the man. To hear her tell me that she knows the layers I hide beneath the skin, hit me in my chest. She's not wrong. I know I've been short with her since I walked in and saw her sitting at Sam's old desk, but I have to be. She's my employee, and I can't take advantage of that. Not only that, but part of me was mad. Mad that the first woman in a hell of a long time who garnered my interest was now off-limits. That's enough to push any man to be broody, as she called it.

She moves, and I shift with her. I'm sure she's going to wake up, but the sounds of her quiet breaths tell me she's still sound asleep. We're now lying on the couch, her back to my chest, and my arms around her. It's been too long since I held a woman all night long. I didn't think I missed it. *Until now.* Then again, maybe it's just Sawyer with her green eyes and soft skin. She's the difference. Placing a kiss to the back of her head, I close my eyes and let the soft sounds of her breathing lull me to sleep.

It feels as though I've barely closed my eyes when the sun shining brightly through the door forces me to open them. It takes me a minute to realize where I am and who I'm with. Glancing down, Sawyer has her face buried in my chest and the blanket from the back of the couch covering her face. Her arms are wrapped around me and mine around her. I wait for the panic to take over. But it never comes. Instead, a slow smile pulls at my lips. I've barely slept, yet I'm wide awake and ready to tackle the day.

Gradually, I pull the cover from over her eyes so I can see her. I want to soak up this moment, one I'm sure to never have again. My hand goes to her hair. As I let the silky locks fall through my fingers, I should be worried this will wake her up, but that's not a hardship. Then I'll get to see those bright green eyes. As if thinking about them causes her to wake, her eyes flutter open.

"Hi," she says shyly, a light blush coating her cheeks.

"Morning." My voice is gruff from sleep.

She blinks a few times before her eyes widen, and she tries to scramble off the couch. "Don't go," I say, my voice gravelly.

She instantly stops moving. "I'm sorry. I didn't mean to fall asleep on you or drink that much." She pauses. "I should call Hadley to come and get me."

"No." It's sterner than I intended it to be. "I mean, I can take you. Let's go grab some breakfast, and then I'll take you to Jase's to get your car."

"You don't have to do that." This time when she tries to sit up, I let her. She stands and pulls at the hem of my T-shirt that's already hitting her just above her knees. "I'm so sorry, Royce," she whispers.

"Hey." I stand and wrap my arms around her in a hug. She feels good next to me like this is where she belongs. "There is nothing for you to apologize for. We fell asleep."

"I—" she starts, but I place my finger to her lips to stop her.

"We fell asleep, Sawyer. That's it. Now, there are spare toothbrushes under the sink. Go change, and I'll take you to breakfast, and we can get your car."

"Bossy Royce is back," she says, pulling out of my hold and making her way down the hall.

I watch her go, wearing a smile larger than I can ever remember. She brightens the day, and to have her here in my space, prancing around my house in my clothes.... Yeah, a real bright fucking day indeed.

"This place is awesome. Do you come here a lot?" Sawyer asks just as Rosie steps up to the table.

"Mornin,' Royce. 'Bout time you brought a pretty lady in with you." She turns her attention to Sawyer. "Rosie, nice to meet you. What can I get you to drink?"

"Um, orange juice and a glass of water, please."

"Comin' right up." Rosie moves to the table a few over from us and asks for their drink order.

"I guess that answers my question." Sawyer chuckles. "I take it this is your stomping ground?"

"Maybe." I shrug. "This place is a gem. Off the beaten path, so most tourists never discover it. I come here often enough. Mostly on the weekends for breakfast." Often enough is about every weekend. Rosie works the morning shift, so she and I have become quite well acquainted.

"All alone?"

Is she fishing? Or maybe just confirming what Rosie let slip? "I've never brought anyone here," I say as my phone rings. Reaching into my pocket, I see Marshall's name on the screen. I never send my brothers to voice mail, and although I'm tempted to do so now, I swipe my finger across the screen to answer. "Hello?" I ask, holding a finger up to Sawyer as I mouth "Marshall," letting her know why I took the call.

"What are you doing right now?" he asks.

"Uh, just getting breakfast, why?"

"I was thinking about taking the boat out today. You in?"

I glance across the booth at my dining partner. "Nah, got things to do today."

"What? What things? You work too much, Royce." My baby brother begins to lecture me.

"Not work."

He pauses. "What's her name?"

It's on the tip of my tongue to lie to him, but that feels wrong. Sawyer should never be the dirty little secret. "Sawyer," I admit.

"Damn it, Royce. You said you weren't working."

"I'm not. I'm having breakfast."

"Breakfast before the office does not qualify as not working."

"I'm not going to the office."

"Are you feeling all right?" he asks.

I can't stop the laughter from escaping. "Never better." That's another truth that my dear brother will think is a lie. He's not used to seeing me or hearing me this happy. Not since before the incident with Jennifer, my ex-wife.

"Where are you?" he asks again. From the sound of his voice, he's worried he might need to come and get me. I think my baby brother thinks I've lost my mind.

"I'm at Mabel's diner."

"Who are you with? Stay where you are, I'm on my way."

"Marshall."

"Royce, I mean it. Stay put."

I'm laughing so hard, I can hardly speak. "M-Marshall," I try again.

"What the hell is going on with you?" he asks, perplexed.

More laughter, and I can't seem to stop. I'm sucking in air as my laughter consumes me. "I-I'm f-fine."

Sawyer, who is smiling, scoots her glass of water across the table, and I take a long drink, trying to calm down. "I'm fine," I say now that I'm more composed. "You don't need to come and get me," I say, wiping the tears from my eyes.

"So, you're at the diner, and you're fine?" he asks slowly, for verification.

"Yes."

"Are you alone?"

"No." I wink at Sawyer. "Sawyer is with me."

"Are you working?"

"No, we're not working. We haven't been working, and we have no plans to work today." Although I normally work on Saturdays, I'd much rather try to think of ways to get her to spend the day with me.

"Let me talk to her." By the tone of his voice, he's not the least bit convinced that Sawyer is here with me.

I shrug and hand the phone to her. "Marshall wants to talk to you."

"Me?" she asks. I nod, and she takes the phone from my outstretched hand. "Hello." She's quiet while she listens. "Yes. I'm at Mabel's with Royce having breakfast." She's quiet again. "No. W-We're not working." Her voice is soft, almost fearful.

I know what's coming. I know that my brothers and Jase are never going to let me live this down, but the past two weeks, I've been driving myself insane. I want her, but I can't have her. She's all I think about, but I can't have her. Despite what I said, there are no rules against me pursuing her. However, it would be awkward, and I would need to find a new assistant if it doesn't work out. Sitting here with her, watching as she talks to my brother, convincing him I haven't lost my mind, I don't care anymore.

I want to get to know her.

Who am I kidding? I want her. But I won't go there, not until I know that this, whatever it is, can work between the two of us. That means that my brothers, Jase, Gail, my family, they're all going to find out, and I'm okay with that too.

"Umm, I don't know. I think you should ask your brother." She listens, and then she smiles. The room is brighter just by her being in it. "Sure, here he is." She hands the phone back to me as Rosie delivers our breakfast.

"Listen, our food was just delivered, so I'm going to get off here and eat," I tell Marshall.

"I don't know what's going on, but if it's what I think it is, I say go for it."

I glance over at Sawyer. "Yeah," I agree.

"Damn." He chuckles. "This is not how I expected this call to go. All right, so are you and your girl in for the lake?"

My girl. I really like the sound of that. "I don't know. Let us eat, and I'll see if Sawyer is up to it. What time are we meeting?"

"Two."

"I'll let you know."

"You better." He hangs up, muttering her name, and I grin. It's not often I can shock my brothers. I have no doubt that the others will know before I take my first bite of eggs. At least I got to shock one of them.

"Everything okay?" she asks.

I realize I'm staring off into space. "Yeah, Marshall's being pushy about the lake. We don't have to go if you don't want to."

She swallows hard and takes a sip of orange juice. "Do you want me to go?"

"Yes." I don't even think about it because I'm certain of my answer. Teasing from my brothers and best friend be damned. I want her there. With me.

"We're breaking the rules." She offers me a huge grin.

"There are no rules, Sawyer."

"No, but it's deeply frowned upon." She changes her voice to sound masculine and fails miserably.

"All right, smartass. Are you in?"

"You sure about this?"

"Yes."

"Okay. I need to get my car and shower, but I've got nothing else planned."

"Good, right?" I ask as she takes another huge bite of her pancakes.

"So good." She holds her hand over her mouth. "I'm going to have to come here more often."

Hopefully with me. Instead of speaking the words aloud, I dig into my food as well. I'm going to need my energy for a day that's sure to hold a lot of teasing from my brothers, and me trying to keep my dick from giving my true feelings for Sawyer away.

CHAPTER ELEVEN

Sawyer

ROYCE DROPPED ME off at my car over two hours ago. He insisted that he pick me up for whatever it is we're doing today. Going out on a lake, on a boat, I think is what we're doing. Honestly, when I was talking to Marshall, I was only half listening. I was waiting for broody Royce to make an appearance, but he never showed. I'm not exactly sure what's going on, but a day on the lake sounded fun. I already know that Marshall and Conrad are fun to be around, and if the boss man himself is telling me I should go, well, that sure beats sitting at home alone in a new city all weekend.

I don't know why he was so insistent that he pick me up, but I conceded. As soon as I got home, I rushed to the shower and shaved everything. I slathered on about a pound of lotion and picked out my cutest bikini. It's not too revealing but still makes me feel sexy. I throw on some cutoff jean shorts and a tank top, before deciding that I better pack a bag, just in case. I toss in a towel, some suntan lotion, another pair of shorts and a tank top, and a bra and panties. I don't know that I'll need dry clothes, but it's better to be prepared. I add a brush, a couple of hair ties, and call it good. I want to be ready for whatever I'm getting myself into today.

Pacing my small living room, I mentally go over what I've packed. If we're just lounging, maybe I should bring my Kindle? I race back to the bedroom, grab my Kindle from the nightstand, pull the charger from the wall, and spy my cell charger, and decide to grab it as well. I don't know that I'll be able to charge them on the boat or at the lake, but as I said, I don't know what I'm getting into so better to be prepared.

I startle at the knock at the door. I will my heart to slow its rapid pace as I take careful steps toward the door, giving it time to slow its tempo. Not only that, but I don't want to look too eager. Hand on the knob, I turn and pull open the door, and my breath hitches in my lungs. CEO Royce is broody and sexy. Friend Royce, in his worn jeans and T-shirt, is every woman's fantasy. Going-to-the-lake Royce, he's… mouthwatering. He's in a pair of cargo shorts and a sleeveless T-shirt. Not just any sleeveless shirt. No, this one is homemade. An old threadbare T-shirt that he's cut the sleeves off; it not only showcases his arms and the gorgeous ink but his abs. His abs have abs.

"Sawyer." My name is a growl.

Blinking hard once, twice, three times, I pull my eyes up his body to meet his eyes. "Hi," I manage to croak.

His heated gaze bores into me, and I have to shift my feet to ward off the arousal I feel from just one look. "Sawyer," he says, his voice even sounds like sex. He reaches out and traces his index finger over my shoulder, causing goose bumps to break out against my skin. He slides his hand under the strap of my bag and gently removes it from my shoulder. "I'll take this," he says huskily.

"Thank you." I manage to find my voice. "I wasn't sure what I was getting into, so I packed a towel and some different clothes."

"You're perfect," he says, letting his eyes roam over me.

There is not one single part of him that's touching me, but I feel him everywhere. "I'm all set," I say, ignoring his statement. I don't know what to say to that. Thank you? You're too kind? You're my boss, and we're breaking the rules? Yeah, I should have gone with that last one, but to be honest, I like this Royce. He reminds me of the man I met on the plane, with an added edge of sexiness. Not that he didn't give off the sexy vibe on the plane, but today he's taking that to a whole other level. I'm kinda hoping he sticks around. At least for today.

Stepping outside, I pull my door closed, making sure it's locked. When I turn to face him, he gives me a lazy smile, laces his fingers through mine and leads me to his car. I slide into the buttery soft leather seats and try not to moan. Like his brother Owen, Royce drives a car that is sexy and sleek. I don't know what model it is, but I do recognize the Jaguar emblem on the front. I guess what they say is true. You get what you pay for. I've never been in a car with the leather this soft. I was wearing jeans this morning, but now, the soft leather against my bare skin has me shifting in my seat. It feels more intimate. Then again, maybe that's just Royce, and his laidback persona, and the sexy-as-fuck clothes. Definitely the clothes.

"Your tattoos, do they have meaning?" I ask, staring at his sculpted arms, and the ink that adorns them.

"Some do, some don't."

"You and your brothers, you're not your typical businessmen," I state.

"What makes you say that?"

"The ink, for one. At least you and Grant. I don't know if the others have tattoos."

"They do. You'll see some of them today. Marshall, Owen, and Conrad all have theirs hidden, Grant and I are the only two who have gone far enough that they can be seen on a daily basis, no matter what we're wearing." He moves his arm so his hand rests on my leg. "You know you want to touch them," he teases.

More like trace them with my tongue. "You seem so… straight-laced at the office. These are a total contrast to that."

He shrugs. "I like them. Just because I have tattoos doesn't mean I'm not a professional."

"No, I didn't mean it like that. It's just… another side of you. One that at first glance, if not for the obvious ink some people would miss, the artistic, carefree side that you seem to keep locked away."

"Another layer?"

"Yeah, definitely another layer to add to my Royce Riggins list."

"Oh, you have a list?"

"Yep."

His hand wraps around my knee, and it feels like a bolt of electricity. "Let's hear it." His eyes are on the road, but they might as well be on me with the way I'm blushing right now. "We've been over this."

"I guess we have. You think you're going to see another layer today?"

"Probably."

He chuckles. "I hope you're writing these down. I'd hate for you to forget one," he teases.

"Oh, I have it right here." I hold up my phone to show him. He throws his head back in laughter. The sound fills the car, and I would give anything to be able to bottle the sound and take it home with me. I could listen to him laugh for hours. The corners of his eyes are crinkled just a bit, and his smile is not only wide but genuine. Sexy Royce just got bumped to the top of the list as my favorite.

He leaves his hand on my knee the remainder of the drive, and I open my mouth a hundred times to ask him what's going on, but close it, only to repeat the process over again. He's my boss, but there is an underlying attraction there. Has been since the day we first met. I know it's not breaking the rules, but I love my job, and I don't want this, whatever this is to interfere. Then again, if I had to choose, Royce or the job, I'd choose Royce. I can work anywhere, but I've never felt this overwhelming attraction before in my entire life.

We pull onto a long drive. "Where are we?" I ask, taking in the lush trees and the beautiful landscape that surrounds us.

"My parents' place."

"Wait." My hand goes to his arm. "I thought we were going to the lake."

"We are. They have a lake on the property."

"Are your parents going to be there?"

"They live here."

"I know but—" He pulls his car to a stop outside of a large building. "What is this, Royce?" I point to his hand on my knee, then to my chest, and then at him. "What's going on?"

He leaves the car running, thankfully, because it's a scorcher here today in Tennessee. Unbuckling his seat belt, he turns to face me. "I can't answer that, Sawyer. Not really. I know that ever since the moment I laid eyes on you, you've been all I can think about. I know that I don't like that you hung out with my brothers. I know that I like you in my car next to me, in my house, in my arms. I like it all. I know that you work for me and that complicates the hell out of things, but the way you make me feel when I'm with you...." He shakes his head, averting his gaze.

"Tell me. How do I make you feel, Royce?"

He lifts his head, and those hypnotizing eyes of his seem as though they are peering into my soul. "Alive. You make me feel alive."

"I'll start looking for a new job," I blurt.

"What? No. You're not looking for a new job. Look, let's just... spend the day out on the lake. We're friends and coworkers, right?"

"And this?" I ask, placing my hand over his.

"This is me not able to resist you, but I promise you, once we step foot out of this car, I'll be on my best behavior. We're peers, who are getting to know each other better."

I raise my eyebrows, and he laughs. "Fine, we're more than that, but today I'm going to be good for you. Who knows, by the end of the day we may be ready to kill each other. We've only ever really hung out on the plane."

"I've been with you all day today."

"Not all day. This will be good. We can test the waters, so to speak. What do you say?"

"I'm here, aren't I?"

"You'd really look for another job?"

I nod. "I feel it too, and I don't know exactly what *it* is, but I know it's like nothing I've ever felt before."

"Come on then." He gives me a boyish grin. "The lake is calling our name."

"Wait." I pull on his arm to stop him. "Who is going to be here today?"

"My brothers and us. Sometimes Mom and Dad come along, but I don't know if they are today or not."

I swallow hard. "So your entire family is here?"

"Yes, but you've met everyone but Mom and Dad."

"Royce, I should go."

"No. What you should do is climb your sexy ass out of this car. We're going to have a great day. I promise you."

"Okay. Coworkers, right? That's our plan and our story."

"Yeah, baby," he says, his voice soft. "That's our story. Now, come on, you." He reaches for his handle, and I do the same. He pops the trunk and grabs both of our bags, and reaches his hand out for mine. I shake my head, and he frowns.

"Really, Royce?" I shake my head.

"Fine," he grumbles. "This way."

I follow along behind him and into the building. As soon as we walk in, I hear voices, which sounds like a lot of people cutting up and having a good time. We walk down a short hallway and through another door that leads us to an open space and a huge boat. It's big enough for at least twenty people and nicer than anything I've ever been on.

"There they are," Marshall calls out. He jumps down off the

boat and walks toward us. He doesn't stop until he has me in a hug. "Glad you could make it."

"Let her breathe," Royce snips.

Marshall grins.

"Sawyer!" Conrad comes walking around from the other side of the boat. "Bring it in, woman." He holds his arms open wide, and only when he's close enough to hug me does Marshall step back, releasing his hold on me. "You ready for some fun in the sun?" he asks.

"Come on, we'll show you the boat." Grant swoops in and takes my hand, guiding me to the other side of the boat. "Watch your step," he says, climbing up behind me.

"Wow. This is incredible."

"You spend much time on a boat?" he asks.

"No. Not really. I mean, I've been on one but nothing like this."

"Dad's pride and joy." Grant grins.

"Other than Mom, of course," Conrad says, joining us on board.

"It's incredible."

"You ever drive a boat?" Marshall asks, climbing on board with two large bags in his hands.

"Uh, no." I laugh. "I'm not sure I should be trusted at the helm of a boat."

"Oh, come on, it's fun. I'll show you."

"Don't pressure her," comes from Owen as he climbs on, bags in hand.

"Hi, Owen," I greet him.

"Sawyer." He gives me a grin, which is not very Owen-like.

"You need anything before we head out to the lake?" Royce asks, stepping off the ladder with our bags in his hands.

"Um, I should probably use the restroom before we leave."

"We have one below deck," he assures me. "Unless you need to go now?"

"No, just thinking ahead." I laugh nervously.

"It's clean too," Marshall adds. "Mom makes sure of that."

I look around to see if maybe their parents are going to join us. "Is it just… us?" I ask hesitantly.

"Yep." Conrad smirks.

"Oh, I should let the five of you do your thing."

"No," Royce speaks up before anyone else can. "You'll have fun," he says, his tone lighter.

"You're an invited guest," Owen assures me.

"Okay. Well, what can I do to help? We could run out and get food, and I can cook," I offer.

"Food is covered, and we just brought the rest of it on board." Royce points to the bags that his brothers just carried on board.

"Okay, well, um, I don't really know what to do?"

"You have a bathing suit on under that?" Conrad points at me.

"Yes."

"That's all you need. We'll take care of the rest. Just enjoy some sun and a relaxing day on the water."

"That I can do." I move to one of the side seats and perch on the edge.

"Hey." Royce stops next to me. He bends and places his index finger under my chin, bringing my eyes to his. "Today's going to be a good day. Just relax and have fun. Oh, and try to imagine it's just the two of us." He winks.

"Yeah, not a good idea with your brothers on board." The words are out before I can stop them. His eyes smolder, and he leans in a little closer, but the spell is broken when Grant walks behind him and smacks him on the ass.

"Get moving, big brother."

"How are we getting to the lake?"

"It's just about a mile out on the property. We'll ride back here, and one of these guys will drive the truck."

"That would be me." Owen raises his hand. "These goons have

already cracked open a beer." He shakes his head, but there's no malice in his tone. "Sawyer, you're welcome to ride in the truck with me. In the air conditioning." I look up at Royce for direction, but he's looking at his phone. "Sure. Thanks, Owen."

"What?" Royce's head pops up.

"She's riding in the truck with me."

"You can ride there." Royce points to where I'm sitting.

"Yeah, but Owen offered to let me ride in the truck." I stand and glance over at Owen. It's hard to tell what he's thinking with that beard covering his face, but it doesn't hide the twinkle in his eyes. He was being nice by offering me solace in the cab of the truck with air conditioning, but he also seems thrilled to be getting under his big brother's skin. I don't see this side of Owen at the office. I smile; it's good to see him opening up.

"Ready?" he asks, reaching for my hand.

Something that sounds like a growl comes from Royce, but we both ignore him as Owen goes down the ladder first, so that he can "spot" for me. Again, I'm assuming this is another dig at his brother.

I shouldn't encourage him, or any of them really, but I'm secretly thrilled to see Royce and his reaction to me with his brothers. It's yet another layer of him. I don't know that I would go as far as calling it jealousy, but he definitely doesn't like the current situation.

"Owen." Royce's deep voice has me staring up as my feet hit the ground. "She's not yours." He points at his brother.

A thrill races through me at his words. I glance down at Owen, and this time, I see his white teeth through the beard as he grins up at his brother.

"Not yours either if I recall." He turns that grin on me, and I'm hit with those Riggins genes. He really is handsome, but he doesn't make me weak in the knees like Royce does. "Ready?" he asks.

"Yep. Let's do this." I make my way to the passenger side of the truck and climb in. I try not to let it show that Royce trying to warn his brother away from me is affecting me like it is. My insides are like a swarm of bees buzzing around. He turns me inside out without even trying.

"He's not impressed." Owen chuckles.

"No fraternizing with the employees," I remind him.

"Right," he says in an exaggerated tone. "Today is going to be a hell of a lot more fun than I originally thought." With that, he hits the button to raise the garage door, and we're driving down an old dirt road to what I assume leads us to the lake.

It's too late for me to back out now, but I'm beginning to wonder what in the hell I got myself into.

WHEN I WAS ten, and my father told us he was building a lake, I didn't think about what it was going to cost, or the logistics of getting it done. My brothers and I were pumped to be able to go fishing and to swim anytime we wanted. It never failed every time we would go to a public lake someone would end up talking Dad's head off about a business venture they wanted him to join, or asking for a loan. He decided the only way he was going to get uninterrupted time with his family was to build a lake. He wanted it big enough so we could use the boat, to ski and tube, and use the Jet Skis.

Now that I'm older, I understand the magnitude of the financial investment he made. Not that we couldn't afford it, but he and my mother gave my brothers and me our own hangout. We spent every summer out on this lake growing up. We still try to do it as often as we can now that we're older and have responsibilities. When Jennifer and I got married, this is where I wanted it to happen, but she refused. She hated the lake. Hell, she hated everything and anything that had to do with the outdoors. That should have been my first sign that we weren't meant to be.

I've never brought anyone here, just my ex, and she never went out on the boat with us. My brothers occasionally brought a girl with them, but it's usually a huge get-together, not just us. Our buddies know they have an open invitation, but as we got older, everyone started getting busier. Day jobs, wife, kids, adult responsibilities, and for the most part, it's the five of us and sometimes Mom and Dad. Not today. Today Sawyer is here.

And I can't keep my eyes off her.

"You know," Grant says from his spot next to me, "if you keep it up, this vein right here"—he taps the center of my forehead with his index finger—"might burst right open."

"Fuck off," I grumble.

"Seriously, what's up with you?" he asks, his voice suddenly serious.

"I'm fine." We both know that I'm lying.

"Want to try that again, big brother?" He smirks, taking a sip of his beer. I stay quiet, not because I want to ignore him, but I know if I start talking, that all the shit I've been holding on to is going to spew out of my mouth. "No? Okay, how about we start with why you were with her?"

"She was at Jase and Sam's last night."

"And that explains why she was with you today how?"

Here we go. "She drank too much, and I took her home. She didn't have her keys or her purse, so instead of going back to Jase's to get them, she stayed at my place."

"And you gave Marsh and Con a hard time for dancing with her." I can hear the humor in his voice.

"Nothing happened."

"Oh, I believe you. That vein in your forehead tells me that all on its own. What I'm not certain of is whether or not you wanted something to happen."

"I met her. Before her first day at the office, I met her."

He nods. "Where?" There is surprise in his tone.

"The plane." I go on to tell him how we met and how I felt something for the first time in forever.

"So, what's stopping you?"

I turn to look at him. "She works for us."

"Lame-ass excuse if you ask me. I've never seen you act this way, not even with she who shall not be named."

"It's fucking with my head."

"Don't let it."

"Yo, you two coming or what?" Marshall calls over to us. He's standing on the side of the boat. Owen and Conrad are already in the water, and Sawyer stands next to him.

"You going to let those three swim with your girl?"

My girl is standing beside my baby brother in a barely there teal bikini. Okay, so it covers her everywhere, but all that smooth exposed skin is also fucking with my head. I want to wrap her up in my arms and feel her skin against mine. I want to kiss her lips, and—I shake out of my thoughts. I can't go there.

"Count me in," Grant calls out just as Owen climbs back on the boat.

I watch as Grant runs and jumps into the lake, splashing Sawyer, making her laugh. I want those laughs. I also know me, and I can't do anything halfway. If I start something with her, I'm all in, and I don't know if that's the right thing to do.

"You not swimming?" Owen asks, running the towel over his head.

"Yeah, I'll get in eventually."

"You used to be just like them, you know?"

"What?" I turn to face him.

"You were the fun-loving brother, until Jennifer. She took the light from your eyes, and even now, four years later, she's still taking it."

"That's crazy."

"Is it? Come on, Royce. You can admit that she didn't want

anything to do with this place. In fact, there wasn't much that the two of you seemed to have in common, if anything."

"Yeah, I should have listened when you told me not to marry her," I agree.

"She just seemed… off to me. I didn't want you to get hurt."

Owen and I are closest in age. He's two years younger than me, and until my ex, he was the most serious one of all of us. He always has been. That's just his personality. "That ship has sailed," I tell him.

"Has it? She brought you down, took the light before the divorce, and she's still taking it. What's worse is you're letting her. You stopped living. I get it. What she did sucked. She fucked you over, but you had a prenup, and there were no kids involved. Did it suck? Absolutely. Should it define you and the rest of your life? No."

"What would you do, Owen? She works for us."

"You're the only one who seems to be hung up on that."

I think about that, and he's right. Even Sawyer admitted that she was willing to look for a new job to see where this might go. "I want her," I admit.

"No shit, we can all see it. The real question is, what are you going to do about it?" He nods to where Sawyer still stands on the side of the boat. She has yet to get into the water, and I can't help but wonder if she's waiting on me.

"I told her I would be on good behavior today." Owen raises his eyebrows, and I can't hold in my chuckle. "I might have held her hand on the way over here."

"Oh, big steps, brother." He smiles, scratching at his full beard. "Just relax, and whatever happens will happen."

"Relax? Do you know what that word means?"

He laughs. "I know exactly what it means. I've been in the water already, and I'm the DD, so I'm relaxing responsibly."

"I'll see what I can do," I say as I tip my beer to my lips and finish it off before tossing it into the trash. With careful steps, I make my way to the edge of the boat, to Sawyer. "You not swimming?" I ask her.

She looks up at me, and even though she has on sunglasses, I can imagine the green in her eyes bright and sparkling. "I was waiting for you."

Something tightens in my chest, and I fist my hands at my sides to keep from pulling her into my arms. "Together?" I ask her.

She holds her hand out for me, and I don't hesitate to take it as we step on the edge. "On three." She nods and removes her sunglasses, tossing them on the seat. "One. Two. Three." I count us off, and we jump in at the same time. Once we hit the water, her hand is released from mine, and I feel the disconnect. I also feel panic. I surface and open my eyes looking for her. I don't see her and feel the panic start to rise. "Where is she?" I call out to my brothers. Before they have time to answer, I feel her wrap her arms around my neck from behind, and she wraps her legs around my waist.

"Looking for me?" she asks.

"She's right behind you," Marshall replies with a shit-eating grin.

"Helpful," I mutter. Below the water, my hands grip her thighs, holding her to me.

"Is this okay?" she whispers in my ear.

I want to turn and hold her close, but this will do for now. "You tell me, Sawyer. Is this okay?"

"I don't want to let go," she confesses.

"Then, this is more than okay." I take off swimming with her wrapped around me, and her laughter fills the air. It's as if the sound reaches inside my chest and grips my heart. I let Owen's words replay in my mind, and he's right. I used to be a fun-loving guy like the rest of my brothers. Hell, even Owen has been more laidback than me today. I want to be that guy again. I'm tired of being angry, and I miss the companionship of a woman for more than just a night. I miss women in general. It's been far too long since I've allowed myself even the simplest pleasure of a hook-up.

"Cannonball!" Grant shouts as he launches himself over the side of the boat, splashing us all.

I'm ready to yell at him for it, but Sawyer lets go of me and climbs up the ladder. I'm quiet as I watch her. She disappears, and then I hear her feet slapping against the deck as she runs and, just as Grant did, launches herself off the boat. She lands close to him, water splashing up and covering his face. He coughs, obviously not prepared, and I grin.

"That's it!" Grant swims after her, but she's faster and swims to me, wrapping herself back around me. "He can't save you."

"He can," I answer for her.

Grant's smiling at the two of us. "He won't be by your side all day." He takes two fingers and points at his eyes, then points them at Sawyer. "I'm watching you, blondie," he teases.

That's how the entire day goes. We break to grill some burgers before going back in the water. It's just the boat today, but I can't help but imagine the two of us out here on the Jet Skis—anything to keep that smile on her face and keep her wrapped around me.

"Owen is going to have to drive us home," I tell Sawyer as we get back to the garage and start to unload the boat. "I had four beers." I'm kicking myself in the ass for having one, but it was damn nice to just let loose and have some fun.

"I only had one, and that was when we first hit the water. That was hours ago. We've eaten since then and everything."

"You kids have fun?" My dad's voice greets us. Turning, I find him and Mom holding hands walking into the garage.

"You two should have come with us," Owen says, greeting Mom with a hug and a kiss to her cheek.

"Oh, you kids don't want us hanging around."

"You know you're always welcome," Conrad tells her. "Besides, then Sawyer would have had another woman to talk to. She was outnumbered." My brother grins, and I feel Sawyer stiffen beside me.

Mom's eyes scan until they land on the two of us. "Sawyer." She lets go of Dad's hand and walks toward us. "I've heard so many great things about you." She steps into Sawyer's space and wraps her in a hug. "Gail, Sam, and the boys, all of them have had nothing but great things to say."

"Thanks, Mrs. Riggins."

"Oh, none of that Mrs. business. Call me Lena."

"Thank you, Lena," Sawyer corrects. "It's nice to meet you."

"This is my husband, Stanley." Mom turns and motions for Dad to join them.

"It's a pleasure." Dad offers her his hand. "You keeping these boys in line?"

"They were very well behaved," she assures our parents with a slight laugh.

"Come in and eat. I've got fried chicken and all the fixings," Mom tells us.

I chance a look at Sawyer, and she shrugs. "We'll be right in," I tell Mom. I finish helping my brothers clean up the boat, making sure we have all the trash and wet clothes. "We're headed in to change," Conrad says.

"We've got our stuff here." I hold up my bag and Sawyer's. "We'll be right in."

"Take your time." Marshall winks. "We'll cover for you."

"Jackass," I mumble, but his laugh and that of my other brothers tell me they all heard me. I wait until it's just the two of us before sliding my arms around her and pulling her into a hug. "I had such a good day with you."

"Me too. It was fun." She pulls out of the hug. "Thank you for the invite."

"Are you okay with dinner with my family?"

"Are you?" she counters.

"Yes." I don't even think about my reply. I'm always ready for more time with her. I'm in trouble with this girl. Deep, deep trouble.

"We're friends."

Reaching out, I slide my hand behind her neck and lean down, placing my forehead against hers. "I want to be more than your friend, Sawyer."

Her hands rest on my chest. "It's been a weird couple of days. Let's give it some time and make sure you still feel that way."

"I'm not going to change my mind."

"Good." Green eyes smile up at me. "Where can I change?"

"There's a bathroom through the door." I point to the door to our left. "But I can help you here, and it's just us." I let my hand slide down her bare back, nothing but the strap of her bikini top in my way of feeling her soft skin.

"Go change." She pushes away from me and removes her bag that I still have over my shoulder and saunters off to the bathroom. I swear she adds some extra sway to her hips just for my benefit, but I'm good with that. I soak up the sight of her until I can no longer see her.

Dropping my bag to the floor, I slip out of my swim trunks and pull my dry clothes out of my bag. I'm not worried about being seen. My brothers have seen it all before, and to be honest, I wouldn't be upset if Sawyer caught me. Maybe she'll be tortured the way her body on display and snuggled up to mine in the water has tortured me all day today.

"Ready?" she asks, not even five minutes later. She's in a tank top and cutoff shorts, her wet hair is up in some kind of knot on top of her head. She has no makeup on, and I love her like this. Just Sawyer. She's never looked sexier to me than she does in this moment.

"Stop looking at me like that, Riggins. Your mom has fried chicken with my name on it. Come on." She holds her hand out for me, tossing her bag over the opposite shoulder. I take her hand and lead her up to the house. She pulls free once we reach the front door, and even though I hate it, I don't pressure her. Instead, I place my hand on the small of her back and lead her into the house.

THEY HAVE A piece of my heart—all seven of them. Tonight is the first time since I lost my parents that I've felt as though I was a part of a family. Lena and Stanley welcomed me into their home, to their table, and treated me as if they've known me for years. Royce and his brothers were cutting up all through dinner, recapping our day out on the lake, and every once in a while, Royce would slide his hand under the table and give my thigh a soft, reassuring squeeze. It's almost as if this entire day has been a fairy tale.

"I hope you all saved room for dessert. I made apple pie."

"I hope you made more than one," Owen comments. Lena gives him a look that says "you know I did," and disappears into the kitchen. Not a minute later, she's back with a tray carrying two pies that smell like heaven.

"There's two more where this came from. Let me grab the ice cream."

"We love you, Momma!" Marshall calls out.

"Kiss ass," Conrad mutters.

"Come on, man, it's her apple pie with vanilla ice cream," Marshall defends.

"You doing okay?" Royce asks, leaning in and placing his lips next to my ear.

I can't stop the goose bumps that break out across my skin. He notices immediately and traces his index finger over my bare shoulder.

"Yes." I nod as if he needs to see the visual acceptance that I am indeed doing okay.

"Uh-hm." A voice clears. Royce gives me a lazy grin and a wink, making him seem so carefree before turning to face whichever of his brothers who deemed it necessary to break into our moment.

"What's up?" Royce leans back in his chair and throws his arm over the back of mine, his fingers softly caressing the bare skin of my shoulder.

This man is trying to kill me.

In front of his family.

"Dig in," his mom says, and I can only assume that she busted us… snuggling, flirting, canoodling? Is that a thing these days?

The apple pie is delicious and hit the spot after that meal and a long day out on the lake. I insist on helping Lena clean up, and she comments how nice it is to have another woman around. I'm tempted to ask her how often other women are here eating with them around their table, but I bite my tongue. It's none of my business, but I am curious.

"You two need a ride?" Owen asks.

"Nah, Sawyer only had one, and that was hours ago. She can drive us home."

Us. Home. Royce doesn't seem the least bit fazed at how that sounds.

"You're letting her drive your car?" Conrad asks.

Royce shrugs. "She's of legal age and has a driver's license."

"Yeah, but—" Conrad starts, but Owen reaches out and smacks him on the back of the head, and he closes his mouth.

I glance over at him. "What am I missing?"

"Nothing," Royce assures me. "You ready to head out?"

"Yes." I turn to face his parents. "Thank you so much for your hospitality. Today was so much fun, and the food was delicious."

"You're always welcome," Lena assures me.

"You keep those boys in line." Stanley points at me, wearing a kind smile.

"Thank you," I say again when Lena steps forward and wraps me in a hug. "It was so nice to meet you."

"All right, don't scare her off," Royce says, pulling on my hand, making his mother release me from her hold.

"I'll see you tomorrow for dinner," Royce tells his parents.

"Oh, Sawyer, are you coming tomorrow? There's always plenty," Lena offers.

"Thank you," I say politely. I assume it's some kind of family gathering. "I have a lot to do to get ready for the workweek." That sounds better than I'm not sure your son wants me here.

"Like what?" Marshall asks.

"Marshall," Lena scolds him. "You don't pry."

"She started it." Marshall winks at me, making me laugh.

"Laundry, the grocery store, cleaning my apartment, the list goes on and on."

"I can come help with all of that. You don't want to miss one of Momma's Sunday dinners."

"Yeah, that's not going to happen," Royce speaks up before I have a chance to.

I stiffen at his blatant refusal of my attendance. He notices and squeezes my hand. When I look up into his eyes, they tell me a different story. "If she needs help, I'll do it. But don't pressure her," he says, not taking his eyes off mine. "Let her make her own choice." He breaks the connection and looks over at his brothers.

"I'll see you guys tomorrow. Mom, Dad, thanks for everything."

Just like that, hand in hand, we walk toward the door, where Royce picks up both of our bags before guiding us out to his car. He doesn't let go of my hand until we reach the driver's side door. Digging into the pockets of his cargo shorts, he pulls out his keys.

"You sure you're okay with me driving? We can catch a ride with Owen."

"You sober?"

"Yes."

"Okay, then. I am too, but you had one and I had four. Even though it was hours ago, you win. You okay with that?"

"Yeah, but uh, my car is at my place, and you can't drive so…." I let the unspoken question trail off.

"So you'll stay with me."

"I can call a cab."

"You can stay with me." He places his hands on his hips like he's rearing for a fight.

"People are going to start talking."

"First of all, I don't give a fuck. Second, let them talk. All I'm worried about is how you feel. Stay with me."

"Royce," I murmur. I want to stay with him. It's crazy and irrational, but I've enjoyed my time with him. "I don't think dinner tomorrow is a good idea."

"You have that much to do?"

"No," I confess. "I just don't think it's a good idea. I don't know what this is, and I work for you, and two days ago, that was a deal breaker for you, and now it's not?" It's more of a question than a statement. I don't really know what he's thinking.

"I can't answer that, Sawyer. I wish I had the words and the answers. All I can do is be honest with you. Let's go to my place, and we can talk," he says as the door behind us slams, and the voices of his brothers filter through the night air.

"Okay."

"Okay," he agrees, leaning in and kissing my temple. Stepping back, he opens the door for me and then tosses our bags into the back seat before walking around the front and sliding into the seat next to me. "It's just a car," he says when he sees me gripping the wheel.

"A car that I'm sure costs more than I make in a year. Just a car," I add, muttering under my breath.

"It's insured. Just relax." He reaches over and places his hand on my thigh. I glance down, and the ink that adorns his fingers is a dark contrast to the ink-free skin on my legs. And very apparent I need to spend more time in the sun. The dome light in the car dims, bathing us in darkness. "Press the button, babe." He chuckles.

"Right." Placing my foot on the brake, I press the ignition button, and the engine roars to life. I turn to look at him. I can barely make out his features in the darkness of the car. "Is your seat belt on?"

"Yes, dear," he says, humor lacing his voice.

"Please, Lord, don't let me wreck this car," I mumble under my breath.

I feel his hot breath against my cheek. "Relax, I'm right here." His lips press against my neck right under my ear.

"Not helping, Royce."

"Take us home."

Home. He's different tonight. After a day with his family, he's more carefree and affectionate. Just more layers to the sexy, intriguing man that has taken over my thoughts since the moment he saved me from a panic attack on the plane. I know he's my boss, and a relationship is frowned upon—his words—but I want all of his layers. I want to peel back each one and examine them. I want to know all of him.

The drive back to his place is quiet. I'm sure he notices that my attention is on the road and not wrecking the expensive sexy beast of a car of his. Although it's quiet, it's not uncomfortable.

"Go ahead and pull into the garage," Royce says, hitting a button on the dash when we pull into his driveway. The garage door lifts, and slowly I pull inside.

"You're fine, Sawyer," he assures me. "You have plenty of room."

"I don't want to rip off a mirror," I say, concentrating on side mirrors, making sure I indeed have plenty of space.

"You're cute."

"Am I pulled up far enough?" I ask him.

"Yeah, you're good." He hits the button again, then reaches over, puts the car in Park, and hits the button to turn off the ignition. "Let me turn the light on so you can see where you're going." Quickly, he climbs out of the car, and within seconds, the garage light is turned on, and he's standing next to my door, opening it for me and offering me his hand. "Let me grab our bags." With one hand tightly clasped around mine, he opens the back door and retrieves our bags.

"I can toss these into the washer, so you have clothes that don't smell like lake water tomorrow."

"Thank you," I say as we step into the mudroom.

"This way." He leads us through the house, and down, and into his bedroom. "This house has two laundry rooms. I only ever use this one since I'm the only one who lives here. I don't have any detergent in the other one." He leads us into the closet and through a door that takes us to what has to be the largest laundry room I've ever seen.

"Is there a specific way I need to wash any of these?" he asks, unzipping my bag and pulling out my clothes.

"I can do that," I say, reaching for the bag, but he's already got it emptied and into the washing machine.

"Can they all be washed together?"

"Yes. Thank you, Royce."

His reply is a cheeky grin. "Let's get you out of those clothes, and we can toss them in too." He places our bags on the island in the laundry room and leads me back to his closet. "T-shirt," he says, pulling a random shirt off a hanger, "and how about some boxer shorts?" he asks.

"You wear boxer shorts?" I blurt the question and quickly place my hand over my mouth, horrified that the words left my mouth.

A slow, sexy grin tilts his lips. "I own boxer shorts, but I'm more of a boxer brief kind of guy. That is when I wear them."

I swallow hard. "Ar-Are you wearing them now?"

He smirks. "Nope."

"Dear God," I murmur.

His grin could light up all of downtown Nashville. "What about you?"

"M-Me?" I stammer.

"It's only fair. You know what I have on. Better yet, maybe you should show me." He taps his finger to his chin as if he's thinking about his options. "Yes, definitely show me. I'll go first."

He reaches for the waistband of his gym shorts, and I hesitate, only a margin of a second before shouting, "No!"

The sound of his deep, rich laughter surrounds us. "Get changed, beautiful. I'll wait for you out there." He points over his shoulder before he turns on his heel and leaves me to change. Alone. In his closet that is bigger than my bedroom in my apartment.

I make the world's fastest wardrobe swap, and toss my clothes into the washer before starting it. I linger in the closet, not sure of what's waiting for me when I walk out that door. The attraction is thick, and the more time I spend with him, the more I want him. I want his layers, but I also want his hands all over my body. And his mouth, and… well, you get the idea.

With that want, comes the fear of the unknown. Trusting him, letting him in, and then there is the elephant in the room. He's my boss.

"Sawyer, you okay in there?" Royce calls out.

Time to face the music. "Yes," I say, stepping out of the closet.

His eyes rake over me, and I feel naked under his gaze. "Come lie with me." He holds out his hand. I don't hesitate to take it and follow him to his bed. I open my mouth to ask if this is a good idea but quickly close it. I want him. Whatever that looks like, I'll deal with the consequences later.

CHAPTER FOURTEEN

Royce

SAWYER CLIMBS ON my bed, and the sight just about brings me to my knees. My cock is already throbbing painfully at the sight of her in my clothes, and now lying on my bed, thoughts of stripping her out of them is front and center in my mind.

"Royce?" Her voice is soft. Uncertain.

"Just admiring the view," I tell her with an easy smile. It's not entirely untrue. She's a fucking goddess lying on my black and gray comforter. She looks like she belongs there with her blonde hair splayed out.

She pats the bed next to her, and I don't waste another second, taking this opportunity to get close to her. "You got some sun." I gently touch the tip of her nose.

"I'm sure I look like Rudolph. I usually do in the summer. I don't tan that easily, hence the ghost-white legs I'm sporting."

"You have fair skin," I say, running my hand over her arm.

"Curse of being a blonde, I guess."

"Beautiful," I whisper, lifting a lock of her hair and rubbing the silky strand between my thumb and index finger.

"Careful, Riggins. That's the second time tonight you've used that word. Your sweet side is showing."

I can't help but smile at her. "I'm always sweet." I try to say it without laughing but fail miserably.

"What are you doing here?" she says, changing her voice to sound deep.

"What are you talking about, crazy girl?"

"That's what you said to me that first day. You'd just walked around the corner from the elevators and said, 'What are you doing here,' in your bossy alpha CEO voice."

"I only have one voice."

"Not true. You were brooding. Don't get me wrong. It was hot. Sexy even, but the polar opposite of the man I knew you to be."

"And now? Who am I now?" I'm almost afraid to ask, but she's not wrong. I tend to be over the top at the office, and although I never thought about it until she mentioned it, I do tend to be different things to different people. That's normal, though, right?

"Complex," she says, resting her hand against my cheek.

I place my hand over her wrist and turn my head, pressing my lips in the palm of her hand. "I was married," I blurt. She doesn't say anything. Her eyes are trained on mine as she lets me process my thoughts. "It was good, or at least I thought so until it all came crashing down around me." Her thumb smooths a line under my eye. "Our marriage wasn't perfect. She hated the lake, and pretty much everything else I enjoyed, but I loved her. I once thought that love was all you needed."

"What happened?" she asks softly.

"She complained that I worked too much. It was a constant battle with us, but I had just taken over the reins as CEO, and I thought I had something to prove. To myself, you know? I always knew it would be me who took over for Dad, and I wanted to prove to me and everyone else that he made the right decision. That I could handle being the head of Riggins Enterprises."

"She wanted more time with you."

I nod. "I thought so too, so I decided to surprise her. I left the office early and picked up dinner and some flowers. I wanted a night with my wife. I wanted to show her that she was—Anyway, I got there, and the house was quiet. I made my way upstairs to our bedroom and heard moaning." She gasps, but I keep on. "I pushed open the door and found her and her best friend, Sandra, naked in our bed. They were… let's just say there were toys and lots of things I can never unsee."

"I-I don't know what to say to that."

"Apparently, they had been sleeping together for years. Jennifer used me as her cover. She signed a prenup and thankfully left quietly. She never apologized. Her exact words were 'why are you home early?'" I shake my head, warding off the memory.

"Not to poke fun, but isn't that kind of every man's fantasy? You know two women in his bed?" There is a sparkle in her eyes, one that tells me she's trying to lighten the mood.

"No. Not this guy."

"Really?" she asks, surprised.

"I don't share, Sawyer." She swallows hard.

"No sharing. Got it."

"She crushed me. Our marriage wasn't perfect, but I loved her. At least I thought I did. Looking back, I'm not so sure. We dated in college, and marriage seemed like the logical next step."

"Did you, I mean, what about sex?"

"I hate talking about this, let alone to a beautiful woman lying in my bed." That's not just a line. I hate talking about my ex-wife, period. I hate it even more that we're doing it now. However, something tells me that this is important. I need her to understand. She's always talking about my layers, and this is one of them. I want her to have this missing piece, or layer if you will.

"We don't have to." She's quick to give me an out.

"It's okay. I want you to know." I take a minute to think about how to describe my sex life with my ex-wife. "We had sex, often, and it was good, but it was always missing that… spark. I chalked it up to being together for so long and being comfortable. They say that the new wears off, and I thought that's what happened with us. Now that I'm away from the relationship, looking back, I realize that it was never there." Not like it is here. In this moment, lying in bed next to her. The sparks are igniting between us. Her touch is like fire to my cheek, and I want to go down in flames with her.

"Spark is important," she agrees, her voice barely a whisper.

Needing to touch her, I raise my hand and rest it against her cheek. "I never felt like this with her," I confess. She's quiet, but her green eyes tell me what her words aren't. She feels it too.

"Royce?" Her voice is soft, but we're lying so close to one another she might as well be shouting.

"Yeah?"

"Will you do me a favor?"

"Anything." I mean that with all that I am. I would do anything for her. I can't explain why I feel this way. My heart beats faster when she's near, I've done nothing but think about her since the moment we met, and lying here with her next to me, nothing has ever felt this right.

"Kiss me."

Fucking finally! "My pleasure." Moving in closer, I can feel her breath as it brushes across my face. Making eye contact, I give her the chance to take it back. I wait for one, two, three heartbeats before pressing my lips to hers. Soft. So fucking soft and sweeter than anything I've ever tasted. Moving my hand from her face, I brace myself on the bed and hover over her, and our bodies are now aligned without ever breaking the kiss.

When a soft moan filters from her lips, I swallow it down. I could do this for hours. I've never reveled in the act of just kissing a woman. Not because it was going to lead to sex, but because I felt like I couldn't breathe without doing so.

Her hands grip my shirt, and I'm cursing the fact that it's in our way. I need to be closer to her, to feel the soft press of her body against mine. I settle for deepening the kiss. She meets me stroke for stroke as our tongues taste one another for the first time.

"Off," she mumbles against my lip while pulling at my shirt. "Take it off," she insists, sliding her hands under the hem. She rakes them over my abs, and I feel her touch everywhere. My cock that's already more than on board with the direction of our night twitches against the zipper in my cargo shorts.

I refuse to stop kissing her. Her lips against mine is the equivalent to taking what feels like my first deep breath in months. Years. Ever. When she gets the shirt to my neck, I brace all of my weight on one arm, letting her pull it out, and repeat the process with the other. The seconds our lips are separated induces panic inside me like I've never known.

I need her.

I crave her.

With my shirt out of the way, she places her hands on my cheeks and pulls me back to her. This time she takes control, and I'm willing to concede happily as long as she doesn't stop kissing me. She nibbles on my bottom lip before soothing the ache with her tongue and forging her mouth to mine yet again.

Heaven.

"More" is her breathy plea.

"Sawyer," I murmur her name, letting my lips trail across her cheek and down her neck. "Tell me what you want," I whisper in her ear.

"Y-You," she pants, her back arching off the bed.

"I'm right here," I assure her, kissing my way to the swell of her breasts not concealed by my shirt.

"I-Is this another—layer?"

I can't stop my chuckle. "The one that shows that I'm insanely attracted to you? Sure," I concede.

"No. The teasing. You're a tease, Royce Riggins," she says, her green eyes dark and wild with need. With pleasure.

"This is going to complicate things."

"I don't care. Let's complicate them. Make the water muddy, mix oil and vinegar, however the hell you want to state it. All I care about is that you find your way inside me. Sooner rather than later."

Fuck.

"Saying no is the right thing to do." I don't know if I'm trying to convince her or myself.

"That's where you're wrong." She runs her hands over my shoulders. "The right thing to do is to take care of this ache. The one that you've created inside me. Only you can take it away."

"We can't go back from this."

"Who says that I want to?" Her hands slide behind my head, and she pulls me back into a kiss.

Soft lips.

Hot breath.

"I need you naked," I say just as my phone rings from its spot on the nightstand. I ignore it and continue to kiss her. If there is exposed skin, my lips are there, exploring her. Tasting her.

"You should probably get that," she says when my phone stops ringing only to begin again.

Resting my forehead against hers, I take a minute to catch my breath. That's the effect she has on me. My phone stops ringing, only to ring again. "Damn it," I curse, rolling off her and reaching for my phone. "Hello," I snap.

"Royce. We have a problem," Grant says.

"What's wrong?" I'm instantly on alert.

"Tony. We have him on video going through the lot and slashing the tires on all of the rigs. He took a baseball bat to the building windows. Security was able to detain him. I don't know what the hell took them so long to allow him to do so much damage. Scott called and said that he just got there and the place is a disaster. News crews are there, and Tony is screaming wrongful termination."

"He wasn't terminated. He still fucking works for us," I seethe.

"I'll call Sawyer and have her arrange the company jet. Shit," Grant murmurs. "Does she even know how to do that yet? Maybe I should call Gail."

I turn to look at Sawyer. "Do you know how to arrange the company jet?"

She nods. "Sam gave me instructions. I have them on my phone. She said I would need the information at odd times so to keep it on me."

"No," Grant replies.

"I was asking Sawyer."

"You're still with her?"

"Yes."

"And it took you forever to answer your phone." If it is possible to hear someone smirk, it would be Grant at this moment.

"Fuck off," I grumble.

"Where do you need to go?" Sawyer asks, her phone in her hands.

"Idaho, plant 82. There's an issue. I need to get there sooner rather than later," I tell her.

Her eyes widen, but she nods and gets to work preparing the company jet. Her fingers fly across the screen before she places her phone to her ear. She climbs off the bed and moves toward the bathroom as she speaks softly into the phone.

"She's taking care of it. Are you going with me?"

"Yeah," he agrees. "I'll meet you at the airport. I'm going to call Owen on my way and let him know what's going on."

"I'll text you what time to be there."

"Thanks, and, Royce?"

"Yeah?"

"Sorry to ruin your night."

"We were just talking."

"Keep telling yourself that, brother." He laughs as the line goes dead.

Tossing my phone on the bed, I run my hands over my face and fight the urge to scream. This is part of my job as CEO—I handle this shit—but this is a first for me. It's the first time an employee has come in raging mad, and the first time that I dread leaving the office. Who am I kidding? It's not the office I don't want to leave. It's her. Sawyer.

Her hands land on my shoulders, and I lift my head. She's standing in front of me, and I can't resist wrapping my arms around her and resting my head against her belly. "I'm sorry."

"You have nothing to be sorry for. This was out of your control, and it's your job to handle whatever it is that you have to handle. It must be major for one of your brothers to call you at this hour."

I look up at her. "How did you know it was one of my brothers?"

She runs her fingers through my hair, and I pull her even closer as my legs part wider, making room to bring her into my space. "That's a layer. You have this way you speak to them. You're not as stern as you are with your employees, and you're more vocal. You don't hold back your frustration or the foul language." She smiles softly, and I swear I can feel her hands reaching into my chest and gripping my heart.

"I'm sorry that I have to go." I run my hands up the back of her thighs. "I hate that I'm losing this time with you."

"You have a job to do. I'll be here when you get back."

Acceptance. I only have my failed marriage to go off, but I've never had this kind of acceptance when it comes to my job. "Will you miss me?" I ask, my lips quirking up at the question.

"Yeah, Riggins. I'm going to miss you." She kisses the corner of my mouth, then pulls out of my hold. "The jet will be ready in an hour. You need to get packed, and I need to call a cab."

"What?" I reach out and snag her wrist, pulling her back into me. "You don't need to call a cab. You can stay here and sleep." I hate the thought of her in my bed alone, but what's worse is thinking about her leaving and going back to her place. Even though I'm not going to be here with her, I want her here.

"I can go home, Royce. I'm a big girl."

"I know, but it's late, and I would feel better knowing that you were here in my house tonight. Not out in a cab, all alone." I give her what I hope is a puppy-dog look. I've never used it on anyone but my momma.

"Fine." She rolls those beautiful green eyes, but there's a smile playing on her lips. "I'll stay."

"Good. Now, I need to grab a shower and pack."

"Anything I can do to help?"

I rake my eyes over her. "No. If you come near that shower, I'm going to be late."

"You are the boss." She smirks.

"Make yourself at home, beautiful. I'll be right out." I kiss the corner of her mouth and stand from the bed and rush to the bathroom to take the world's fastest shower. I have an hour, and the airport is only ten minutes away. The faster I get my shit handled, the more time I have with her before I need to leave.

Fifteen minutes later, I'm showered and packed. When I exit my closet, Sawyer is in my bed, under the covers. Her hair is pulled up on top of her head, and I'm two seconds from calling Grant and telling him to handle this clusterfuck on his own. "You look like you belong there," I say, and her eyes pull away from her phone to look at me.

"Sorry," she says sheepishly. "The air conditioning was a little cool." She starts to get up, but my words stop her.

"No. Stay." I take a seat on the edge of the bed. "In fact, stay as long as you want. I hope only to be gone a couple of days."

"I can't stay here. I'll lock up when I leave, but I need to go home and do laundry and grocery shop. All the things I said I needed to do earlier."

I nod. "Fair enough. I'll call you."

"Do you even have my number?"

"Yes, Sawyer, I have your number. You're my assistant." *Yet, she feels like more.*

"I was just curious. You've never used it."

"I'll call," I say again. I've not even stepped one foot outside of these walls, and I already miss her. I went on countless business trips during my marriage, and never once did I feel this way when I had to leave.

"Go. You're going to be late."

"Come here," I murmur, reaching for her. My hand slides behind her neck, and my lips press against hers. This kiss is different from all the others. It's not hurried or ignited by the chemistry between us. No, this one says I'm sorry I have to leave, and I'll miss you. Both I find to be true.

"Have a safe flight. I'm sorry I won't be there to calm you down." She smiles.

"Maybe you should come with me." As her boss, I can demand it, but I know as well as she does, I don't need her there. Grant and I can handle this, and anything we might need can be handled remotely.

"Owen, Conrad, and Marshall need me," she says, her face serious. "I can't abandon them."

"What if I need you?"

"Do you?"

I stare into her eyes, and I swear I could get lost in them. "Yeah, beautiful. I think I do." My phone rings, and I don't have to look to know that it's Grant making sure I'm on my way. "I need to go. The keys for my SUV are in the kitchen. Drive it home tomorrow. Don't call a cab."

"You're going to be late," she reminds me.

One more kiss of her sweet lips and I force myself to stand and walk away from her. By the time I'm pulling out of my garage, Grant calls again. "What?" I snap.

"You coming?"

"I'm on my way."

"Shit, I forgot you had to take Sawyer home."

"She's still at my place. She's staying tonight, and before you ask no, I don't want to talk about it. Do you have an update?"

He laughs. "Yeah, so the head of Idaho security just called." He spends the ten-minute drive catching me up to speed on what's going on, and it's a good thing. I'm not sure that if I was left to my own devices that I wouldn't have turned this car around and gone back to her.

Back to Sawyer.

MY PHONE VIBRATES from its place next to me on my desk, and a thrill races through me. I have a pretty good idea of who the message is from. Royce kept his word and called me early Sunday morning to tell me they'd arrived, and he was going to be busy "taking care of the shit storm," which were his words. He also said he'd text me later. Later ended up being late Sunday night as I was ready to fall asleep.

It's Friday, and although I haven't heard his voice since that first late-night call. The trip to Idaho took longer than they expected. They wanted to stick around and make sure everything was settled before heading home. He's been texting me every day, and I've gotten into the habit of keeping my phone out of my desk so that I don't miss him. Well, miss his texts. I already miss him. The office just isn't the same without his brooding.

My phone vibrates again, but I ignore it. I need to get this spreadsheet finished for Owen, and I'm afraid if I start down the texting rabbit hole with Royce, I'll never finish it and get out of here on time. Hadley and I are having dinner, and I don't want to be late.

I'm so engrossed in my task I don't notice Marshall standing in front of me until he clears his throat. "Oh." I look up. "I'm sorry. I was in the zone." I chuckle. "What can I do for you, Marshall?"

"You can answer your phone before you give my brother an ulcer."

"What?"

He points to my phone that buzzes with what I assume is another text message. "Royce is flipping out that he can't get a hold of you."

"I'm working."

"You work for him." He grins, crossing his arms over his chest.

"I can assure you that he doesn't need me right now. I've arranged for the jet to be ready for takeoff, and confirmed that everything is a go."

Marshall nods. "You're right, but what you didn't account for is that my brother refuses to leave until he talks to you."

"What? That's crazy. I texted him earlier, and everything was all set."

"Look at your phone, Sawyer."

Heaving a sigh, I grab my phone and swipe the screen and read his messages. I changed his contact name earlier this week. He's no longer Royce plane guy. To me, he's just Royce.

Royce: Headed to the airport.

Royce: Getting ready to board.

Royce: Sawyer?

Missed Call: Royce Riggins

I glance up at Marshall. "Three messages and a missed call. None of them appear to be urgent."

"Call him."

I roll my eyes, and his grin grows wider. Hitting Royce's contact, I place the phone to my ear. "Sawyer," Royce's greeting is rushed.

"What's wrong?"

"I didn't hear from you."

"I'm working, Riggins," I tease.

"As your boss, you should answer your messages and your phone when I call."

"I'm sorry, *boss,* what did you need?"

He sighs. "Don't be like that."

"Did you need something, *Mr. Riggins?*" He doesn't get to act a fool because I was doing my damn job.

"Fuck," he curses under his breath, but I hear him loud and clear. "What are you working on that's so important?" His tone is softer, but there is still an underlying edge to his voice.

"A project for Owen, and I want to get out of here on time tonight. Hadley and I are having dinner with Sam."

"So, I don't get to see you?" he asks, his voice low.

"I didn't know you wanted to see me." I don't bother to lower my voice, even knowing Marshall is listening to every word.

He huffs out a breath. "I want to see you."

"I have plans."

"Cancel them."

"No."

"Sawyer, it's been a damn week since I've laid eyes on you."

"And it's going to be at least another day. I'm not going to change my plans."

"Where are you going?"

"Oh, no, you don't. I'm not telling you so that the alpha CEO Royce can show up."

"Sawyer," he all but growls into the phone.

"Is that all? I really need to get this completed for Owen."

"Come to my place after." It's not a question. It's a demand.

"No."

"What do you mean, no?"

"You're a grown man. If you don't know the definition of the word no by now, we have an issue," I say, and Marshall loses it and bursts into laughter.

"Sawyer, they're waiting on me."

"I'll talk to you on Monday, Mr. Riggins," I say, and end the call.

"Holy shit, did you just hang up on him?" Marshall asks in disbelief.

"Yep," I say, popping the *p*. I place my phone face down on my desk, just like before, and go back to working on the report for Owen. Marshall is standing in front of me when his phone rings.

"Yeah?" he answers.

"I'm standing at her desk," he replies. He listens before saying, "I don't think she wants to talk to you, bro." Another pause. "Hold on." He pulls the phone away from his ear and hands it to me. "He wants to talk to you."

I take the phone from him and fight the urge to roll my eyes. Again. "Sir," I say in greeting.

"I fucking miss you." His gravelly voiced confession causes goose bumps to break out on my arms. "Please, Sawyer. Can I see you tonight?"

"There he is," I whisper.

He chuckles. "I'm sorry for being an ass. It's been a long week, and all I can think about is getting home to you."

"You should have started with that."

"So, you'll come by? Or I can come to you. Just tell me when and where."

"I'll come to you." I chance a glance at Marshall, and he's smirking. "Have a safe flight."

"I'll see you soon," he says softly, ending the call.

"How did you do it?" Marshall asks once I pass him back his phone.

"How did I do what?"

"Get my brother out of the trance he's been living in the past several years."

"Has he? Been living in a trance?"

"He's been a shell of himself, but he's coming around, and I see a lot of the old Royce in him. We have you to thank for that."

"I'm just his assistant."

"Come on, Sawyer, we both know that's not true. He was flipping the fuck out because he couldn't get a hold of you and knew he wouldn't be able to during his flight."

I don't have a reply to that, so I stay silent and simply shrug. I try to appear unaffected, when my heart is pounding in my chest, and the fluttering in my belly intensifies. I've missed him too, so damn much.

"It's okay. We're all good with it. In fact, we encourage it. You're bringing our brother back to us."

"It's frowned upon," I remind him with a wink.

Marshall throws his head back and laughs. "It's frowned upon because Royce likes his routine, but he didn't always use to be that way. He changed with his divorce. He was pissed when Jase started dating Sam because he trusted her. They were friends. We all are. Then you came along, and you flipped his world on its end."

"I don't know about that."

"I think my brother's actions today prove that. Or should we talk about you staying at his house, both with and without him?"

"It was late," I defend.

"I've heard the story," he says, nodding with a smile tilting his lips. "I also know Royce. That's not him. That's not how he operates. His home is a sacred place. He bought it after the divorce, and I've never known a woman other than family, and Sam, of course, to step foot inside his home." He taps his hands against the counter. "Let that sink in, and tell me you're just his assistant. Now, I've got work to do, and you have a project to finish so that my brother can get his Sawyer fix."

"Marshall!" I scold, laughing.

"Have a good weekend, Sawyer," he calls out, already walking down the hall toward his office.

Shaking out of my thoughts, I dive back into the report for Owen. He rarely asks for help, and I want to get this done for him, so maybe, just maybe he doesn't have to work so hard this weekend.

Two hours later, I'm hitting Send on an email to Owen. It's a few minutes before four, and I'm relieved to have that off my plate, and Owen's as well. I'm answering some emails when Conrad stops at my desk.

"Have a good weekend, Sawyer," he says with a wave.

"Thanks, Conrad, you as well."

"Oh, keep my big brother out of trouble, will you?" He smirks.

I open my mouth, but quickly shut it, only to open it again and shut it just as quickly. "He called all three of us when he couldn't reach you. Marshall gave us a report on the outcome." He winks.

I shake my head. "You Riggins boys are something else."

"I tried to warn you," Gail says, coming around the corner. I didn't even hear the elevator ding.

"You did," I agree.

"I just wanted to check on you. I haven't been up here much this week. I've been dealing with the crisis in Idaho from an HR standpoint."

"Things are going well. It's been quiet with Royce and Grant both gone."

She nods. "The office will be back to crazy next week," she assures me.

"Ladies, I'm heading out." Conrad waves at us, giving Gail's shoulder a soft squeeze before disappearing around the corner.

"So, any questions? Anything I can help with?" Gail asks me.

"Nope. I think I'm good."

"She's doing a great job," Owen says, joining us. He has his bag over his shoulder. "Thank you for the report, Sawyer. You saved me a lot of work this weekend."

"You're welcome. It's my job, and I'm happy to help."

"I'm heading home. I told Jase I'd stop by and look at some financials for him. You ladies have a good weekend." His eyes scan back to me. "You call me tonight if you need a ride."

I nod. "Thank you, I don't plan on needing a ride."

"Offer stands." He waves.

"Bye," Gail and I say at the same time.

"Well, you should head on out too. It's been one of those weeks," Gail says with a sigh.

"I have a few more emails I want to take care of, and then I'm headed out as well."

"Perfect. You're doing great, Sawyer. I'm so glad you're here." With a wave, she turns and walks back around the corner.

When I hear the elevator doors open, then close, I sit back in my chair and sigh. I love this job. I feel at home, and even when Royce is his bossy self, I still love it. I worry that whatever this is between us will cause me to have to look for a new job. However, on the flip side of that, I could have Royce as a permanent part of my life.

"Ouch," Marshall says.

I look up to find him standing beside my desk, twirling his keys around his fingers. "Whatever it is you're thinking, stop. It looks like it's physically causing you pain. It's all going to work out."

"The youngest brother yet so wise," I muse.

He chuckles. "I had to watch the four of them growing up. You learn a few things when you have five men because we can't leave out Dad, to look up to."

"I like it here."

"Good. We like you, and we all know Royce likes you." He wags his eyebrows.

"Go." I point toward the elevators. "Have a good weekend, and stay out of trouble."

"Don't do anything I wouldn't do," he sings as he walks backward toward the elevator. "Or do." He shrugs, turns on his heel, and disappears around the corner.

Shaking my head, I dive back into my emails and decide to go ahead and print each of their schedules for next week and place them on their desks for Monday morning. I'm sure to write the date and time the schedule was printed with my initials and drop them off on each of their desks. It's possible it could change. In fact, I'm sure of it, but I like for them to have a hard copy of what their week looks like. With Royce and Grant both gone, they didn't need theirs, so I grab the one from this week from their desks to toss into the shred bin and replace it with the one for next week.

Back at my desk, I shut down my computer, grab my phone and purse and head out for the weekend. It's been a long week of missing Royce, and I'm excited to see him tonight. However, first, I'm having dinner with the girls. Sam's doctor cleared her for light outings as long as she's not on her feet. It took some creative convincing for Jase—her words not mine—but he finally agreed if he was the one to drive her to the restaurant and drive her home. Originally, we were going to do it at their place, but Sam needed out of the house.

"Why do you keep checking your watch?" Hadley asks me. She's sitting next to me in a booth, while Sam and her future sister-in-law, Logan, sit across from us.

"No reason," I say.

"Nope, not buying what you're selling, girlfriend. Spill it," she says, taking a drink of sweet tea.

"Fine." I roll my eyes dramatically. "I'm meeting up with Royce after this."

"Oh." Sam leans in, placing her elbows on the table. "This is a new development. Tell me more."

I can feel the flush creeping up my neck. "We're… getting to know each other. He called and said he missed me this week. I missed him too."

"And?"

"And he wanted me to cancel tonight and I told him no. When he realized I wasn't willing to change my plans, he asked me to come to his place after."

"I knew it!" Sam smacks her hands against the table. "I knew it when I saw the way he looked at you. That man has it bad."

"It's complicated with me working for him." I don't tell them that I confessed to Royce that I was willing to find another job.

"Careful, Sawyer," Sam says, her eyes sparkling with humor. "I think it might be in the water." She rubs at her round baby bump.

"She's right," Logan chimes in. "Although, I don't think it's the water. When you have men that look like ours, it's not a hardship to have their babies."

"There are always kids at your place," Sam comments.

"Yeah, between Kacen and the rest of the band, we have our own little posse." Logan chuckles.

Our food arrives and we all dig in. I enjoy getting to know Sam better, and Logan. Hadley fits in with them, and by the time our waiter is bringing our checks, it feels as though the four of us have been best friends for years.

MY PHONE IS clutched in my hand like a lifeline. And although I know she can't reach me while we're in the air, I've checked the damn thing no less than twenty times, hell, maybe more. I've lost count.

"You know you're not going to miss any calls while we're in the air, right?" Grant smirks.

"Fuck off," I grumble. There is no heat behind my words.

"Didn't you just talk to her?" he asks.

I give him a look that tells him to back off, but he just laughs. "You're different with her."

"I'm not anything with her," I say, shoving my phone into my pocket. It's a bald-faced lie, and we both know it. The problem is that I want to be everything with her. I don't give a fuck that she's my employee, or that I barely know her. I want her—more than I've ever wanted anyone. I've never felt this intense connection I seem to have with her. Not even with my ex, and that fucks with my head. I thought I knew Jennifer. I thought I loved her, and I was wrong. What if I'm wrong about Sawyer too?

"Let me ask you this. How often do you think about her? Why were you so insistent that you talk to her before we took off? Why have you checked your phone a hundred times in the last hour knowing damn well nothing is going to come through while we're in the air?"

I don't even have to think about my answers, but I don't give them to him. Not that I need to. I'm sure he can see it written all over my face. "I'm not the best judge when it comes to women," I say, surprising him if the look on his face is any indication.

"Jennifer deceived you, Royce. She had us all fooled."

"I should have known better. She hated everything I loved. Hell, she never once went out on the boat with us, or even just with me. Sawyer, she's all in, and it's fucking with my head."

"I don't think it's your head that's the problem."

I glare at him. "Leave my cock out of this."

"I meant your heart, but now that you mentioned it, I'm sure Royce junior is just as affected as the old ticker. Sawyer's beautiful."

"Grant," I growl, and he chuckles. It's a low and deep sound, much like my own, but in this moment, it's grating on my nerves.

"See what I mean? You know I've got your back, I'd never do that to you, but you can't even stand to hear me tell you that your girl is beautiful."

"She's not mine." She's not, but that doesn't mean I don't want her to be.

"Why the hell not?"

I open my mouth to reply and stop. I can only think of one reason. Fear. I'm not afraid of her, but of my judgment. I thought Jennifer was the one, and I was only living a lie. I never felt like this for my ex-wife—cagey needing to hear her voice. If I'm wrong about Sawyer, I know I'll never recover. I'm a shell of the man I used to be, and losing her would be the equivalent of losing all of me.

"Sawyer is a catch, Royce. Are you willing to step back and let another man stake a claim? How are you going to feel when you've missed your chance? How are you going to handle someone keeping her bed warm at night?"

"Enough," I growl.

"There it is." He grins.

"What the fuck are you talking about?"

"That determination I see written all over your face."

"You don't know what you're talking about."

"Tell me that the thought of her with someone else doesn't piss you off. Tell me it doesn't have you seeing red."

I run my fingers through my hair. "You know it does."

"Then do something about it." Grant gives me a pointed look. "You are the only one who can take that step. She's not going to. You need to tell her what you want."

"I want her, damn it. Are you happy? I want her more than my next breath," I say, sucking in a lungful of air and slowly exhaling.

"Then make it happen. You're ruthless when it comes to your job. Why should you not be any other way when it comes to all aspects of your life? You take charge, that's who you are. You let the lies and deceit of one woman steal your happiness. You realize that, don't you? She didn't just destroy your marriage. She's still controlling your life. She's not your wife, but you hang on to her betrayal, and you're not living. What happened to the man who wanted to be a husband and father? Hell, we've all said we hope to be half the man our father is. Yet, here you are, letting her take that from you."

"If you could buckle in." The flight attendant appears before us. "We're preparing to land."

With a nod, Grant and I secure our belts. I hate to admit it, but he's right. I've let Jennifer's betrayal shape my future. I'm letting her keep me from going after what I want. I'm letting her keep me from Sawyer. Now it's up to me to decide what I'm going to do about it.

I'm pacing. I called Sawyer as soon as the plane landed. She didn't answer so I texted her. I've read her reply to that text a hundred times in the last two hours.

Sawyer: Dinner with the girls. I'll stop by when we're done.

That's it. She didn't give me a time, or tell me where she was. No, all I have is that she's coming here when she's finished hanging out with her friends. Hence the pacing. I've showered and caught up on a few emails, but I can't really focus. I'm too amped up to see her. It's been too long since I've laid eyes on her. I've never missed someone like this. I went away for college, just to Ohio. I missed my family, but not like this.

It didn't feel like there was a knot in my stomach, and with each minute that passes, it gets tighter and tighter. Being away from my family didn't feel like that.

Nothing ever has.

My phone that's gripped tightly in my hand rings, and I fumble to answer it. "Hello."

"Hey. We're heading to Mom and Dad's for a bonfire, you in?" Conrad asks.

"No."

"Whoa, who pissed in your cornflakes this morning?"

"Sorry," I say, running my fingers through my hair. "I'm waiting on Sawyer."

"Bring her with you."

"I haven't seen her in a week."

"And?" I can tell by the tone of his voice he's enjoying this way too much.

"And, no. I'll catch you guys for Sunday dinner." Maybe. Depends on if I can convince my girl to go with me. After going without her for a week, I know without a doubt it's going to be hard to leave her side for the foreseeable future.

"Maybe I'll call Sawyer and invite her, and then you'll have to come if your girl says she wants to go."

"She's not my girl," I say as there's a knock at the door. "I gotta go." Ending the call, I toss my phone on the couch and take a deep breath. I can't attack her as soon as I see her. She's going to go running for the hills. I make my way to the door and pull it open, but she has her phone to her ear. Her green eyes sparkle from the porch light, and she waves at me.

"I don't know. I just got here. Let me see what he wants to do. Are you sure I won't be imposing?" she asks.

"Is that Conrad?" I ask her. She nods. I reach out and take the phone from her. I hit End Call and slide it into my back pocket.

"Hey." She smacks at my chest, and I place my hand over hers, keeping it held over my heart. "I was talking."

"I already told him no, right before you knocked on my door," I tell her as I take a step back. I don't let go of her hand, so she has no choice but to follow me. I push the door shut and then step forward, causing her back to press against it. Bracing one hand on the door, I remove the other from hers that's still pressing against my chest and cradle her cheek in my palm. "I fucking missed you," I say, bending and lightly pressing my lips to hers.

"Hi," I say softly, pressing my forehead to hers.

"That was a nice hello," she replies. "But that wasn't nice to hang up on your brother."

"I needed to kiss you."

"Well, now that you have, do you want to go?"

I start to say no because what I really want is to have her all to myself, but it hits me that my ex never wanted to spend time with my family. A bonfire to her would have been the equivalent of a root canal. "What do you want to do?" I pull away so I can get a good look at her.

She shrugs. "It sounds like fun."

"Fun, huh?" I drop my hand from the door and settle my hands on her hips. "How about this? We can go on one condition."

"What's that?" she asks suspiciously.

"You stay here tonight. I've gone an entire week without you, and I can't go another night."

"You've lived thirty-two years without me, Riggins."

"I know, baby. Trust me, I know. So, do we have a deal?"

"I don't know," she muses. "I might need more convincing."

Bending, I place my hands on the back of her legs and lift her. Instinctively, she wraps her legs around my waist and her arms around my neck, and we're moving. I carry her further into the house until we reach the living room. I drop to the couch, with her still wrapped around me. She wiggles, grinding against my cock that's already begging for her.

"You keep moving around like that, and the deal is off," I growl against her lips before kissing her hard. It's sloppy and uncontrolled, exactly how she makes me feel. Nothing in my life has been routine since that day on the plane, and I'm finding I don't care. Not as long as I get her like this.

Bracing her hands on my shoulders, she pulls out of the kiss. "I-I can't think when you kiss me like that."

"Good." I lean toward her, and she laughs, placing her hand over my mouth.

"Behave," she playfully scolds me before dropping her hand.

"I don't ever want to go that long without seeing you ever again," I confess.

"Good thing I work for you." She winks.

"This is more than that. You know that, right?" This conversation is long overdue.

She shakes her head. "I don't know what this is, or who we are to one another. What I do know is that your kisses set my body on fire, and I know that I missed you too," she says softly. Her hand rises to rest against my cheek. "More than I thought possible."

"We're staying in," I say just as my phone rings.

"You better get that. They're just going to keep calling." She chuckles.

"Cockblocker," I answer.

Marshall's laughter carries through the line. "You bringing your girl or what?" he asks.

I raise my eyebrows at Sawyer, and she nods. "Yeah, we're on our way." I didn't really want to go, but she seems excited, and as long as I get to spend time with her, I'm all in. I end the call without correcting him—telling him she's not my girl. I want her to be, and seeing her tonight, after being away from her for so long, solidified that decision for me. I don't know how this is going to end, but I know that I don't want it to. I want her. I don't care that it could get all kinds of complicated if this doesn't work, but if I'm being honest, I can't see a situation that we can't work out. I can't see me ever letting her go.

"You ready to go now?" I ask her.

"Yes." She drops a kiss to my lips and climbs off my lap.

My cock is throbbing, and I don't hide the fact. A blush coats her cheek when her eyes land on my lap. "Umm." Green eyes meet mine.

"All you," I say, adjusting myself before standing. "Let me grab a couple of things, and we'll be ready to go." I dart off to my room and grab her a sweatshirt. It's summer but sometimes the night air can get chilly by the water. I also grab a blanket from the hall closet, just in case.

"What's all that?" she asks as I meet her in the kitchen.

"Just in case." I place a kiss on her lips. "We're going to take my truck."

"You have a truck?"

"I'm a country boy. Of course, I have a truck."

"Country boy? You're in a suit and tie on the daily, Riggins."

"That's *work* me, and I was raised loving the outdoors. You can't live in Tennessee and not have some country boy running through your veins." I snag my arm around her waist. "Just another layer, baby." She grins, and I would do anything to keep that smile on her face.

"Show me the beast," she says, pulling out of my arms.

"What makes you think it's a beast?"

"You don't do anything halfway, Royce Riggins."

"Nope." She's right. "Come on." With her hand locked in mine, I lead her out of the house to the attached garage, out the side door, and to the external garage. My truck is a long bed and doesn't fit in the house garage. Not to mention my car and SUV are parked there.

"Not as bad as I thought," Sawyer says when I open the back door of my truck, tossing the sweatshirt and blanket inside.

I chuckle. "I'm glad that you approve. Let me help you up." I open the passenger door for her, and before she can protest, I have my hands on her hips, lifting her into the truck. "Buckle up, baby."

As soon as I'm behind the wheel and we're on the road, I reach over, take her hand, and lace my fingers with hers. I'm inwardly cursing that I didn't buy a bench seat. Regardless, my hands are on her, and that's enough to calm the raging storm that was coursing through me earlier tonight.

"You sure this is okay?" she asks when I park next to Grant's truck at the lake.

"Yes."

"What are they going to think? I mean, if they ask me, what do I say? About us?"

The cab of the truck is dark. Nothing but the light of the fire behind us offering a dim glow. Turning in my seat, I place my palm against her cheek. "You tell them that it's none of their business. You tell them that you're mine."

"Am I yours?"

"Yes."

"Royce, there are so many things—" she starts, but I lean in a little closer and press my lips to her to stop her.

"We'll figure it out. I want you to be mine, Sawyer."

"Does that mean you're mine?" she counters.

That twisting feeling is back; only this time, it's my heart that feels constricted at her question. "Yeah, baby. I'm all yours," I assure her with another kiss to her lips. "Now, let me show you what it's like when you get all five Riggins brothers together for a bonfire and a few beers."

"How are they getting home?"

"They'll stay at Mom and Dad's, or Owen will drive them home."

"He doesn't drink?"

"Very rarely. He likes control, and he can't have that when he drinks." I watch her closely, waiting for more questions.

"They're going to come knocking," she says.

"You know them too well." One more kiss and I reach for the door. "I'll come get you down."

"I can manage."

"Don't care. I want my hands on you." I give her a look that tells her to stay put and hop out of the truck.

She listens, and with my hands on her waist, I lift her from the truck. I don't set her on her feet until I've kissed her sweet lips once more. Hand in hand, we make our way to the back of the truck, and over to the bonfire my brothers are sitting around.

FOUR SETS OF eyes turn to look at us, and I grip Royce's hand tighter. I should be doing the opposite, letting him go under their stare, but I don't want to lose my connection to him.

"'Bout time you got here," Marshall calls out.

"Wow, this is not what I expected." My eyes widen in surprise.

Royce stops and gives me his full attention. "We can go," he says softly, just for me.

"No, that's not what I meant. You said bonfire, and I imagined a big fire in the middle of a field."

"That's what this is."

"No, this is stunning. An actual stone fire pit, Adirondack chairs, pebbled rock all the way around, picnic tables, this is more… fancy than I pictured."

He smiles down at me, pushing my hair out of my eyes. "That's all Mom. She comes down here sometimes. A few years ago, we decided to have a fire after several days of rain, and it was a muddy mess, Mom got on the phone the next day, and this was the result. We can come here no matter if it's muddy and not be slopping around in it. Of course, there's the walk from the truck, but we can all back in and get close enough that it's just a few steps.

"It's amazing."

"Thank you," he replies, softly pressing a kiss to my forehead. Whistles and catcalls fill the night air, and I'm glad for the dark of night so they can't see my blush. "You did that in front of your brothers," I whisper, mortified.

"I'm not hiding you, hiding us from them. We're in this, right?"

I stare up at him, and there is no way I can deny him, not when my mind, my body, and my heart are all screaming yes. I nod, unable to speak over the lump in my throat. I don't know what this means for my job, but right now, with his arm over my shoulders as we walk closer to the fire, I can't seem to find it in me to care.

"Sawyer, you can sit with me." Conrad pats his lap, and Royce growls, causing a chorus of laughter to fill the night.

Royce leads us to an empty chair. He sits and pulls me down onto his lap.

"This is new," Owen comments.

"This is official," Royce replies.

Marshall whistles. "That's big, brother."

Grant holds his bottle of beer up in salute before taking a big swig. "Good to see you pulled your head out of your ass," he says, his eyes locked on Royce.

I can feel Royce nod from behind me. His arms wrap around my waist as he pulls me closer. With the slant of the chair, it leaves me leaning against his chest. "Mom and Dad coming?" Royce asks, continuing to hold me like this in front of his brothers like it's no big deal.

"Nah, Mom said they were calling it an early night," Owen tells him.

"Ack," Marshall says like he has a bad taste in his mouth. "We all know what that means," he says with a sour look on his face.

"Hey, just you wait. When you're their age, you're going to only hope that you have their—" Grants stops there. "Yeah, never mind." He shudders.

"How in the hell do you think we all got here?" Owen asks with a laugh.

"No. No, no." Conrad holds his hand up. "We're not going there."

"Con," Owen says.

Conrad turns to look at him. "Our parents have sex, and by the fact that the five of us are sitting here tonight, they have a lot of sex," he says with a straight face, but the white of his teeth is showing from behind his beard.

"Ah, man, you had to go there." Conrad stands up, tosses his empty beer bottle into a tote, and grabs a new one from the cooler.

"Good for Dad," Royce says.

"Not you too," Marshall grumbles, and I can't help the giggle that escapes me.

"Laugh it up, Sawyer," Grant tells me. "Don't think your parents don't still do the deed." He smirks.

"Fuck," Royce hisses.

"I lost my parents a few years ago," I tell the four sets of eyes watching me, aware the mood suddenly shifts. "You might not want to think about them doing… that, but I promise you you'll miss even these conversations when they're gone." My intention isn't to put a downer on the evening, but my words are honest.

"Fuck, sis." Owen stands, and before I know what's happening, I'm pulled to my feet even with Royce's protest, and Owen wraps me in a hug.

Hot tears prick my eyes at his comfort. All too soon, he's pulling away, and I'm thrust into the arms of yet another Riggins brother. Grant passes me to Marshall, who passes me to Conrad, and finally there waiting for me is Royce. The five of them passed me around to hug after hug, and some of the shattered pieces of my heart from the loss of my parents piece themselves back together. They've opened their arms and their family to me. I wish

I could find the words to tell them what that means to me. What *they* mean to me.

"Let's take a walk." With his arm around me, we walk away from his brothers. "I'm sorry, Sawyer."

"Why are you apologizing? They didn't know. They didn't offend me. It's just hard to talk about sometimes, but your brothers… they're amazing."

"I just hate the thought of you in pain. I hate I wasn't there for you."

"You didn't even know me then."

"I didn't say it made sense," he says, pulling me in close and pressing his lips to my temple.

"Where are we going?" I ask as we get further away from the fire, and the voices of his brothers.

"I just wanted some time with you."

"Are we going to get eaten by a wolf?" I ask when I hear howling off in the distance.

"Not a wolf, probably a coyote, and no, you're safe with me."

"What about bears? There are bears in Tennessee, right?" I ask, my eyes scanning our surroundings, but with nothing but the moonlight to offer me assistance, I don't see a thing.

"Yes, there are bears, but we've only seen them a few times on our property. I think we make too much noise for their liking."

"We should go back," I say, already worried.

"We're here," he says, holding me close, not letting me slip away from him and run back to the fire.

"Where's here?" I ask, looking up at him.

"Here." He points out in front of us, and I gasp at the beauty of it. There's a long dock that leads to what appears to be a gazebo floating in the middle of the water. There are strings of lights all around lighting the gazebo.

"Is it floating?"

"Nah, appears that way, though. That's how Dad planned it. It's kind of like an island, I guess. More of a peninsula."

"Wow."

"Come on." He drops his arm from my shoulders and laces our fingers together as we walk toward the gazebo.

"How are these lights working?" I ask, and then immediately apologize. "I'm sorry. I'm asking so many questions."

"Don't apologize. I'm glad. This place means a lot to me and my family. There's a small solar panel on the top of the gazebo that powers the lights."

"That's so cool." My eyes take in the beauty of the lights softly shimmering off the lake, and the peacefulness of the water. It's breathtaking.

"I agree," he says, pulling me into his chest. "Dance with me."

"What?" I laugh. "There's no music."

"We don't need it. Just our bodies aligned, and we can make our own music," he says, surprising me but dipping me over his arm, placing a kiss on my lips. Sweet Royce has my heart pounding in my chest, and I know that tonight, this moment is one I will never forget.

"Oh, playful Royce," I say, laughing as he lifts me upright.

"Your Royce," he murmurs, his lips molding with mine.

My hands slide around his neck and I stand on my tiptoes to reach him, but he saves me the trouble when he lifts me in the air, and I wrap myself around him like a monkey. "So much better," I say, placing a kiss on his neck.

"I'm not willing to leave this to chance, this connection we have. I know that talking is going to kill the mood, but my marriage ended because she hid truths from me, truths that would have prevented our nuptials altogether. I want us to always be open and honest with one another."

"I'm listening," I say, lifting my head. His mouth is so close to mine. I crave his lips on mine, but I know this is important to him.

"I don't share, Sawyer. When I say you're mine, and I'm yours, I mean that with all that I am. I know there are a lot of uncertainties, and you're worried about the fact that you work for me, but we can figure that all out as we go. I'm committed to this, to you, whatever that might be."

"We're us," I murmur, fighting back the tears that are welling in my eyes. Sweet Royce is almost too much for my poor heart to handle. His words cause my body to ache for his, while my heart swells in my chest.

"We're us," he agrees. His lips press softly to mine as he sways slightly with me still in his arms. His hands grip my ass, and my hands are buried in his hair. The kiss is slow, sensual, with nothing but the sounds of the night surrounding us. Gentle and slow, his lips tease mine. Stroke after stroke of his tongue against my own, and I'm on fire for him.

"I want you," he murmurs, peppering kisses across my cheek and down my neck.

I tilt my head back, giving him more access. "Y-You have me," I tell him, chills racing down my spine as his lips connect with my collarbone.

"Not here. Not the first time."

"You love this place."

He nods. "You deserve better."

"No. I deserve the best of us. We get to decide what that looks like."

"Tell me what you want, Sawyer."

"I want this ache that you've caused to go away. It's been there since the day we met."

"We need to go," he says, turning, but my words stop him.

"What do you want, Royce?"

"I want this ache that you've caused to go away." He pulls me down against his hard length, and I can't help but wiggle my hips. "It's been there since the day we met."

I look down at the hardwood of the gazebo. "Too bad we don't have that blanket," I muse.

"Wait." He carries me to the built-in bench and sets me there. He walks to the other side and lifts the bench seat. "I've never used these, so I forgot they were here. Mom likes to have blankets out here for the chilly nights. She had Dad install the waterproof box so they would stay safe from the elements and the critters." He pulls out a thick quilt and grins. "Don't worry, she washes them frequently." He shrugs before laying it out on the floor of the gazebo. He then reaches in and pulls out another blanket.

"I don't think we need that. It's still pretty warm."

"Yeah, but I'm not risking us getting caught and someone seeing you."

"Will we? Get caught, I mean?"

"No. There is no one out here but my brothers, and it would need to be an emergency before they would come after us, and they'd call first."

"You sure?"

"Positive. I wouldn't risk you like that." He holds his hand out for me, and I go to him without a second thought. "You sure?" he asks.

I don't reply. Instead, I reach for the hem of his shirt and push up until I've pulled it over his head and drop it to the wood floor beneath us. Dropping to my knees, I work at the button of his shorts and pull them down his legs. He toes off his shoes and kicks his shorts to the side.

"You're wearing too many clothes, babe." He gives me a tender smile that I feel all the way to my soul.

I lift my arms in the air, giving him the invitation to undress me. He takes his time, letting his fingers trail over my sides before he has my tank off, and he's tossing it to the pile of clothes. He leads me to the bench and places his hands under my arms, lifting me so that I'm standing before him.

"Much better," he murmurs. His fingers deftly unbutton my shorts, and with a gentle tug, they fall around my ankles. "Hands on my shoulders." I do as he asks. "Lift." He taps first my left leg, then my right as he removes my flip-flops and my shorts. "Fucking perfect," he says, leaning in and kissing me through my panties. His hands are everywhere, my thighs, my hips, the small of my back. He cups each of my breasts that are still covered with my black lace bra, testing their weight in the palm of his hands.

"Royce," I breathe his name.

His hands slide around my back, and he unhooks my bra. Slowly, painfully so, he slides the strap over each shoulder before pulling away from my body. "Jesus," he whispers, just as his mouth captures one hard nipple while his hand seduces the other.

"Royce." All I can do is say his name, well, unless you count the grip my hands have on his hair holding him to me. His mouth… it's magical.

His lips trail over my stomach, and my body quivers at the contact. "You cold, baby?" he asks, not bothering to stop the pursuit of his lips and tongue against my skin.

"Y-You know I'm not."

"These are sexy as fuck," he says when he reaches my panties.

"They'd look better on the pile of clothes over there." I nod in the direction I think our clothes are. I don't really know and don't care at the moment. I just need to feel all of him against all of me.

"I think I'll keep these," he says, sliding his index fingers under the waistband of my panties and tugging them over my thighs and down my legs.

I don't wait for him to tell me to lift my legs. I kick them to the side and jump off the bench I've been standing on.

"I wasn't done with you."

"Get naked, Riggins," I say, standing stark naked with my hands on my hips. I've never been this vocal with a man about what I want. However, with Royce, he makes me feel safe and protected.

"You're so sexy." He reaches for me, but I step out of his reach.

"Now. I need you naked now."

He chuckles but makes quick work of removing his boxer briefs.

"Finally," I mumble, settling on the quilt he has spread out for us. "You coming, Riggins? Or is this going to be a party for one?"

"Not a chance of that," he says, bending to grab his wallet from his shorts. I watch as he pulls out a small foil packet, and then takes his spot next to me, pulling the second quilt over us. He props himself up on his elbow, letting his free hand roam over my body. "I can't tell you how many times I've imagined touching you."

"Less talking more touching," I say, desperate to have his hands all over my body.

"Oh no, I need time. These hands need to roam over every curve, memorize every inch of your flawless skin."

"There'll be time for that later."

"I'm not rushing this, Sawyer."

"Another layer," I mutter under my breath, making him laugh.

"You think so?"

"Yeah, teasing Royce."

"Your Royce," he immediately replies, and a swarm of butterflies take flight inside me.

I place my hand on his cheek. I don't say anything, but I don't need to. I know that the need and desire that I see in his eyes are staring back at him. We both want this with a need that's indescribable.

"Make love to me." It's a bold move, especially since I used love, but that's what this feels like. It's intimate and personal, and it's too late to take the words back, not that I want to. I just hope it's not too much.

By the look in his eyes, he's on board.

THERE IS A slight tremble in my hands that I hope she doesn't detect. I want to touch her everywhere, taste her everywhere, but my girl asked me to make love to her, and although I don't know if this is love, I can't deny her anything. Besides, I'm all about taking things slow. I want to savor this time with her.

My hand roams over her stomach, not stopping my exploration until I reach her pussy. I slide two fingers through her folds, and she moans, a sound from deep within her chest. "You're wet for me."

"Please," she murmurs, lifting her hips.

"I need you ready for me, babe. I don't want to hurt you."

"I can take it. Just… take this ache away, Royce. I need you. All of you. Right now." Sawyer's words are choppy as I slide one digit inside her.

"Oh, God."

"Royce," I correct her. I only want her screaming my name.

Her eyes fly open, and the corner of her mouth tips up to one side. "Royce," she says, almost on a moan.

My cock twitches where it rests against her thigh. She reaches for me. Her small hands stroke lightly, as she tests the feel of me in her palm. I'm not a saint. I've slept with more women than I care to admit, but never in my life have I felt this… magnetism that seems to flow between us. My cock grows harder at her touch, so much so that it's painful. As bad as I want to bury myself deep, I also want to take my time. I want to cherish the gift of this beautiful woman lying beside me.

Dropping my head, I press my lips to hers. She bites down on my bottom lip, and my cock twitches in her hand. "We should hurry," she breathes. "In case they come looking for us."

"They won't."

"B-But what if they do?"

"I'll give you what you want, under one condition."

"This again." She rolls her eyes playfully. The smile on her lips tells me she's not as upset as she wants me to believe.

"When we get home, I get to take my time with you. I get to trace every inch of you with my tongue. I get to memorize every curve," I say as my fingers continue to lazily pump in and out of her.

"I've already agreed to stay with you," she reminds me, her breath catching.

I nod. "Yeah, baby, you did. But now you have to promise to let me cherish you." She sucks in a breath. "What do you say, Sawyer? Do we have a deal?"

Her hand falls from my cock, and she cradles either side of my face. "That's not what I expected you to say."

"No?"

She shakes her head. "So many layers, Royce Riggins."

"That's all you, babe. You bring out so many different emotions inside me."

"I want them all."

It's my turn to agree with a nod. I kiss the tip of her nose and sit up. I reach for the condom and slide it on before diving back under the covers and hovering over her. Her grip's on my bicep as I line myself at her entrance. "Eyes on me, beautiful," I say as I slowly ease myself inside her.

Her legs lock around my waist, and her fingernails dig into my arms. "Oh," she moans, closing her eyes.

"Sawyer." Her eyes snap open. "Eyes on me. I want you to see me. I want you to know who's inside you."

"Only you, Royce Riggins. Only you."

I rock my hips, and she bites down on her bottom lip. "Jesus, Sawyer," I murmur, burying my face in her neck. I'm about to lose my shit. That's a first for me. I've never in all my life felt something as incredible as her.

My mind flashes to a conversation I had with my dad after my divorce. He asked me if I had ever felt magic? I told him he was crazy, that magic didn't exist, and he just gave me a lazy smile. "That's where you're wrong, son," he'd said. "When you experience the magic, you'll know it. That's when you know it's real. That's when you know you found her. I could see it in you. She wasn't your magic son."

"Magic," I murmur in her ear. It's as if the stars have aligned, and everything is right in my world. All because of the woman lying beneath me. I don't have an explanation for how I feel about her. It's been a hot minute, yet my heart beats faster for her, and the thought of losing her has panic welling up inside me.

"Hey." Her hands roam over my back. "Talk to me."

I'm buried balls deep inside her and realizing that she's the missing part of me. She's the reason for all the layers she's always yammering on about. She brings out every single emotion. And every part of me wants her. All of me.

"You okay?" I ask her.

"Are you?"

"Never better," I say, pressing my lips to hers. "Never felt anything like this, like you in all my life."

"I'm a sure thing, Riggins," she says when we come up for air. "No need for all the flair for dramatics."

"Are you calling me dramatic?" I ask, pulling out and pushing in deep. A moan escapes from her chest.

"Y-Yes," she replies.

"Yes, what, baby?" I ask as I pull out and push home once again.

"Yes, you're being dramatic."

"That's what you do to me," I confess. "I don't talk during sex. I sure as hell don't think about my future when all I should be thinking about is my release, but with you, my mind wanders. My cock is buried in your wet heat, and your body is wrapped around mine, and all I can think about is the next time I get you like this. Not just the next time, but the time after that, and the time after that, hell, fifty years from now."

"Those are big claims, Riggins."

"It's the magic."

"You feeling okay?" She laughs, placing her hand against my forehead.

"Your pussy is magic, Sawyer," I say, pulling out and pushing back in. It's the start of a rhythm that takes our breath and our ability to speak. We're both chasing the high.

"Faster," she pants, and who am I to deny her anything?

I lose myself inside her. I let the chemistry that's been sparking between us since that very first day take over, as I give her all of me. It's not long before she's tightening around me.

"Please, don't stop. I'm close... so close," she breathes as her nails dig into my back. I bend my head to kiss her neck, and as soon as my lips reach her skin, she tightens around me even more, at the same time as she cries out my name. Not able to hold back, I follow her over the edge.

With my arms braced on either side of her head, I rest my forehead against hers. "You've ruined me," I tell her.

Her soft laughter fills the night air. "Yeah? The spell I cast on you must have worked." She grins, her hands tracing up and down my back.

"Magic, baby. That's the magic." I kiss the corner of her mouth and pull out of her. I quickly tie off the condom and toss it to the side for now. I lie down on my back and pull her into me.

"I wish we could see the stars," she says after a few minutes of silence.

Tossing the cover off us, I smile as she shrieks. I stand and pull her to her feet. I reach down for the quilt before guiding her to the railing of the gazebo. Stepping behind her, I wrap the quilt over my shoulders, pulling her into my chest, and wrapping it around the both of us. "I give you the stars," I say, kissing her neck.

"Wow," she breathes. "They're so bright. It's so quiet and peaceful out here."

"I love it here. Always have. This place holds so many special memories from my childhood. And now…" I hold her a little tighter. "…it holds something special for us too."

She manages to turn in my arms, and my cock comes to life, pressing hard against her stomach. "Are you telling me you have a sentimental side, Royce Riggins?" she teases. Her green eyes are sparkling under the rope lights and the light of the night sky.

"Only when it comes to you and my family."

"I'm honored to be included in that."

"My sweet Sawyer." I brush the hair back from her eyes. "You're at the top of the list." Her reply is to rest her head against my chest, right over my rapidly beating heart, and wrap her arms around my waist. I hold her close, sure to keep the blanket held tight around us, shielding our naked bodies from the cooling night air.

We stand here in silence, just holding one another. My mind is replaying tonight, hell every moment I've ever spent with her. Not that I need to. Tonight proved to me that Sawyer Gibson is my magic. She's everything I never knew I needed or wanted. Standing here under the moonlight and the star-filled sky, I vow I'll do whatever it takes to make her mine. For now and for always. She doesn't realize it yet, and it's too soon to tell her, but Sawyer stole my heart tonight. Here, in my favorite place, on my family's property, I found the love of my life.

"Thank you for tonight," she says, smiling up at me. "I'll never forget this as long as I live."

"There will be many more just like it," I assure her. *I'll make sure of it,* I silently promise.

"We should probably be getting back. I'm sure your brothers have already come to their own conclusions as to what we've been doing," she says, looking down.

"Hey." I lift her chin with my index finger. "They know I would never have brought you here if you didn't mean something to me. That's now what we do. We don't bring casual dates here. The five of us, we love this place. They know me, and they know that you're not just some random woman."

She nods and pulls out of my hold. I don't stop her. Instead, I drop the quilt and begin to get dressed as well. Once dressed, I grab the condom and shove it into my pocket, and together we fold the quilts and place them back in the box beneath the bench seat.

"I feel like we should take them with us to wash them," she says once I shut the lid to the seat.

"I'll come back out tomorrow and make sure it gets done. If we take them with us now, my brothers are going to give you even more shit. I'm fine either way, but I figured you wouldn't want that kind of attention."

"No, I don't." She steps forward and slides her arm around my waist. "I know what happened here tonight makes things awkward, but, Royce…" she looks up at me, "you're worth it."

This woman has effectively brought me to my knees. I swallow back the lump in my throat, kiss her forehead, and guide her back toward my brothers and the fire. There are so many emotions racing through me, and I can't seem to settle on just one. The only thing I can be certain of is that Sawyer Gibson is mine.

"We were getting ready to send out a search party," Conrad says once we're back in their line of sight.

"I know this land like the back of my hand," I remind him.

"Oh, we know." Grant smirks.

"The search party was to save Sawyer from you," Marshall chimes in.

"All good?" Owen asks. His eyes are on Sawyer. I don't take it personally. He knows I would never hurt her. I'm proud that my brothers, my best friends, are looking out for her, even when it comes to me.

"Yes. This place is gorgeous." She looks up at me. "Magical even." There is a small smile playing at her lips, and I have half a mind to lean down and take her lips with mine.

Owen's eyes find mine, and he nods. I know what that nod means. My brother approves. None of them liked my ex-wife, but I was too blind to what I thought we had to see between the lines. This time, my eyes are wide open. I'm not letting my head choose for me. Instead, I'm following my heart. My head tried to talk me out of it, but my heart won.

"Beer?" Owen asks.

"Nah, I'm driving us home. Babe?" I raise my eyebrows in question.

I have no doubt there is a light pink shade of her cheeks from my calling her babe. "Yes." She nods. "Thank you." Owen reaches into the cooler and hands her a beer.

"You cold?" I ask her.

"I'm fine."

I nod, leading her back to the same chair we were sitting in earlier, and pull her into my lap. To my surprise, my brothers don't give me shit. Instead, they welcome Sawyer into the fold of our family. They include her in conversation and ask her about her life. They share stories about me when I was younger, the havoc the five of us used to wreak. It's the best night of my life. Hands down. The beautiful woman in my arms gave me a piece of herself, and in turn, I gave her all of me. I have never felt this kind of peace or contentment. I owe that all to her.

We spend hours sitting by the fire, drinking beer, and sharing memories. Sawyer tells some of her own, vacations with her parents, her college days. I soak up every tiny morsel she's willing to share with us.

By the time the fire has died down, it's well into the morning hours, and Sawyer has long since passed out against my chest. With a wave to my brothers, I carry her to my truck and drive us home.

"Royce." Her sleepy eyes blink open before closing again.

"I got you, babe. We're at my place. I'm taking you to bed." She nuzzles into my neck as I carry her bridal style to my room and place her on the bed. "Let's get you into something more comfortable," I say, pulling off her shoes. She sits up and raises her arms in the air, allowing me to pull her shirt off. I move onto her shorts before reaching behind her and unclasping her bra. Her ample breasts are on full display, and I'm cursing the fact that I didn't turn on the lamp. "Let me get you a shirt to sleep in."

"No, just you," she says over a yawn. She lies back on the bed and snuggles into the pillow. "Will you hold me?" she asks, her voice low.

"Give me just a minute." Kicking off my shoes, I strip out of my shirt on my way to the bathroom. I toss the condom in the trash, wash my hands, and throw my shorts into the dirty clothes basket. Sliding into my bed with us both in our underwear causes my cock to stir, but she's exhausted, and the truth is, so am I. Pulling the cover over us to ward off the chill of the air conditioning, I wrap my arms around her and tug her close. For the first time in over four years, I fall asleep with a woman next to me in my bed, and my final thought before sleep claims me is I want to do this exact thing every night.

WE SPENT MOST of the day yesterday in bed, and I don't feel the least bit sorry about it. Royce tried to convince me to stay in bed all day, but all I could think about was washing the quilts from the night before. It took me a few hours to convince him, but eventually we made our way to his parents' place. We grabbed the quilts, and took them back to his place to wash them. Once they were done, we dropped them off and picked up some takeout. The rest of the day was spent in his bed.

Today, however, I had things to do. Laundry and grocery shopping for the week were at the top of the list. Royce went to the store with me, and picked up some things for his place as well. After dropping them off, we unloaded my groceries and snuggled on my couch in between loads of laundry. Every day with him is better than the one before.

"We have to be at Mom and Dad's at five," he tells me casually.

"For?" I ask, but then I remember their Sunday dinners.

"Sunday dinner."

"That's a family thing."

"You're right, it is. And as far as I'm concerned, you're my family. Sunday dinners are just as sacred as the lake. It's serious members only," he says, his eyes boring into mine.

"You really want me to go?"

"Yes. And before you ask, Mom will be thrilled, Dad and my brothers too. You already know Mom cooks for an army, and you've already claimed your seat at the table next to me."

"That was one meal."

"It's your spot, babe." He grins. "What do you say? Will you come with me?" He bats his eyelashes and we both know that I can't say no to him.

"Yes," I say before I can talk myself out of it.

Two hours later, we're walking into his parents' place. The smell of the grill hits me as soon as we walk in.

"It's about time you two got here. We were going to start without you," Lena says, coming around the island and giving first me, then Royce a hug. "Go on and make your plates." She waves her hands toward the spread she has laid out.

Not needing to be told twice, all four of Royce's brothers grab a plate and dig in. Royce and I stand, his front to my back, his arms around my waist just watching them.

"Y'all look like you've never seen food before." Royce laughs.

"It's Mom's potato salad," Grant defends. "You know if you don't get it, it will be gone."

Lena comes to stand next to us. "I have two more bowls in the fridge," she says, leaning her shoulder into mine.

"Bless you, woman." I smile at her.

"I've learned a thing or two over the years. Feeding five teenage boys, I had to always be prepared."

"I imagine there was never a dull moment."

Her eyes sparkle. "Not one, and I wouldn't trade those memories for anything. Now, you two go make your plates." She motions for us to follow her.

She and Stanley start making theirs as well. The four of us head to the dining room, and sure enough, everyone is in their same seats as the first time I was here. The conversation flows and so does the laughter. You can feel the love that they have for one another inside these four walls. It's exactly like I want my home to be, my family. Maybe one day I'll be a permanent part of this one. My heart skips a beat at the thought.

Today is the first day back to the office since things have changed between us. Royce told me last night when I made him take me home not to worry, that it will be business as usual, but I'm still stressing about how he's going to act toward me. Don't get me wrong, broody CEO Royce is hot as hell, but I prefer my Royce. The sweet, caring guy I spent the weekend with.

I barely slept last night. I don't know if it's because, after two nights of sleeping next to him, my body already notices his absence or the fact that I couldn't seem to turn my mind off worrying about today. Hence the reason I'm here an hour early. I stopped and picked up some pastries that I know all the guys will enjoy, and instead of setting them up in the break room, I place them on the counter by my desk, along with a small stack of plates and napkins. I want to see their faces when they enjoy the flaky, buttery sweetness.

The elevator dings and my head lifts to see who it is. Royce, dressed in his suit and tie, comes around the corner. His outfit is a definite contrast to the man I spent the weekend with. He's staring at his phone, but when his eyes lift, and he spots me, a slow smile crosses his face, and he slides his phone into his pocket.

"I fucking missed you," he says, not stopping until he's behind my desk, sliding his hand behind my neck and bending to press his lips to mine.

I expect it to be a quick peck on the lips, but he demands more as his tongue surges past my lips to battle with mine. "R-Royce," I murmur, pulling away.

"I wasn't done, baby," he says, and kisses me again.

"Should I call HR?" a deep voice filled with humor says from behind us.

"You should go away," Royce says, grinning down at me. He stands to his full height and turns, giving us a clear view of Conrad.

"Morning, lovebirds. Are these fair game?" he asks, pointing to the pastries.

"Y-Yes." I clear my throat and sit up straighter in my chair. "They're for everyone."

"I like this one, big brother." Conrad winks, helps himself to a pastry, and takes a huge bite.

Royce's hand is still behind my neck, and his thumb is gently caressing the sensitive spot behind my right ear. The elevator dings, and this time, it's Owen, Marshall, and Grant stepping off at the same time.

"Wow," Grant says. "Looks like we missed our invite to the party."

Conrad points at me and holds up his half-eaten pastry. "So good," he mumbles as he takes another bite.

"Thanks, sis," Marshall says, digging in.

I swallow hard at the nickname, sis, the same one that Owen used Friday night. These men have quickly accepted me as a part of their lives, and being around their family brings tears to my eyes. It's something I've missed terribly since my parents have been gone.

"You good?" Owen asks. He's the most observant man I've ever met.

I nod. "There's a copy of this week's schedule on each of your desks." I need to get into work mode. I can't forget that I'm not a member of the Riggins family.

"Thanks, babe." Royce places a kiss to the top of my head, grabs a pastry, and strolls to his office.

Grant looks at Royce retreating back and then turns his gaze on me. "I don't know what you're doing, Sawyer, and I don't care. You're bringing our brother back to life. Keep that shit up," he says, holding his hand up for a high-five.

I can't help but laugh as I slap my hand against his. "I'm just me, Grant."

"Well, 'just you' are doing great things for him."

"He's right," Owen agrees.

"And these." Marshall holds up his second pastry. "These do great things," he says, taking a huge bite, "for me."

"Eat up. If you leave them here, I'll eat them, and my ass doesn't need all that." I point to the box and make a circling motion.

"Sawyer!" Royce snaps. My head whips to look at the doorway of his office. "I don't want to hear that shit come out of your mouth. Ever."

"I can feel my ass expanding just looking at them," I say in reply.

He stalks toward me. He doesn't stop until he's bending over me, bracing his hands on the arms of my chair. "You're perfect." He kisses the corner of my mouth and stands to his full height. "Don't you all have something better to do than harass Sawyer?"

"Your girl brought us breakfast." Conrad smirks.

Royce looks down at me. "See what you started. You're never going to get rid of them."

"They're not so bad."

He shakes his head, a smile tilting his lips. "I got shit to do." His hand reaches out and tucks my hair behind my ear. "Lunch today?" he asks.

"You have a lunch meeting," I remind him, and he curses under his breath.

"Go, get to work. That is why we're here."

"Fine," he grumbles. "Don't be bothering her all damn day." He makes a point to look at each of his brothers before walking away and disappearing into his office.

"So bossy," Marshall mutters, reaching for his third pastry.

I smile as each of them, pastries in hand, head to their offices. I should have known there was no need to worry. These Riggins men are one of a kind.

This week has flown by. Royce had a packed schedule, and I've barely seen him. We had dinner Monday night, but he ended up having meetings that ran late Tuesday and Wednesday, and I already had plans to have dinner with Hadley last night. Royce tried to convince me to come over after, but Hadley came back to my place, and we stayed up way too late talking about anything and everything. Her wedding is just a couple of months away, and we had a lot to catch up on. I'm so excited for my best friend. Derek is a great guy, and anyone who sees the way that he looks at her can tell how much he loves her. They are definitely my example of couple goals. I want that one day.

I can't help but think about Royce. We've shared stolen kisses, and any excuse he can find to touch me while we're at work he takes full advantage of. I can't help but wonder if he could be my future. If he will one day look at me the way that Derek looks at Hadley. My phone ringing pulls me out of my thoughts.

"Riggins Enterprises, this is Sawyer."

"Hi, Sawyer, this is Sasha, Mr. Peterson's assistant. Something has come up, and he's going to need to reschedule his meeting this afternoon with Mr. Riggins."

My eyes quickly scan the books, and I see a Mr. Peterson on Royce's schedule for three o'clock. "Would you like to go ahead and reschedule?" I ask, hoping she'll volunteer the reason for canceling before I have to ask her.

"Yes, however, we're not sure when. Mr. Peterson has had a death in the family. Can I call you next week once I know more?"

"Certainly, and please give Mr. Peterson our condolences." Ending the call, I click on Royce's calendar and remove the meeting. I then pull up my email and send him one letting him know why the meeting was canceled, before diving back into typing a few letters that Grant dictated yesterday. I'm focused on what Grant is saying, which is why I startle when I feel Royce's hands on my shoulders. Tilting my head back, I smile. "Hey."

"Hi, beautiful." He bends to place a kiss on the tip of my nose. "I got your email."

"Gives you a little catch-up time," I say, swirling around in my chair to face him.

"My thoughts exactly. We leave in thirty."

"Wait. What do you mean we leave in thirty? It's two o'clock in the afternoon." I'm sure I'm looking at him like he's lost his mind.

"It is, and I'm using my time to catch up."

"And that includes us leaving because?"

"Because it's been a hell of a week without you. Stolen kisses here at the office are not going to cut it. I need you in my arms."

"We're having dinner tonight," I remind him.

"Change of plans. Our night starts in thirty."

Grant walks past and stops when he sees Royce at my desk. "Hey, man, got a minute? I got Scott on the line for an update on Idaho. Thought you might want to sit in. I saw your schedule was clear."

"Fuck," Royce sighs. "Yeah, I'll be right there." With a nod, Grant turns to head back to his office. "I'm sorry. I'll make this quick."

"Royce, I can't leave. We can't just slip out early."

"I'm the boss."

"And I have responsibilities."

Another heavy sigh leaves his lips. "Fine. Come with me." With my hand in his, he leads me to Grant's office. Peeking his head in the door, he says, "I'm going to hop on the call from my office." With that, he turns and leads us to his office. Once inside, he shuts the door and takes a seat behind his desk, pulling me into his lap.

"What's going on?" I ask, looking over my shoulder.

"What's going on is that I can't wait a minute longer to hold you, so you're going to sit with me while I take this call. Then, I'll give you thirty minutes to wrap up whatever it is that you need to do, and we are out of here for the weekend."

He doesn't give me a chance to respond before he hits the conference button on his phone, and Grant's voice fills the room. Not willing to make my presence known, I lean back against his chest, and he wraps his arms around me. I feel his lips press to my temple. He keeps one arm around my waist, while the other rests on my thigh. I'm wearing pants today, and I make a mental note to never wear pants to work again. Only skirts from here on out. Anything that gets me closer to him and gives me the chance to feel his skin against mine.

"Thanks for your hard work, Scott. I think the two of you can take it from here," Royce says, not bothering to say goodbye before he taps the button on his phone that ends his connection to the call.

I move to stand, and I'm surprised when he lets me. Although that's short-lived when his hands land on my hips. He turns me to face him and lifts me from the floor, setting me on his desk. "I missed you this week," he says, circling his arms around my waist.

"You've been busy," I say, placing my arms around his neck.

"I don't like it."

Ah, broody Royce. "Well, there's not much we can do about that. You're a big boy now with a multi-million-dollar company to run. It can't all be fun and games."

"Sassy," he says, pressing his lips to mine.

"Hey, Royce." I recognize as Marshall's voice as he walks into Royce's office.

"You didn't lock the door," I hiss.

He grins. "I've got nothing to hide."

"Me!" I shriek. "Me on your desk specifically." I try to stand, but he's not willing to let me go. Instead, he tilts his head to the side to look at his brother. "What's up?"

"Sawyer, have I told you how glad I am you're here?" Marshall asks.

"What?" I turn to look over my shoulder.

"This guy. He's much more relaxed when you're around." He points at Royce.

"Until my time with my girl that I've been missing all week gets interrupted by my little brother. What's up, Marsh?" Royce asks with no heat in his tone.

"I have the final mock-up of the new marketing campaign for Idaho, the rebranding of sorts. Thought you might want to take a look at it."

"Sure, send it over, but I doubt I'll get to it before Monday," he says, running his hand up and down my back. I'm not even sure he realizes that he's doing it.

"You're taking the weekend off?" Marshall asks, and his surprise is more than evident in his voice.

"Yes." Royce's gaze is locked on mine. "I'm taking the weekend off. In fact, Sawyer and I are heading out early."

"I can't. I have some letters I need to finish for Grant," I tell him.

"What about me?" Grant asks from behind me.

I give Royce an "I'm going to kill you for putting me in this situation at work" look, and his grin only grows.

"Sawyer and I are heading out, starting our weekend early," Royce explains.

"She doesn't want to go. She has some letters she's typing for you," Marshall adds.

"Yeah, but I asked you to date them for midweek next week. So, they don't need to be done today," Grant tells her.

"Haven't you ever heard do today's work today, because you don't know what tomorrow will bring?" I ask, exasperated with the Riggins men in the room.

"It's all about balance, sis," Grant says. I'm not looking at him, but I can hear the smirk in his voice.

"See, babe. It's all good. Go close down and do what you need to do. We leave in thirty."

"Royce—" I start, but he presses his lips to mine, effectively shutting me up.

"Please. I miss you."

He gives me the saddest look I've ever seen. "Pouting Riggins?"

"If that's what it takes, yes."

I can't help but laugh. "Fine, but this is not going to become routine. I'm still an employee of this company. I can't just go making my own hours."

"You can when you're mine."

I don't have a reply for that. Especially not with two of his brothers within earshot. Instead, I push back on his shoulders, and this time he lets me. With his hands on my hips, he lifts me from his desk. I ignore all three of them as I leave his office and make my way back to my desk. I try to act irritated and hide my excitement at the same time. I've missed him too, and I can't wait to spend some time with him.

WHEN I TOLD Sawyer we had plans this weekend, what I meant was I wanted to stay locked away at her place or mine, shutting out everything but the two of us. I should have been more specific because when my brother called and said everyone was going out to the lake, Sawyer chimed in and told him we would be there. It's not that I don't want to see my brothers or my parents, but seeing her at work and not being able to hold her is torture. Last week, I had to practically drag her out of the office early. This week, I had hoped to do the same, but it didn't happen. Instead, Sawyer stayed to help me with a few reports and ordered us dinner. We were at the office until after seven last night.

I promised her no more working on the weekend—that I had plans for her, and she was all mine. All of that is true, and I should have been more specific. I should be lying with her naked body next to mine. Her bed or mine; I'm not picky. Although I admit, I do enjoy having her at my place. It feels more like home when she's there. Instead, we're headed to my parents' place for another Saturday of sun and fun on the lake.

"Come on," she says from the passenger seat of my truck. "It'll be fun. You love the lake."

"I do, but I wanted some time with you."

"I'm right here."

"Naked time."

She throws her head back and laughs. The sound fills the cab of my truck and has my heart beating a little harder inside my chest. "We had naked time last night, and this morning," she reminds me.

"I can't help that I crave your body next to mine," I say, keeping my eyes on the road.

"My sweet Royce," she whispers, reaching over and placing her hand on my arm.

"I'm always sweet."

"Uh-huh, you are, but sometimes you take it over the top, and it makes my belly flutter. Like a swarm of butterflies are having a party in there or something."

Checking my rearview mirror, I move the truck to the side of the road and put it in Park. Taking off my seat belt, I turn and lean over the console. I take her face in my hands and press my lips to hers. Hearing her description just now, it's exactly what happens every time I'm near her. Knowing that she feels the same way, I had to kiss her. I needed my lips on hers, her taste on my tongue. Waiting wasn't an option.

A blaring horn pulls us out of the kiss. I turn to look, and I see Marshall's truck flying by us. "I feel it too," I say, turning my attention back to Sawyer. "All of it." I take her hand and place it over my heart. "You feel that?" She nods. "That's what you do to me. Just looking at you causes my heart to race." Another blaring horn, and this time I don't bother to turn to look. I'm positive it's another one of my idiot brothers. "We should go," I say as her phone rings. I pull away, giving her space to answer.

"Hello," she says as I lock in my seat belt and pull back out on the road.

"Hey, Had." She listens. "Sorry, Royce and I are going to his family's lake today. We're taking the boat out."

"Hey." I reach over and place my hand on her thigh. "Invite them."

"Hold on a minute." She covers the speaker of her phone. "Are you sure?"

"Of course, I'm sure. We have friends out there all the time. Besides, I think it's time I met your best friend."

"Are we there?" she asks, smiling.

"We've been there. Tell her to join us. You can text her the address."

"Hey, Had, why don't you and Derek join us?" She listens. "No intrusion at all," she assures her. "I'll text you the address. Come on, and you've been dying to meet Royce, so now's your chance." Another pause. "Yay. Okay, I'll text you the address. See you soon." She ends the call and glances over at me. "Thank you for that. She's been hounding me to meet you."

"Why didn't you say anything?"

She shrugs. "I didn't know if we were there yet. I wasn't sure what this was exactly." She waves her hand between us.

"This is everything."

"Everything," she repeats.

The final mile to get to my parents' place is quiet. I park next to the building where the boat is stored and put the truck in Park. Removing my seat belt, I lean over and do the same for hers. Reaching next to me, I move my seat as far back as it will go. "Come here, Sawyer."

"What?" She looks at me with a confused expression on her face.

"Come here, baby." I tap my lap.

"You're crazy."

I nod. "About you. Now come here." Without further prompting, she climbs over the console and straddles my lap. My arms wrap around her waist. "You and me, we're official. I don't care what you call it or how to label us, but we're together. You're mine, and I'm yours. Never question if I want to be involved in your life. I don't care if it's to tell me you bought a pair of shoes on sale, or if it's spending time with your best friend and her fiancé, I'm your guy, Sawyer. I want all the good, all the bad, and everything in between."

"If the employees of Riggins Enterprises could see you now." She smiles at me. "That silver tongue of yours hits me here." She taps her chest over her heart.

"This tongue?" I ask, leaning in close and licking the column of her neck.

"Y-Yeah, that'd be the one."

I chuckle. "This tongue has so many talents," I say, and she swats at my shoulder.

"You're terrible, Royce Riggins."

I shrug. "Grab your phone, babe. We need to send Hadley the address. I'll text my brothers and tell them we'll join them out at the dock once they get here."

"Are you sure this is a good idea?"

"Yes. Trust me." I kiss the corner of her mouth.

"Okay. Here." She hands me her phone. I'm not being nosey, but I see their text thread, and it makes me smile.

Hadley: How's the hottie boss?

Sawyer: Still hot. LOL

Hadley: You're falling for him.

Sawyer: Yes, and it scares me.

Hadley: Just roll with it. You can't have a reward without risk.

Sawyer: Says the girl who's engaged to her soul mate.

Hadley: How do you know he's not yours?

Sawyer: A girl can dream.

Quickly, I type out my parents' address telling them to park at the building and to look for a black four-door truck, and I plan for the two of us to sit here and wait for them. It gives me the perfect opportunity to steal a few kisses. "Done, now, where were we?" I ask, sliding my hand behind her neck and pulling her lips back to mine. Her body relaxes as she grinds her hips. There's a knock at the window. "Shit," I curse, just before the door flies open.

"Sawyer, is he holding you hostage?" Conrad asks. His grin tells me that he knows damn well what he interrupted.

Sawyer's cheeks turn a light shade of pink. "No. We're waiting on Hadley and her fiancé."

"Awesome. We're all packed up and ready to go."

"I have a cooler in the back, and Sawyer made some cookies and brownies. She insisted we stop and pick up some more food too."

"Sis, you don't need to do that."

"I feel like I'm mooching off all of you. I wanted to contribute."

"This one—" Conrad points at Sawyer, but he's looking at me. "—you better nail that shit down, brother, or I might."

"She's mine," I growl. I didn't mean to sound so possessive. I know my brother and his words were meant in jest, but the thought of her not being mine sends fire through my veins.

"You're good for him." Conrad winks and saunters away just as Sawyer's phone alerts her to an incoming text.

"They're here. They were not far from here when she called; she just didn't realize it."

"Fucking Conrad," I mumble under my breath.

"What are you rambling on about?"

"He stole my time with you. I had plans for you."

She laughs. "Royce, it was a few minutes at best. I'm yours, remember? You get all my time. Besides, I like your brothers, all four of them. I don't mind spending time with them too."

"Hell, I do." I kiss her one more time just as an SUV pulls in beside us.

"Come on. It's time to meet my family." She's smiling, but that's the moment it really registers that Hadley really is all she has left, and they aren't related. I have four brothers who I know have my back, no questions asked, and both of my parents, my best friend. My list is long, but Sawyer's, hers isn't. Hadley is it. I'm suddenly nervous about meeting her, and I've never been nervous about meeting someone a single day in my life. I'm also determined to share my life with hers, share my family with her. I want to give her what she lost way too young.

She climbs off my lap and out of the truck. I adjust my cock that was under the impression that he was getting time with her, and follow after her. Stepping up behind Sawyer, I place my hands on her hips.

"Had, Derek, this is Royce. Royce…" She tilts her head back to look up at me. "This is my best friend, Hadley, and her fiancé, Derek."

"Nice to meet you." I remove one hand from her waist, and offer it to Derek first, and then Hadley. "Glad you guys could make it." The bright smile from Hadley and the friendly nod from Derek have my nerves calming instantly. First impression, they're laidback just like my Sawyer.

"This place is beautiful," Hadley comments.

"I'd never want to leave," Derek adds.

"Thanks. This is where I grew up."

"You should see the lake," Sawyer tells them.

"Come on, hop in the truck. My brothers just took the boat and the Jet Skis down to the dock."

"You fish?" I ask Derek.

"Yeah, not this year. We've been busy with wedding planning."

"Sounds like you needed today. There is nothing better than a relaxing day on the water," I tell him with a chuckle. "We have a small shed by the dock with fishing gear. Help yourself," I say to him as we all climb into my truck.

The four of us make small talk during the short drive to the lake. I hear a gasp and can't help but smile as we arrive at the dock.

"Wow," Hadley breathes. "This place is beautiful."

"My parents really outdid themselves," I tell her.

"They have this huge fire pit, and there's a gazebo, which feels like it's on an island," Sawyer gushes. I don't get the feeling she's bragging. It's more of an "I'm falling in love with this place," and hopefully, the man who introduced her to it.

"How do you ever leave this place?" Hadley asks. "I'd want to build a cabin right over there"—she points to the right at an open field—"and just stare at this view every day."

"Right?" Sawyer agrees. "It's breathtaking."

I'm seeing my childhood playground all over again through her eyes, just as I did the first time Sawyer was here. Growing up, we took it for granted, but I love that my brothers and I still come here. This is home to us, the place where the five of us feel most comfortable, where we feel free and alive. Knowing that it does the same for Sawyer makes me care for her even more than I already do.

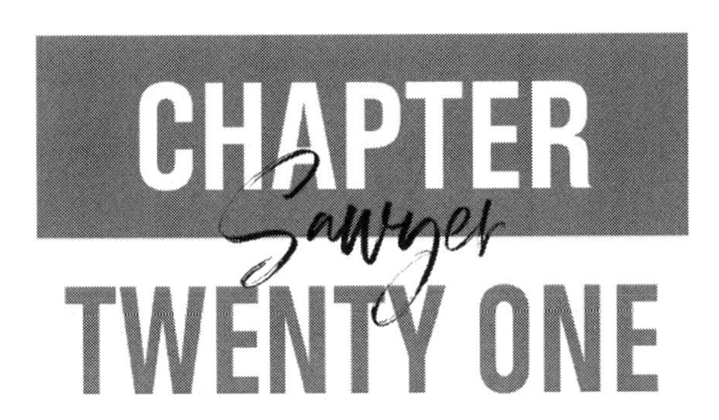

"YOU GOT A little something…" Hadley points to the corner of her chin, a mischievous grin tilting her lips.

"Stop." I laugh.

"Seriously, Sawyer, you can't seem to pull your eyes away from him."

"Them." I turn to look at her. She and I are sitting on the man-made beach in Adirondack chairs, while the guys try their hand at fishing. We've just finished eating dinner of grilled hamburgers and hotdogs. "All six of them," I say, including Derek. "This is every woman's dream, eye candy for days," I say, laughing.

"True, but I know your eyes, like mine, are only interested in one particular flavor."

"Fine, he's hot as hell. Those abs and his ink on full display, do you blame me?"

"Nope," she says, popping the *p*. "You know I love Derek, and he's the only one for me, but the Riggins brothers, they're definitely easy on the eyes."

"The six of them all shirtless in board shirts should be illegal," I add. We both burst into laughter.

"Yo, what did we miss?" Grant calls over.

"Oh, nothing," I call back.

Royce looks over at me. One look is all it takes for my body to heat. I watch him as he reels in his line, and says something to Derek before dropping his pole to the grass and heads my way, Derek on his heels. When Royce reaches me, he holds out his hand, and I don't hesitate to take it. He places a chaste kiss to my lips, takes my seat, and pulls me down on his lap.

"You give up on fishing?" Hadley asks Derek as he does pretty much the same thing that Royce just did with me.

"I'd rather be here with you."

"Me too," Royce whispers in my ear.

"Royce, thank you so much for having us. Today was exactly what we needed to relax. Wedding planning is stressful."

"I told you that you should have eloped." I point at her.

"We'll leave the elopement up to you."

I shrug. "I'm not against it. I don't really want the frills, not anymore." Royce's arms tighten around me, telling me that he understands my change of heart. What he doesn't know is that I used to want the fairy-tale wedding, but I just don't know how I'll feel about that with my parents not being here. I blink back hot tears. I miss them so damn much.

"Where's the gazebo you told me about?" Hadley asks.

"Follow that path." Royce points to the cleared path. "It comes out on the other side of the lake, and the gazebo is there."

"Is it safe?" Hadley asks.

"See." I turn to look at Royce. "It's a valid concern." He chuckles, and I can feel the vibration of his chest against my back.

"It's safe," he assures them.

"Mind if we take a walk?" Derek asks.

"Not at all, man, go right ahead. Just stay on the path, and it will lead you right to it."

Turning to the side, I lean my head on his shoulder. "Are you mad?" I ask once Hadley and Derek are out of earshot.

"Mad about what?"

"I told her about the gazebo. I mean, I didn't tell her *all* about the gazebo. Just that you took me there and how romantic it was. It's enchanting."

"No, I'm not mad at you. She's your best friend, and nothing happened that night that I'm ashamed of." The gentle touch of his fingers tracing up and down my spine cause chills to break out across my skin. "You cold, babe?"

"No. It's just you and the effect you have on me." I lift my head to look at him. "Thank you for today. I know you didn't want to come, but having Had and Derek here has been great. I'm glad you all finally got to meet."

"Me too. It wasn't that I didn't want to come. I just selfishly wanted all of your time."

My heart thunders in my chest. He has this way of being direct with his words, but their meaning hits me right in the heart. I've met so many layers of this man, and although different, they make him the amazing, kind-hearted person that he is. I don't know how I was the lucky one to be seated next to him that day, and furthermore, getting a job at Riggins Enterprises, but I've smiled more since that day on the plane than I have in too many years.

"What are you thinking about?"

"You. Us."

"Yeah? My favorite subject."

"I find that I look forward to each new day. Before I moved to Nashville, I was missing that. I lost my parents, and my job was miserable. I'm kicking myself in the ass for not leaving sooner."

"I'm glad you didn't. Don't get me wrong, I hate that you put up with that jackass for as long as you did, but I'm glad you waited. I'm glad that it was you who sat next to me on that plane.

I'm glad it was you who took over for Sam, and most of all, I'm glad it's you sitting here curled up in my lap."

"There's nowhere else I'd rather be."

He wraps his arms around me, and I feel his lips press to my forehead. "I'm falling hard, Sawyer. So damn hard."

"Can we make a deal?" I pause and feel him nod his agreement. "I'll catch you if you catch me."

"Come here." His hand slides to my cheek, and I lift my head, allowing him the opportunity to press his lips to mine. "Promise," he murmurs. Moving my head back to his shoulder, we lie together, unmoving, and watch the sun set over the water. It's the perfect day, and the company's even better.

"I'm heading out," Owen says, standing. We're all sitting around the fire just talking.

"Be careful," I tell him. I stand from Royce's lap and give him a hug.

"We should get going too," Hadley says, standing from her spot on Derek's lap. "Thank you so much for having us. It was such a fun day."

"We'll have to do it again." Royce stands and shakes Derek's hand, then pulls Hadley into a hug.

"I'm so glad I got to see you both," I say, hugging first Had then Derek.

"We should plan to get together again soon," she tells me.

"Just tell us when," Royce says, sliding his arm around my waist.

"You guys heading out too?" Marshall asks.

"You ready, babe?" Royce asks.

"Yes," I say, covering a yawn.

"Yeah, we're heading out. I'll come out tomorrow and help bring the boat and Jet Skis into the garage."

"Nah, we're staying." Conrad holds up his beer bottle. "We'll take care of it."

"Are you sure? We don't mind helping," I tell them.

"Nah, we've got it," Grant assures us.

"Night," I say, going to Grant and giving him a hug, making my way toward Conrad, and then Marshall before making my way back to Royce.

"See ya later." He waves to his brothers, tossing his arm over my shoulder and leading me to his truck. He walks me to the passenger side and opens the door for me.

"You do this for all of your dates?" I tease him, climbing up in his truck.

"I haven't dated since college."

"Oh, I just assumed after your divorce…" I let my words trail off.

"I hooked up. It was random sex, and even more random in occurrence. It's been over two years."

"And you never brought anyone here?"

"Just my ex-wife, and she hated it. She never would have enjoyed today."

"Well…" I lean out of the truck and place my palm against his cheek. "I can't think of a better way to spend such a gorgeous day. Thank you for sharing this with me." I kiss his lips.

"You're going to fall out," he says, stepping close and sliding an arm around my waist as he deepens the kiss.

"Nah," I say when he pulls away. "I know you've got me."

"You're damn right." He kisses me one more time before pulling back and shutting the door. The drive to his place is quiet, and I'm fighting exhaustion. He leads me inside and upstairs to his bedroom. "I need to shower, get this lake water off me."

Without a word, he leads me to the bathroom. I watch as he reaches in and turns on the water, then gets to work stripping me out of my clothes. I waste no time stepping under the hot spray. I reach for the shampoo, but his hand stops me.

"Let me."

My hand falls to my side, and I tilt my head back, letting him take care of me. My heart swells in my chest, and I can no longer deny what it means. I'm in love with him. This sexy multi-layered man has stolen my heart.

"Rinse." His husky voice pulls me out of my thoughts.

Turning to face him, I tilt my head back, close my eyes, and let the water rain down on me. I feel his hands on my body, which causes me to raise my head. His soapy hands are traveling over my body. I stand still, letting him do his thing, relishing the moment.

"Turn for me," he murmurs.

Doing as he asks, I turn to face the shower wall, and his hands repeat the process all over again. I'm no longer exhausted. How can I be with his hands all over me? "Your turn," I say, reaching for the body wash, and stepping around him.

"Sawyer, sweetheart, I don't know if I can handle your hands on me right now." He looks down at his hard length that's standing between us.

"No?" I ask as I run my now soapy hands over his chest.

"Fuck me," he mumbles, tilting his head back, letting the water fall over his face.

I take my time running my hands over every inch of him. When I reach his hard length, I stroke him a few times, and a groan from deep in his chest fills the room. "Rinse," I say, my voice gravelly.

Doing as I ask, he turns to give me his back, letting the water rinse away where my hands just explored. Like he did with me, I repeat the process over the muscles of his back, enjoying the feel of his skin beneath my fingertips. When I've had my fill, and the entire backside of his body is covered in soap, I tap him on the shoulder. "You can turn," I tell him.

Slowly he turns, and what I see has me freezing in place. His hand is wrapped around his hard length as he strokes himself from root to tip. "Your hands on me," he grits out.

I watch with rapt attention as he leans one hand on the shower wall to brace himself, while he continues to stroke himself. Backing up, I take a seat on the far end of the shower and spread my legs. On instinct, I reach down and run my fingers through my folds. I've never watched a man pleasure himself, and I'm so turned on that I need to cure this ache inside me.

"Fuck, Sawyer," he pants.

Glancing up, I see his eyes are locked on my hands between my legs. I notice that he's started to stroke faster, and that spurs me on to give him a show. Lifting one leg on the bench to give him a better view, I pleasure myself, mimicking him stroke for stroke.

"I want to fuck you, but this... this is the hottest fucking moment of my life. Don't stop. Please, don't stop," he says with a desperate plea.

I don't stop, just like he asks. I keep pace with him and refuse to take my eyes off his hand as he strokes himself. I agree that with him, this is the hottest moment of my life, but I can't seem to find the words to tell him that. I'm too enthralled with watching him and giving myself the pleasure that my body seeks.

"Sawyer, I'm close, baby."

I nod. I'm tilting on the edge of euphoria, but I can't find my voice to tell him. All I can do is stare wide-eyed as his hand moves faster, his legs quivering. My hand shakes, but I don't stop. I'm chasing the high that only this moment can give me.

"Fuck!" Royce growls as he finds his release. Watching him has me calling out his name as pleasure rocks my body. My eyes are closed as I slump back against the shower wall. The exhaustion from before the shower seeps in, and I'm ready for bed. "Come here." His soft words have me opening my eyes in time to witness him sliding his hands under my body and lifting me into his arms, bridal style. "Let's get you cleaned up." Back under the spray, he sets me on my feet but makes sure to keep a hold of me. He takes over and cleans me up before shutting off the water and lifting me into his arms again.

"I can walk," I tell him. I'm tired, but not so much so that my legs no longer work.

"Just let me do this."

Not one to complain when a sexy man wants to take care of me,

I keep my mouth shut and let him do his thing. Ten minutes later, we're both dried off, my hair is brushed, and we're climbing into bed. Royce pulls me close to him, and I rest my head on his chest, with his arms wrapped around me. It's not long before I'm drifting off to sleep, and just before sleep claims me, I think I hear him whisper the words, "I love you," but I'm not sure.

IT'S BEEN FOUR months today since I first laid eyes on the love of my life. I don't know what I did to have her be on that flight next to me, but it turns out to be the best thing that ever happened. We are in sync at work, and my fears of dating my assistant have long since been squashed. She knows me. Sometimes I think better than I know myself. She can anticipate what I want or need at the office, and at home, that's where I take over. I pamper her because she deserves nothing less.

She's now a permanent fixture at my parents' table for Sunday dinners, and if I have my way, it will never change. It took me meeting Sawyer to finally see through the clouds that my family claimed I was living in. I wasn't living. I've smiled more since meeting her than I have in years. Even the years that I was married. I knew already that marrying Jennifer was a bad idea. It ended in disaster, but it wasn't until Sawyer that I realized exactly how wrong we were for each other. Sawyer and I never argue, and we both have this need to always be with the other person.

Not for fear of what might happen if either of us are away, but because that's what makes us happy.

I'm going to marry her.

I just need to tell her that I love her first, and then buy the ring. Small details for a love like ours. I see it in the way she looks at me. She loves me. I can feel it in my bones. I've whispered it to her a few times when I knew she was asleep, but I wanted to give it time. To say that I was jaded by my divorce is an understatement. I wanted to make sure it wasn't the newness of having a female companion that actually wanted me that was making me feel this way.

It's not.

It's all Sawyer and the way she makes my heart pound in my chest just by entering a room. She's pretty much staying at my place all the time now. Her toiletries are on the counter in my bathroom, and her clothes hang beside mine in the closet. I don't hate it. No, I love it, and I want it to be permanent. I have a plan. I just need to set it in motion.

"Hey," she says from the doorway of my office. "Hadley and Derek invited us over to see their new place on Saturday."

Shit. "I told Owen I'd help him at his place on Saturday." I didn't know about the invitation, but I did already make plans with my brother. "You should go, though. I know you've been wanting to see it."

"Are you sure? I hate to go without you."

Just another reason she's nothing like my ex. Jennifer wouldn't have even extended the invitation to me. She would have simply told me where she was going to be. Even then, I'm not certain she would have been telling the truth.

"Of course, I'm sure. She's your best friend. We can meet back at my place that night." She nods, but I can tell she's not thrilled with the idea. "Come here." I move back from my desk, pushing my laptop back and patting for her to sit. She doesn't hesitate to shut my office door and come to me. "Tell me," I say once she's perched on my desk.

"It's silly."

"No, it's not. Not if it's how you feel. Tell me."

"I just—I wanted you to be there."

"I'm sorry, babe. I don't want to cancel on Owen." It's not a complete lie, but it's not Owen's plans I'd be canceling. I think about moving the date, but I don't want to. I want to proceed with my plan. I don't want to wait any longer. I'll make it up to her. "I'll make it up to you. Maybe we can invite them over next weekend?"

"But you won't get to see their place."

"Babe, she's your best friend. That's not going to change." Reaching up, I palm her face with my hands.

"I know," she sighs. "I'm being selfish, and I've just gotten used to it being us, you know?"

"I do know, and I'll miss you," I say, kissing her softly.

"Dinner at my place after," I suggest. "Invite them," I say, hoping that will make up for me missing lunch at their place.

"You sure?"

"Yes. In fact, why don't you recruit them to help you move in?" I toss it out there.

"What?" she asks, surprised.

"I want you to move in with me. I want to be with you every second of every day."

"I—" she starts, but closes her mouth, making me chuckle.

"Think about it, Sawyer. You don't have to decide this minute."

She nods just as there's a knock at my door. "Come in," I call out, not bothering to give Sawyer time to move. Anyone who is on this floor knows that this is more than likely what they're going to find if she's not at her desk.

"You decent?" Owen asks.

"Barely," I say as Sawyer smacks my shoulder, causing Owen and I both to laugh.

"We still on for tomorrow?" he asks. His calm demeanor gives nothing away.

"Yes." This couldn't have worked out better.

He nods. "Sounds good. I'm heading out for the day. Jase has some numbers he wants me to look over."

"Bye." Sawyer waves at him.

"I guess I should get back to work," she says.

"Let's just head home. It's four. We've worked enough hours this week."

"Royce," she sighs. This is a constant battle with us, me needing her to myself and leaving work early. I've cut my hours since she came into my life, yet the work is still getting done. I know that I would look over reports that I'd already analyzed just to avoid going home to an empty house. That's no longer me. I can't wait to wrap up what has to be done and go home with her. It's all Sawyer.

"Go finish up whatever you need to. Let me know when you're ready." I kiss her one more time before she hops off my desk and walks out of my office. Grabbing my phone, I text Owen.

Me: That was close.

Owen: She doesn't have a clue.

Me: I know. Thanks for going with me tomorrow.

Owen: I've got your back.

Tossing my phone back on my desk, I answer a few more emails before shutting down my laptop. I pack it up along with a contract I've been working on, just in case I get time over the weekend to review it. I doubt it, but it's better to be prepared than to have to come back to the office to get it. I'm ready to go drag Sawyer from her desk when my cell phone rings. Glancing, I see Jase's name.

"What's up?" I ask, leaning back in my chair.

"Just tried to call Owen and he didn't answer."

"He was in my office. What's going on?"

"Nothing, there's a hotel chain in California for sale. The place is beautiful, but they're bleeding money. I was hoping Owen might be willing to take a look at the books before I take the leap and buy it."

"You know he will. He's a whiz at that shit."

"That's the truth. Hey, how are things with Sawyer?" he asks.

"Perfect."

He whistles. "That's a pretty big claim coming from you."

"I get it now. I understand you and Sam. I didn't before, but it all makes perfect sense to me."

"Told you, man. Once you find the right woman, everything changes."

"Like magic."

"Exactly. Just like fucking magic. Hey, there's Owen. I'll catch you later."

Ending the call, I slide my phone in my pocket, pick up my bag of work to take home that I hope I don't touch, and go find my girl.

"I should be home by five or so," I tell Sawyer as we're getting ready for the day. "Did you talk to Hadley to see if they wanted to come over?"

"I mentioned it, but I'm not sure if she's going to or not. I'd say they just want to be in their new home."

"Maybe. Either way, make plans for whenever. This is the only day that I had something not on my calendar." On purpose, but I leave that information to myself.

"Okay," she says, sitting on the bed to pull her boots on.

My girl was excited for the fall weather to wear her boots. I don't understand it, but I don't question it either. It makes her happy, and that's all that matters to me. I make a mental note to get with Sam to order her a couple of pairs for Christmas.

"I'll see you later." She stands and places a kiss on my lips.

"I'm right behind you. I just need to finish getting dressed. My sexy girlfriend distracted me," I say, pulling her into another kiss.

"See you tonight." Her green eyes are sparkling with happiness, and I fight the urge to pound on my chest. I did that.

I wait until I hear the front door close before dropping my towel and quickly getting dressed. Making sure I have my keys, wallet, and phone, I'm out the door to pick up Owen.

Pulling up to his house, I beep, letting him know I'm here, but there's no need because he's stepping out onto his front porch at the same time.

"Hey, man," I say when he climbs into the passenger seat.

"You ready for this?" he asks me.

"Yes."

"I admit. This time around, I couldn't be happier for you."

"Thanks, O," I say, swallowing the lump in my throat. It means the world to me that my family loves Sawyer as much as I do. That's just another contrast from her and my ex. I should have listened to my family, opened my eyes, but I can't change the past. All I can do is focus on my future. Focus on Sawyer.

"So, what does she think that we're doing today?"

"I was vague. I told her I was helping you. She's over at Hadley and Derek's new place. Wanted me to go with her."

"She'll forgive that little white lie." He laughs.

"Yeah," I agree. When she finds out that I couldn't go with her today because I was buying her an engagement ring, she'll understand. Owen and I talk shop on the drive to the jeweler. It's in the heart of downtown Nashville, and I'm relieved that Hadley and Derek live on the outskirts and on the other side of town. There should be no reason I would bump into Sawyer today. That would be difficult to explain.

"You know the others are going to give you shit because they didn't get to come with you," Owen says as we climb out of the car.

"Too risky," I tell him. "If everyone knew, there is a higher probability of her thinking, something is up. You know Marsh and Con can't keep a secret to save their lives."

"At least not other people's." Owen laughs.

"Exactly." I pull open the door and motion for Owen to go ahead of me. "Time to look toward the future." Owen nods, a small smile playing on his lips as he smacks me on the shoulder and enters the store.

"You didn't even need me," Owen says as we're walking out of the jewelry store twenty minutes later.

"Moral support." I laugh as I hear my name called.

"Royce!" I turn to look over my shoulder and walking toward me is my ex-wife, Jennifer. I haven't laid eyes on her since the day we walked out of the courtroom for our divorce hearing. "How are you?" She leans in for a hug, but I take a step back out of her reach. "Aw, don't be like that," she coos.

"Jennifer," I greet her. I wait for the pain, and the anger to take root, but I don't feel anything. Nothing for the woman I once claimed to love, and who claimed to love me. A slow smile crosses my face that I couldn't stop even if I tried. She no longer has a hold on me. The anger I've been carrying around is gone, washed away with the love that I have for Sawyer. If I hadn't just dropped a pretty penny on an engagement ring, it would be the next thing on my list. I love her, and I can't wait to spend the rest of my life with her. I knew that, but this run-in confirms it for me.

"You look good," she says, raking her eyes over my body.

"Where's your wife?" I ask, even though I couldn't care less.

"Oh, Sandra and I separated. She was a phase, and I realized that I missed you."

"What-the-fuck-ever," Owen says from his spot next to me.

"Owen," Jennifer greets him.

She never liked him, or any of my brothers for that matter.

"Satan," he says, and I don't hide my chuckle.

"Is that any way to talk to your sister-in-law?" she asks, her voice sugary sweet.

"In the eyes of the law, you aren't shit to me or anyone in my family," Owen says, crossing his arms over his chest.

"Royce, I've missed you. I think we should get together and talk."

"I have nothing to say to you." I cross my arms over my chest, matching Owen's stance, and her eyes focus in on the bag from the jeweler.

"Oh, is it your mom's birthday?" she asks.

Bitch. We were together all through college and married for four years. She should know when my mom's birthday is. "Nope."

"Whatcha got there?"

"None of your damn business," I snap. I can't believe I gave so many years of my life to a woman who is nothing like me.

"I don't see a wedding ring," she says sweetly. "Then again, I'm sure I would have heard by now if one of the most eligible bachelors in Nashville was off the market."

"There are five Riggins brothers that are off the market when it comes to you," Owen seethes. "Haven't you done enough damage?"

"I was confused."

"Confused?" Owen asks. "You don't know the difference between your girlfriend's pussy and your husband's dick?"

She blanches at his crudeness. "Your brother worked all the time," she fires back. "He never wanted me."

"Enough!" I snap. "We're not doing this. Not now, not ever. We're over. You're nothing to me but a memory. If you'll excuse us." I turn to walk away, not bothering to see if Owen is following. I know he is. My brothers, all four of them, are loyal to a fault, and he has zero tolerance for the woman who is my ex-wife and took me away from them for far too long.

"That woman is vile." Owen is still seething on the way back to his place.

"I can't believe I was married to her," I say, fighting a shudder.

"Tried to warn you," he mumbles under his breath.

"I know. I didn't want to see it." I glance over at him. "Any concerns about Sawyer?" I ask, even though I doubt I'd listen. I thought I loved Jennifer. What I used to feel for her doesn't even compare to how I feel about Sawyer.

"Nah, Sawyer's one of the good ones. One day I want to find me a Sawyer."

"Yeah? You ready to settle down?"

"Been ready, but watching what you went through makes a man question every woman who comes his way. I'll find her," he assures me.

"When you do, you let me know. You have my support, and when you're ready to buy a ring, I'm there."

I see him nod out of the corner of my eye. "Do you know when you're going to ask her?"

"No. Not yet. I know where I want it to be, but I don't have a plan. I have a few ideas. I just need to get them together."

"Well, count me in for whatever you need," he says as we pull into his place.

"Thanks for coming with me today."

"You didn't need me."

"Yeah, but it's nice to have my brother there. This time things are different."

He nods. "Let me know what I can do."

"Will do. Thanks, O."

It's just after three. Hopefully, I beat Sawyer back to my place so I can slip her ring into the safe, and if time is on my side, start planning how I'm going to ask her to spend forever with me.

"Sawyer's home. I'll see what she's thinking and let you know," I tell Jase. He called and invited us over to visit and see the baby.

"Later," he says, ending the call.

Standing, I make my way to the front door. I pull it open just as she's about to reach for the handle. "I missed you," I say, grabbing her and pulling her into a hug. I want to drop to my knees right now and tell her how much I love her and beg her to spend the rest of her life with me.

She laughs. "It was a few hours at best."

"Too long," I murmur as I place a kiss on her neck.

"Am I allowed to come inside?" she asks, humor lacing her voice.

"You can do whatever the hell you want," I tell her.

"Then let me in, Riggins." Stepping out of my hold, she places her hand against my chest and pushes me back as she steps forward. Reaching behind her, I close the door. "How were the newlyweds?"

"Great." She smiles. "Their new house is so pretty. She's just starting to decorate, but it's really cute. I'm a little jealous. My apartment is not as appealing now." She laughs.

"You can do whatever you want here," I tell her.

"What? I can't just redecorate your house."

Our house. "Sure you can. I don't really have an eye for any of that. Do whatever you want. In fact…" I reach into my wallet and hand her my credit card. "…do your worst, baby."

"I love your house," she says, spinning to get a full view. We're still standing in the foyer.

"It's nice, but it could use a woman's touch," I say, pulling her back into my arms.

"Maybe we can do it together?" she asks, eyes full of hope as she stares up at me.

"Done." I place a kiss on the tip of her nose. "What are our plans for the night?"

"I've got nothing. Hadley and Derek are going to his parents.'"

"What about going to see Jase, Sam, and baby Aria?" Her eyes light up. "Jase just called and invited us over. Said Sam needs some girl time."

"You know I'm down for my baby fix." She grins.

Fifteen minutes later, we're pulling into their driveway. Sawyer is so excited she doesn't wait for me to open the door for her. She's bouncing on the balls of her feet in front of my car, waiting on me. "Come on, slowpoke." She waves her hands in a "come here" motion.

"We just saw them at the hospital last week," I remind her.

"A whole week, Royce. Seven long days without my baby Aria fix." She grabs my hand as soon as I'm within reaching distance and hauls me up the steps. She knocks, and Jase tugs open the door a short while later with Aria resting against his chest.

"Aw, gimme." Sawyer reaches for the baby. "Wait, I need to wash my hands. I'll be right back." She darts inside, slipping past Jase. I hear her call out "Hello" to Sam as she makes her way to the bathroom to wash her hands.

"I might have to fight your girl for my daughter," Jase says, a serious look on his face.

"Come on." I laugh, slapping him on the shoulder and walking into the house. By the time we make it to the living room, Sawyer is finished and reaching for Aria.

"Come on, Daddy," she coos to Jase. "Let me have a turn, you baby hog."

"She's my daughter," Jase defends.

"Go cuddle with your fiancée," she tells him. His eyes dart to Sam, and that's all it takes to relinquish his daughter to Sawyer.

"Hold her head," he tells her.

"I've got this, Andrews, now go." Sawyer snuggles baby Aria, taking a seat on the oversized chair. I choose to sit across from her so I can watch them together. I can't help but let my mind wander to her holding our baby girl. I've always wanted kids. Growing up with four brothers, I knew I wanted children, and wanted them to have that same upbringing as I had. I thought that dream was dead and gone, but looking at Sawyer, it's like looking at my future, and I can see it all clearly. That's our life, a house full of kids, constant, happy chaos.

"What's been going on?" Jase asks.

I tear my eyes from Sawyer. "Same old. Opening a new location in Ohio."

"My old stomping grounds," he says with a nod.

"What about you?"

"Doing the dad thing." He smiles, and I swear I'm afraid his face might crack his grin is so wide. "Nothing better, my man."

I glance back to Sawyer and Aria. "Yeah," I agree. I don't know the exact feeling, but I know how my heart swells watching her with Aria. I can only imagine that would intensify ten-fold with our child.

"You need one," Sam says with a sleepy smile.

"We do," I agree.

Sam's eyes widen at my admission of *we*. "You doing okay, Momma?" I ask her.

"I'm so sorry," Sawyer blurts. "I'm such a bad friend, but she's so cute." She smiles down at Aria. "How are you feeling?" she asks Sam.

"Good. Exhausted." She looks over at Jase, and the look they share causes a wave of longing to rush over me. I want what they have.

"Why don't the two of you go take a nap? We can watch the princess for a few hours," I suggest.

"Mom and Dad are coming over tomorrow," Jase says, "to give us a break. They have Logan and Kacen's kids today, and we didn't want all the germs around Aria. Not yet anyway."

"We've got her," Sawyer assures them.

"Babe," Sam says, and Jase gives her his full attention. "She just ate."

"We've never left her."

"We're going to be right here, man. You'll be right upstairs. I promise if we need you, we'll come and get you."

"If she does something cute, you better take a picture," Jase says, glancing over at Aria sleeping in Sawyer's arms.

"Come on, player," Sam says. "Let's go take a nap."

Jase looks torn, but when Sam tries to stand up from the couch on her own, he jumps into action and scoops her up in his arms. "We'll be right upstairs."

"We've got this," I tell him. "Four little brothers, remember?"

He nods, takes one last look at Aria, and then his feet are moving, carrying them upstairs. "Come sit with me." I pat the loveseat next to me. Sawyer carefully stands and comes to take the spot next to me. Once she's settled, I place my arm around her shoulders.

"She's so sweet," she whispers.

"You want kids?" I ask her.

"Yeah," she says wistfully. "At least three. I was an only child, and I hated it. Now that Mom and Dad are gone, it's just me, and I can't help but think having a sibling would have been nice."

"It's not just you, Sawyer. You know that, right? You have me and my family, Hadley and Derek, Sam, Jase, and this little angel. We might not be blood, but we're your family. Fuck, beautiful, you're my entire fucking world."

"Watch that potty mouth around the baby, Riggins."

"She's an infant."

She shrugs. "She's still a precious little baby." She smiles down at a sleeping Aria.

"Sawyer baby, look at me." I wait for her to give me her eyes. "You're not alone. There are so many people who love you." I let what I've said sink in before going for it. "I love you," I tell her, my voice soft. "I choose you to be my family, baby. That's better than blood. I want you. I choose you."

Her eyes mist with tears. "You just said that you love me."

"You caught that, did you?" I ask her.

"Did you mean it?"

"With everything that I am." Leaning over, I press my lips to hers. "Now, tell me about these babies of ours. Boys or girls?"

A single tear falls from her eye, but the smile on her face tells me the tear is from happiness. With my thumb, I wipe under her eye as she begins to talk about two boys and a girl. That's how we spend the next hour and a half. Talking about what life would be like raising kids visiting the lake, a swing set in the backyard. I memorize every word of our conversation and vow to give it to her—all of it. I want the picture-perfect life we just created in our minds. Sure, life isn't perfect. There will be ups and downs, but with Sawyer by my side, we can make it through anything.

"HAS THIS WEEK been the longest ever, or is it just me?" Marshall asks from where he's leaning against my desk. It's Friday afternoon, and he's right; this week has been hectic as we work to open another location in Northern Ohio.

"It's not just you," I tell him.

"I'm ready to go home and just chill."

"What? No big plans for this Friday night?"

"None. I just want to get out of this suit and drink a beer. Maybe I'll order in some wings, or maybe I'll fire up the grill."

"It's too cold outside to grill," I tell him. It's the last week of October, and the Nashville air has been chilly.

"My wings are better," he grumbles.

"I wouldn't know. You've yet to make them for me."

"Tell my brother to bring you over, and I'll fix you up," he says. Something passes in his eyes, but it's gone before I can name it.

"Rain check?" I ask him. "Royce made me promise not to make any plans this weekend. I don't know what he's got up his sleeve." I watch Marshall for signs that he might know, but his phone rings distracting him.

"Hey, Momma." He listens. "Sure, I'll just leave now and head that way." A long pause. "Love you too." He hits Ends and slides his phone back into his suit pocket. "Mom needs help moving a few things in the basement. I'm going to head out for the day, run home and change and head over there."

"What about your wings?"

"Momma's making dinner, Sawyer. I don't pass up my momma's food," he says, rubbing his belly.

"I don't blame you there. She's an incredible cook."

"Who are we talking about?" Royce asks, joining us.

"Your mom."

He nods. "I'm heading into a meeting with Owen and Grant about the new Ohio plant. It should be a couple of hours. Come and get me if anything comes up." He leans down and kisses me. "You're still mine for the weekend, right?" he asks.

"For as long as you want me."

"Forever, Sawyer. I want you forever."

"On that note, I'm out." Marshall waves and heads back to his office.

I smile up at Royce. "Go to your meeting before you're late. I already set up some snacks and drinks in the small conference room."

"What would I do without you?" he asks. "Oh, I'm going to leave my phone with you. The contractor for Ohio might call. I gave him my cell so he can reach me this weekend. We're on a time crunch. Answer and interrupt us if he calls, please," he adds.

"I hope neither of us ever find out," I tell him honestly. "And yes, I'll watch your phone. That's my job."

"You're mine, baby." Another quick kiss to the corner of my mouth. "And you're more than my assistant," he says before he turns and disappears down the hall for his meeting.

I try to calm my racing heart as I dive back into my hundreds of emails I need to answer. "Sawyer, we're out," Conrad says, Marshall hot on his heels. "Mom needs help," Conrad tells me.

"Uh-huh, you just want free food."

He winks at me. "Catch ya later, sis." They both wave as the elevator doors close.

With Marshall and Conrad gone for the day and the other three in a meeting, I should have lots of quiet time to get caught up on these emails, and maybe if I'm lucky, return a few phone calls. I don't know what Royce has planned for us, but I hope it's lots of relaxing.

Grabbing my phone, I pull up my playlist and hit Play. Turning the volume down low, I get to work.

"Excuse me," a female voice snips.

My head whips up as I reach for my phone to hit Pause on my music. "I'm so sorry. I was so engrossed in what I was doing, I didn't hear you arrive. Can I help you with something?"

"Where's the other girl? Sarah, or Sally, whatever her name was?"

"Samantha," I correct. "She's been gone for a few months now. She's got a newborn baby girl," I tell her with a kind smile.

She waves her hand in the air, letting me know she couldn't care less about Sam and baby Aria. "I'm here to see Royce."

"I'm sorry, Mr. Riggins is in a meeting. Can I give him a message?" I ask politely. I have no idea who this woman is, but she knows Royce apparently.

"No," she snaps. "I don't want to leave my husband a message. I'll just text him."

"H-Husband?" I stammer out the word.

"Yes. Royce Riggins, my husband." She rolls her eyes as if having to explain herself is exhausting.

"Your ex-husband," I find myself saying.

"Not that it's any of your concern, but we're working things out."

"Right." I laugh humorlessly. My heart is racing, and I want nothing more than to slap the lies out of her. She hurt my gorgeous multi-layered man, and it takes considerable effort not to do so.

"Listen, if you value your job, you'll respect me. Disrespectful just like Sam. Where in the hell does he find you idiots?" she mumbles, her fingers flying across the screen of her phone.

I brace my hands on the desk, ready to let her have it when Royce's phone vibrates where it sits next to mine. Glancing at the screen, I blanch at what I see.

> **Unknown:** It was so good to reconnect on Saturday. I can't wait to see you again. This time it's going to be different, baby. I can feel it. Miss you.

My knees threaten to buckle as my mind whirls with what I've just read. He was with her on Saturday. He lied to me. I fell for it. He had me convinced that he was helping Owen, and Owen, oh God, he was in on it. The room begins to spin as I grapple for my chair to sit.

"Worthless," she mutters before flipping her hair over her shoulders and stomping off.

I vaguely remember the ding of the elevator and the whooshing sound of the doors closing, but I can't be sure. All I can think about is that he lied. The man I've fallen head over heels for lied to me. He's back with his ex-wife. I didn't believe her, but that message. He wasn't with me Saturday, and he was insistent that he couldn't change his plans. Pain ricochets in my chest as I fight back the hot tears that prick my eyes.

Quickly, I close down my computer and grab my purse. I survey my desk for anything personal. There is a picture of Had and me at college graduation and one of Royce and me. I grab the picture of Had. Everything else can be trashed. As far as I'm concerned, I want to forget he ever existed. Maybe then the pain will lessen.

I'm able to maintain my composure on the ride to the lobby on the main floor. I rode with Royce today, so I'm going to need to hail a cab. I walk outside to do just that and see the hotel across the street. On impulse, I rush across the street and inside. Within fifteen minutes, I'm in a room dropping to the bed and letting the tears I've been fighting coat my cheeks.

The pain in my chest intensifies when I think about Saturday night. Sitting at Jase and Sam's holding baby Aria, Royce told me he loved me for the first time. We talked about what our life might look like in the future with kids. A sob fills the room as the pain of what he's done rushes through me.

I don't know how long I lie here. Long enough for the pillow to be soaked from my tears and exhaustion to set in. My phone has been ringing nonstop, each time it's Royce or one of his brothers. I'm not ready to talk to them. Not yet. When my phone rings, I start to ignore it, but I'm a glutton for punishment. I glance at the screen. This time it's Hadley, and a fresh swarm of tears clogs my throat.

"H-Had," I croak out in greeting.

"Sawyer, where are you?" I can hear her panic in her voice.

"He l-lied to me."

"Who lied to you?"

"R-Royce."

"He's looking for you."

"I left."

"Where are you?" she asks again.

"A hotel."

"You're safe?" she asks, her voice holding less panic than before.

"Yes."

"Okay, good." She sighs in relief. "Tell me what's going on."

I start at the beginning. I tell her about Saturday after I left their place, about baby Aria, and Royce telling me that he loved me. It was the perfect moment of what I thought was raw honesty. It was our moment, and he stole that away from me. All along, he was planning to get back with his ex-wife.

"Sawyer, you know I love you, right?" Hadley asks.

"Yes."

"You're an idiot."

"What?" I wipe at my cheeks.

"Think about all of this, really think about it. Look past what you think is the betrayal and think about what you know about her, what you know about Royce. I don't believe for a single second that man is getting back with her. Sawyer, he's beside himself looking for you. He's a wreck. There isn't a doubt in my mind that that man isn't head over heels in love with you."

"What do you mean?" I'm trying to decipher her words through my tear-fogged head.

"I mean that he's losing his mind worried about you. There has to be an explanation for all of this."

"What? I saw the message."

"Did you see her name on his phone?"

"What?"

"The message. Was her name programmed into his phone?"

I think back to the message. "No."

"Surely, if they were getting back together, he would have saved her number."

"Maybe," I say, letting her words take root in my mind.

"There is no maybe about it. He's here, Sawyer. Looking at him now, I can say with 100 percent certainty that he's not getting back with his ex-wife."

"Then explain it to me." My voice is pleading, and there is hope. I hope that this could be a misunderstanding, that there is a reason for all of this, and Royce is still the man who owns my heart. The man who loves me.

"It's not my place to explain."

"I don't know if I can see him."

"This isn't you, Sawyer. Where is my fierce best friend who kneed her boss in the balls for coming onto her?"

"She fell in love."

"You love him?"

"Yes."

"Then fight for him, Sawyer. Don't let a woman who you already know is a conniving, lying, toxic bitch cause trouble between the two of you."

"What do you know?" I ask her.

"Like I said, it's not my place, but I'm team Royce."

I can't help but laugh at her. "You're right," I agree with her. "I need to hear it from him."

"Where is she?" I hear Royce ask in the background.

"I need some time, but I'll be at his place later."

"You okay?" she asks me.

"Yeah, I will be. Thanks, Had. Although, depending on how this turns out, I might be pounding on your door later tonight."

"My door is always open to you, but I don't think that will be an issue. Once he lays his eyes on you, he's not going to let you out of his sight." There's rustling, and then I hear his voice in my ear.

"Sawyer." His voice cracks. "Baby, where are you?"

"I'm at a hotel."

"Which one? I'm on my way."

"No. I'll come to you. I need a little more time."

"No." I can hear the pain in his voice. "No more time away from you. I let that bitch control my life for years, and I won't lose you over her. No way. It's not happening, baby. Tell me where you are."

"I'll be at your place in a couple of hours."

"Sawyer," he croaks out. "I love you. You, Sawyer."

"I'll see you soon," I say, my voice betraying me, my tears evident.

"Be safe, baby."

"See you soon," I say, ending the call. A new wave of tears rain down my cheeks from hearing his voice. I want to believe him. Hadley believes him. I trust her. I trust him, or at least I did. I let his ex, a vile woman who I know manipulated him, do the same to me. I'm ashamed. I let the tears fall unchecked. I just need some time before I go to him. I need to be prepared that this could be the end of us, and with that thought, the tears fall harder.

My phone vibrates with a text. Wiping at my face, I focus on the screen.

Royce: I love you, baby. Please come home to me.

Knowing that it's time to face the situation, I make my way to the bathroom. Splashing

some water on my face, I stare at my reflection. My eyes are red and swollen, but there is nothing I can do about that. After patting my face dry, I grab my purse, phone, and room key and check out—no more hiding.

I'M SITTING ON the steps of my front porch. My leg is bouncing up and down as I stare at the driveway, waiting, watching, willing her to appear before me. When I walked out of my meeting and saw that she wasn't at her desk, I thought maybe she was in the restroom. Until I realized her computer was shut down, and the picture of her and Hadley was missing. The framed photo of the two of us still in its rightful place.

That's when the panic started to set in.

The churning in my gut told me something wasn't right. I called her over and over and over again, with no answer. My brothers rallied around me, calling Conrad, and Marshall, all hands on deck looking for her. When I arrived on Hadley and Derek's doorstep, I was in freak-out mode. Derek ushered me inside while I fumbled through what I knew. Hadley called her, and on the first ring, my girl picked up.

Fast-forward to now, and the panic is still there. I know she's safe, but will she really show? I swear, I could kill Jennifer with my bare hands. I don't have the mental energy to deal with her and to be honest, I want Sawyer there when it happens. I want her to see that there is nothing between us. I want her to witness the pure evil that is my ex-wife.

I called Owen and told him to expect a phone call. I want him to tell her about Saturday. I told him not to leave anything out. I don't care if it spoils the surprise of proposing to her. The alternative is that I might lose her, and I'll never survive that. I thought Jennifer's betrayal was the worst thing that could happen to me in my lifetime. I was wrong. Losing Sawyer, it would kill me.

Headlights shine as the car slows and pulls into my driveway. I recognize her car right away, and I'm on my feet. She barely has the car in park before I'm ripping open her door and dropping to my knees. "Fuck, Sawyer." I place my head in her lap and fight back the emotion clogging my throat. "You're here," I say, pulling back to look up at her. Her eyes are red and swollen, and the fury I feel for my ex-wife intensifies.

"I'm here," she replies, her voice soft.

"Come inside." Reaching over her, I unbuckle her belt before climbing to my feet and holding my hand out for her. It remains suspended in the air between us. The knot in my stomach tightens, worried she's going to change her mind and peel out of here. Finally, after what feels like hours, she places her hand in mine. I grip it tightly, helping her from her car. As soon as the door is shut, I wrap my arms around her, burying my face in her neck and breathing her in. The feel of her in my arms, mixed with the relief, is enough to bring me to tears. I push them back as I pull away and lead her inside.

The house is quiet, only the sounds of our footsteps as we enter the living room fill the space. I take a seat on the couch and give her hand a gentle tug, and she takes a seat next to me. Without a word, I pull out my phone and do a video call with Owen. "Hey, O," I greet him.

"You find her?"

"Yeah, she's here." I turn the phone so that he can see Sawyer.

"Not cool, sis. You scared the hell out of us," he says, the relief evident in his tone.

"I'm sorry," she says, her voice small.

"I have a story for you," he tells her.

She looks at me in question before glancing back at the screen of my phone. "A story?"

He nods. "You ready to settle in and listen?"

"Yes?" she says, the word sounding more like a question, making Owen laugh.

"It's one you want to hear, trust me. Are you comfortable?"

Her shoulders visibly relax, and I make a mental note that I owe my brother another solid. He's calming her, and although I wish it were me, at least she's here where she belongs, and it's my family who makes her feel safe.

"Yeah," she says. It's almost as if her body melts into the cushion of my couch. The exhaustion plaguing her is evident.

"Royce, give her the phone and give us a minute," his deep voice demands.

I don't argue with him. Instead, I hand her the phone and stand. Leaning over the couch, I place a kiss on her forehead. "I'll go grab you a water," I say, backing out of the room. Luckily for me, my house is an open concept, and even though I'm in the kitchen, I can hear every word he says to her. He knows that, but he wanted to be sure he had her full attention if I know Owen.

"Once upon a time," he starts, and I hear a soft laugh come from my girl. "There was a man and his handsome younger brother." Another small laugh, and I can imagine she's rolling those beautiful green eyes of hers. "The man, he'd had a rough past in matters of the heart. He gave it to a woman who crushed his heart, his soul, and his spirit. Years passed as he walked around a shell of the man he used to be. Then one day, all that changed." He pauses. "You still with me, Sawyer?"

"Yes," she croaks. I want to rush to her, but I trust my brother. He's got my back, and I have a feeling she needs to hear this from him before she hears it from me.

"One day, the man meets a beautiful woman. With long blonde hair and bright green eyes, he was immediately smitten. Fast-forward a few months and the man had fallen madly in love with the woman. Not just the man, but his family. His parents, his handsome brother, and the other three brothers too," he says, and this time I'm the one laughing.

Needing to be closer to her, I head back to the living room and hand her a bottle of water before taking a seat next to her. I don't say anything as I lace my fingers through hers, resting our joined hands on her thigh.

"One day, the man called his handsome brother and told him it was time. The handsome brother knew without question what he meant. It was time to take the next step with the woman who not only captured his heart, she healed him. So, the brothers made plans. They picked a day to make it happen."

"I don't understand," she whispers. Her eyes are glued to Owen, hanging off his every word.

"The brothers made plans for a Saturday afternoon," Owen starts, but I interrupt him.

"I can take it from here," I tell him.

"Sawyer," Owen says. "I don't know if you knew this, but that story, it's based on real-life events, the man is Royce, and the handsome brother is yours truly." He grins, his white teeth prominent through his beard. "He loves you, sis."

"Thanks, man. I'll call you soon." He nods, and the screen goes black. I toss my phone on the table and turn to face her. "I love you, Sawyer Gibson. Not just 'oh, she's a great girl.' No, my heart belongs to you. Less than a week ago, I sat on my best friend's couch and told you that I loved you for the first time. I told you that you were my entire world, and I meant every word." Standing from the couch, I drop to my knees in front of her and pull the ring box out of my pocket. "I asked Owen to go shopping with me that day. There was something that I needed, and I wanted his opinion." Taking a deep breath, I lift the box, opening it. She gasps when she sees the four-carat diamond ring—two-carat square diamond in the center, with two carats of smaller diamonds surrounding it.

"That night, we talked about what our future might look like, and if this ring would have been on me then, I would have asked you sitting on Jase's couch. I want our two rowdy boys and a little girl who looks just like her momma. I want to take them to the lake and make memories with them that they will carry for a lifetime. I want a swing set in the backyard, and I want the constant happy chaos our life is sure to be. I want all of that, baby, but what you don't realize is that without you in my life, the dream no longer exists. It's not just some random woman I see. It's you by my side. It's you who's growing round with our babies. It's you sitting next to me around the fire, while our kids roast marshmallows. Every single scenario of my future is revolved around you. I love you, with all that I am."

"I don't understand."

Closing the box, I place it back in my pocket. This is not how I plan to propose to her. I don't want that to be her memory of the moment I ask her to spend forever with me. "We ran into Jennifer that day. She told me that she and her wife- her best friend—had broken up and she made a mistake. She wanted to try again." She flinches at my words. "I told her that was never happening, baby. She's nothing to me. A blimp in my past, but you, Sawyer, you're my future."

"I'm so sorry," she sobs. "I saw the message, and I thought the worst."

"Shh." I wrap my arms around her and hold her close. "I have one more call to make. One more call, Sawyer, and then I'm going to show you how much I love you." Pulling away from her, I turn and grab my phone off the table. I open my messages and tap the "unknown" number placing the call on speaker.

"Royce, I missed you," Jennifer's fake as hell voice answers.

"Cut the shit, Jen," I say. "I've informed my staff, which includes the security team, you're not allowed on the premises of any of the Riggins Enterprises facilities. Furthermore, if you show up at my home or those of my family, you'll be escorted off by the police, and I'll file a harassment restraining order."

"Ro—" she starts, but I cut her off.

"This is not up for negotiation. You threw me away, and that was the best thing that ever happened to me."

"I fucking knew it," she seethes. "I knew that jewelry bag was for another woman."

"The love of my life," I say, my eyes locking on Sawyer.

"You're my husband!" she screams.

"I have signed and filed divorce papers that state otherwise."

"Don't do this," she says, panic in her voice. "I need you."

"No, you need my money." Silence greets me on the other end. "I don't know what you're scheming, but it's not going to work."

"You have to help us," she says, her tone changing. "We want a baby, Royce, and adoption fees are outrageous."

"Use your divorce settlement."

"I have!" she screams. "We both tried in vitro with a donor, and it didn't take. We want a family," she cries.

"You should have started with that. Scheming and lying isn't a way to get my help, and those lies ruined any chance of me helping you. Stay away from my family, Jennifer," I say, my tone sharp. "You will regret it if not."

"Fuck you, Royce! I hate you."

"Feeling's mutual," I say, ending the call and tossing my phone on the floor.

"She's horrible," Sawyer says softly. "But I feel bad for her."

"I would have helped her," I say honestly. "If she were honest, I would have helped her, but I can't do it, Sawyer. Not when she tried to take you away from me."

"She didn't know who I was."

"She knew. There was no reason for her to say all of that to you otherwise."

"How do you know what she said?"

"Security footage."

She rolls her eyes. "I should have known."

"Con is all over that shit, babe. That's his forte." I stand from the floor and hold my hand out for her. "Let's go to bed. I need to hold you." Without hesitation, she places her hand in mine as I lead her around the house, locking up for the night. Stopping at the door of my office, I lead her inside, and with one hand, type in the combination on my safe. Reaching into my pocket, I retrieve the ring box and place it inside, before locking the door. I turn to look at her. "That ring is yours, Sawyer. I want nothing more than to have it on your finger so that the world knows you're spoken for. However, tonight is not how I want you to remember the moment you promise to be mine forever. I want it to be special. I have a plan," I tell her.

She nods. "Okay."

"I love you," I say, pulling her into a kiss.

"I love you too." With that, I turn off the light, and lead her down the hall to my room, soon to be our room. I need to hold her. In fact, I'm not sure I'll let her out of bed all damn weekend. The hours when I didn't know where she was took years off my life. I'm not ready to let her out of my sight. I don't know that I'll ever be ready.

I'M IN THAT moment in between being awake and being asleep. Royce's arms are clasped around me. I don't think we moved at all once we fell asleep. I let the events of last night replay in my mind. He took his time undressing us both before pulling back the covers. Together, we climbed into bed. He drew me close and simply held me. I expected him to make love to me, but the silence of the room surrounding us, and with the security of his arms locked around me, I fell fast asleep.

"Morning, baby," he says, his voice thick.

I roll over to get a good look at him in the early morning light. "Morning."

"How you feeling?"

"Better."

He nods. "It was an emotional day."

"Yeah. Royce, I'm sorry that I let her get to me. I just couldn't stomach the thought of losing you, especially to her. After everything that she put you through." Anger stirs inside me, thinking about how I acted, how I let her convince me of her lies.

"You're here, where you belong. That's all that matters." He kisses me softly. His hands roam over my body, and just like that, the need I have for him ignites into a burning inferno.

"I need you," I say against his lips.

"Tell me what you need."

"You."

"You can do better than that, baby. Tell me what you need." Grabbing his hand, I guide it between my legs. His fingers trace through my folds. "Look at you, beautiful, wet and ready for me," he murmurs against my lips. He deepens the kiss as he slides a finger inside me. "That feel good, baby?"

"More," I say, nodding.

"More of this?" he asks, sliding in a second finger.

"Y-Yes," I pant.

"I need something too, Sawyer. Will you give me what I need?" he asks.

"Anything," I say, losing my mind from his magical hands.

"Anything?" he asks.

"I'll give you anything. Just please don't stop," I say, gripping the sheets.

His fingers slow, and I groan. "I'll keep going, but I need something from you first," he says, kissing the corner of my mouth.

"Tell me," I say, frustrated.

I open my eyes to find him staring down at me. "Move in with me. Make this our home." My mouth opens, but no words come out. "If this isn't where you see us living, we'll look for something else, but I don't want to wait any longer to start our future."

I blink back the tears that threaten to fall. "I love this house."

"Then help me make it our home."

He's watching me waiting for my reply. The look in his eyes tells me he's worried about what my answer will be. There's something else, though. Something that looks a lot like hope, and that's what has me nodding my agreement.

"Okay."

"Yeah?" he asks, his smile wide.

"I have one condition."

"Name it." Zero hesitation.

"Make love to me. Show me."

"My pleasure," he says, reaching for a condom. I watch as he rips the small packet with his teeth and rolls it over his hard length, before moving to settle between my thighs. Placing his lips next to my ear, he murmurs, "I love you," as he pushes inside of me.

"I love you," I echo as he slides in and out. Over and over, he sets a slow torturous pace as his hands and lips claim every inch of my skin that they can reach. My hands roam over his back as he fills me, in more ways than one.

My heart is full.

"Who has you smiling?" Royce asks from where he sits next to me on his couch.

"Grant." I laugh.

"What's so funny?"

"This." I turn my phone so he can see the screen.

"Ugh," he groans. "Tell my little brother that I'll remember this day," he says as he takes in the image of him as a little boy on my phone.

"It's cute," I tell him.

"I'm naked, pissing in the wind, holding a NERF gun."

"It's cute, and you were what three? Four?"

"I don't know, but I'm sure Mom does." I go back to looking at the image when I hear him talking. "Hey, fucker, can you not send my girl naked pictures of me when I was little?" He pauses. "Remember this, Grant, payback's a bitch." He shakes his head, ending the call.

"Oh, come on, don't be mad. I have pictures," I assure him. "They're packed away in my apartment, but I can show you if it will make you feel better."

"Much. You know what else would make me feel even better?"

"What's that?"

"Let's go to your place and start packing. We can load up the first load."

"You really want to spend the weekend moving?"

"Yes. I want to spend the weekend moving my sexy-ass girlfriend into our home."

I groan. "I hate packing and moving."

"You pack, baby. I'll call my brothers, and we'll have you moved in no time. Actually, I can just hire it to be done." He picks up his phone. "I can have movers there today."

"It's Saturday afternoon."

"Money talks, sweetheart. Now, what's it going to be? Me and my brothers, or movers?"

"Let's just you and I go over and start."

"Deal." He stands from his seat on the couch and stretches his long, tattooed arms over his head. "Let's get moving, babe. Time's wasting."

"Fine," I grumble, trying to act annoyed when I'm secretly thrilled. Something tells me it's not really that big of a secret when he smirks.

Half an hour later, we're in my apartment with boxes in tow. "I don't know where to start."

"Let's start with your clothes. That way, you have everything you might need. We can get the rest later."

"Solid plan," I agree. Grabbing a box and tape, I head down the hall to my bedroom. I hear Royce on the phone, but don't bother to listen in; I've got too much to do. Taping the box, I start opening dresser drawers and emptying them. I don't worry about wrinkles or packing it nice and neat, as I just want it done. There will be time for that later once we get back to his place.

By the time Royce joins me, I have my large dresser emptied. "Wow, you work fast," he says, looking at the three already full boxes. "One more dresser to go before diving into the closet."

"Is there going to be room for all of this at your place?" I ask.

"Our place," he corrects me. "Yes. There is another walk-in closet. I'm sure you've never been inside. It's bigger than mine and has a closet organizer already installed." His phone rings in his hand. "Hello." He pauses. "Yeah, that's it. I'll let you in."

"Who was that?"

"Jase. He and Sam are stopping by to help. My brothers are on their way too."

"Royce, I thought it was just going to be us?"

"Our family, baby. Hadley and Derek are picking up pizza and beer and are on their way."

"This is an ambush," I say, not the least bit upset.

"Yep." He grins. "I told you, baby. This is our future. It's time to start living again." I feel his words, as well as hear them. Until I met Royce, I didn't realize I too was a shadow of the person I used to be after losing my parents. I was going through the motions. I put up with a pig for a boss for far too long. I like to think that my parents gave me the strength to end it that day. I want to believe that they led me to Royce, guiding me toward my happily ever after.

"You good, babe?" he asks, sensing my mood shifting.

"Yeah," I say honestly. "I'm good."

A knock sounds at the door. "That's them. Love you." He kisses my cheek and rushes to let Jase and Sam into my apartment.

I trail after him, hoping to get my baby Aria fix. "Hey," I greet Sam with a hug.

"Hi. Hope you don't mind us crashing your party? Jase's mom is at the house with Aria and insisted that we get out for a few hours."

"And you came here? Go see a movie or out to dinner."

"Nah, we'd rather be here." She claps her hands together. "Where should we start?"

"You can help me in the bedroom," I tell her. She follows me back to my room, and we dive in. I hear Royce's brothers arrive, and not long after Hadley joins us in the bedroom, and within a couple of hours, my entire room is packed.

"Wow, that didn't take long at all."

"That man is determined." Sam laughs.

"That he is," I agree.

She looks down at her watch. "I hate to abandon you, but I need to get home to Aria. I'm sure she's fine, but I'm missing my baby girl."

"I can't thank you enough for helping. Give her a kiss from me."

"Will do."

The three of us make our way to the living room, and what I see stops me in my tracks. The walls are bare, all of my decorations are packed away, and the cabinet doors in the kitchen are open, showing me that they're bare too. "You all work fast. I was going to donate some of that," I tell Royce.

"You still can. Let's get it moved, and you can take your time going through it."

"But why move it if we don't have to?" I question.

"Because I need you moved. I need you living in our house sooner rather than later. We have the space. Keep it, donate it, sell it, trash it, I don't care as long as we share an address."

"What about a last name?" Jase asks, smirking. Sam smacks him in the chest, but she looks toward Royce as if she's waiting on an answer.

"That too," Royce says, kissing my temple.

Jase nods approvingly. "We're heading out. Mom has Aria, and it's been long enough."

"Thanks for coming. We'll get together soon," Royce tells him.

"All right, I've got the truck and trailer, so we're going to start loading this stuff up."

"Today?"

"Yeah." Conrad shrugs. "Why not? We're here. Let's get this done, so my brother can stop whining."

I look at Royce, and he shrugs. "All right, let's start loading." There's no use in arguing with them. They're all five stubborn as hell. Besides, moving in one day? Yes, please. I'd rather have it done. I would have liked to have gone through some of the things I don't want to keep, but this gives me time to mix my things with his and decide for certain what I want to get rid of. At the end of the day, I'm moving in with him, and that's all that matters.

I'm standing at Royce's house, well, our house, staring into the boxes and furniture that's sitting in the extra bay of the garage. "This is not what a four-car garage is for," I tell him.

"It works. I'll move the SUV to the detached garage, and you can take that spot. You have plenty of time to work through your stuff. All of your clothes are in our room."

"Our room," I repeat his words, letting them roll off my tongue.

"Come on, it's cold out here." He takes my hand and leads me into the house.

"I wish everyone would have stayed and let me feed them."

"Had and Derek brought pizza. And they know how much you appreciate it. That's what family does."

My eyes water. I have a family again. "I know but, I need to thank them."

"How about we invite everyone over in a couple of weeks? We can cook, or we'll order in, but you can thank them then."

"Deal." Pulling my phone out of my back pocket, I send a text to Hadley and Derek.

Me: Thank you both so much for all for your help.

Had & D: That's what family is for.

Royce looks over my shoulder, reading the message. "Told you," he says, smirking.

Me: Thank you all so much for helping today.

I hit Send to Owen, Grant, Conrad, and Marshall. Their replies are immediate.

Grant: Anytime, S.

Conrad: You tamed the beast!

Marshall: You kids be good.

Owen: That's what family is for.

"Come on, you." Royce pulls my phone from my hands. "Shower and bed." I don't put up a fight as he leads me to our room. That's going to take some getting used to, but the smile on my face is genuine. I'm exhausted but in the best way. We're on our way to starting our future together. My mind flashes an image of the diamond ring I know he has in the safe. I don't know when he's going to ask me, but when he does, I'm ready to say yes. Fate brought us together, and love is going to carry us into the future.

"I'M STUFFED," DAD says, pushing back from the table. "Delicious as always, dear," he tells my mom. We're sitting around my parents' massive dining room table, having just finished eating Thanksgiving dinner.

"It wasn't just me this year. Sawyer was a huge help." She smiles over at my girl.

"All I did was mash the potatoes. With a mixer." Sawyer laughs.

"It's more help than I'm used to getting." Mom gives each of us a pointed look.

"Hey, now," Marshall pipes up. "Last time we tried to help, you kicked us out of the kitchen."

"You ruined the deviled eggs." Mom points at him, barely containing her laughter.

"We didn't know they didn't need to be cooked," he tells her, making us all laugh.

"Thank you for having me. Everything was delicious," Sawyer tells my parents.

"You're family, Sawyer" is my mom's only reply.

"Hey." I lean over and whisper in her ear, "Take a walk with me?"

She turns and gives me a smile that lights up the room. "Let me help clean up first."

"Nope. You helped cook. These five can help me. You two go on."

"Are you sure?"

"We've got this," Dad tells her.

"Come on." I stand and reach for her hand. I lead her to the door where we bundle up and head outside.

She sucks in a deep breath. "I love it here, Royce. It's so peaceful, and the stars," she says, looking up at the night sky.

My heart pounds against my chest at the realization of what's about to happen. "You want to walk or take the UTV?"

"Let's ride. Can we go out to the gazebo? I bet it's beautiful with all the snow."

"Yeah, babe. We can go to the gazebo." I couldn't have planned this better. She's falling right into what I've already orchestrated. Thanks to the help of my parents and my brother, everything is all set up and waiting for us.

I take the long way around. The UTV has a window and roof, so it keeps the wind off us. I grabbed a blanket from the chest, though, and give it to her to cover up with. Mom is always prepared. I never realized how handy that is, but it's worked in my favor more times than I can count.

I pull up to an old treehouse that has seen better days. "This is our old treehouse." I shine the lights so she can see. "It's too rough to use, but someday when our kids get old enough, we'll build them another one, just like this one."

"Make sure it's big enough for me to sit in there too."

"Yeah?"

She nods. "I want to be able to experience it with them."

"Me too," I say as I continue on. "This is where Owen got Dad's new tractor stuck when he was sixteen. I was eighteen. It was the summer before I was headed off to college. He got the bright idea to dig a mud hole for the four-wheelers. Not a terrible idea, but he did it during a torrential summer downpour. Hence the tractor getting stuck."

"Oh, I bet he was mad."

"Surprisingly, he wasn't. The next day he pulled it out and then proceeded to help Owen make the pit. The six of us then played around all day in the mud with the four-wheelers." I chuckle. "I can still remember Mom's face when we walked up to the front porch covered from head to toe in mud."

"What did she do?" my girl asks, hanging on every word.

"She sprayed us with the water hose, then made us strip right there on the front porch before letting us inside."

Her laugh surrounds us. "I'll have to remember that."

Finally, we approach the gazebo—the moment of truth. I remember being nervous when I asked Jennifer to marry me. Not because I was afraid she would say no, but because in the back of my mind, I wasn't sure it was what I wanted. It was the next progression in life, so I went with it. This time it's different. There are no jitters, no nerves, and nothing but absolute certainty that Sawyer is the woman I want to spend the rest of my life with.

"WHAT HAPPENED TO the lights?" I ask Royce as we walk toward the gazebo with nothing to guide us but the starry night sky.

"Watch your step," he says, helping me up into the gazebo. "These lights," he says as we're suddenly bathed in a soft glow of twinkle lights.

"Wow," I breathe, staring up at them. "These are different than before," I say, noticing the new lights that hang from the ceiling, making them look like hundreds of twinkling stars. "Royce." I turn to look at him only to find him kneeling on the same quilt we used that first night.

"You're right. They are different. These are special, just for you," he says, taking my hand in his.

"They're beautiful," I whisper.

"You're beautiful," he counters. "Sawyer." He swallows hard. "You brought me back to life. You saved me from my past. I was living with the regrets of my past hanging over my head, but you changed all of that. You showed me that I have something worth living for."

I run my shaking fingers over his hair. "You always did," I tell him.

He nods. "But when I met you, it's as if something just clicked into place. I know it sounds crazy, but it's almost like my heart recognized that you were meant to be mine. Every day with you is better than the one before it. I can't think of my future without seeing you by my side. I want to spend every day of the rest of my life loving you. I want to make babies with you. I want the future that we've talked about."

I watch through tear-filled eyes as he opens the ring box and pulls the sparkling diamond out of it. "Sawyer Gibson, will you do me the incredible honor of becoming my wife? Will you live your forever with me, baby?"

I lose control of my emotions, and my tears begin to fall. Dropping to my knees, I kiss him hard. "Yes," I say against his lips. "Yes, I'll marry you."

Loud shouts and clapping greet me. I look up to find his family, along with Hadley, Derek, Jase, Sam, and baby Aria, standing on the bank of the lake, watching us.

"She said yes!" Royce shouts.

"I can't believe you pulled this off," I tell him.

"I wanted it to be special for you. I wanted you to know that you have family and that it's more than just me who loves you. They're our family, Sawyer."

"So many layers, Mr. Riggins," I say, smiling.

"You love my layers."

"Yeah, I do."

Never miss a new release:

http://bit.ly/2UW5Xzm

More about Kaylee's books:

http://bit.ly/2CV3hLx

Facebook:
http://bit.ly/2C5DgdF

Instagram:
http://bit.ly/2reBkrV

Reader Group:
http://bit.ly/2o0yWDx

Goodreads:
http://bit.ly/2HodJvx

BookBub:
http://bit.ly/2KulVvH

Website:
www.kayleeryan.com

With You Series:
Anywhere With You | *More With You* | *Everything With You*

Soul Serenade Series:
Emphatic | *Assured* | *Definite* | *Insistent*

Southern Heart Series:
Southern Pleasure | *Southern Desire* | *Southern Attraction* | *Southern Devotion*

Unexpected Arrivals Series:
Unexpected Reality | *Unexpected Fight*
Unexpected Fall | *Unexpected Bond* | *Unexpected Odds*

Standalone Titles:
Tempting Tatum | *Unwrapping Tatum* | *Levitate*
Just Say When | *I Just Want You*
Reminding Avery | *Hey, Whiskey* | *When Sparks Collide*
Pull You Through | *Beyond the Bases*
Remedy | *The Difference*
Trust the Push

Co-written with Lacey Black:
It's Not Over | *Just Getting Started* | *Can't Fight It*

Cocky Hero Club:
Lucky Bastard

Riggins Brothers Series:
Play by Play | *Layer by Layer*

ACKNOWLEDGEMENTS

To my family:
Your support means the world to me. Thank you for always standing by my side.

Alfred Liebl:
The moment I saw this image, I knew I needed it. Had to have it! LOL. It took me some time to write the story to go with it, but the image brings Royce to life. Thank you for your talent, and a cover worthy image.

Mike Chabot:
Thank you for doing what you do. You brought Royce to life. Best of luck to you in all of your future endeavors.

Tami Integrity Formatting:
Thank you for making the paperbacks beautiful. You're amazing and I cannot thank you enough for all that you do.

Lori Jackson:
You nailed it. I love this new series and the covers. Thank you so much for being patient with me. It was a pleasure working with you.

Lacey Black:
You are my sounding board, and I value that so very much. Thank you for always being there, talking me off the ledge and helping me jump from it when necessary.

My beta team:
Jamie, Stacy, Lauren, Erica, and Franci I would be lost without you. You read my words as much as I do, and I can't tell you what your input and all the time you give means to me. Countless messages and bouncing idea, you ladies keep me sane with the characters are being anything but. Thank you from the bottom of my heart for taking this wild ride with me.

Give Me Books:
With every release, your team works diligently to get my book in the hands of bloggers. I cannot tell you how thankful I am for your services.

Tempting Illustrations:
Thank you for everything. I would be lost without you.

Julie Deaton:
Thank you for giving this book a set of fresh final eyes.

Becky Johnson:
I could not do this without you. Thank you for pushing me, and making me work for it.

Marisa Corvisiero:
Thank you for all that you do. I know I'm not the easiest client. I'm blessed to have you on this journey with me.

Kimberly Ann:
Thank you for organizing and tracking the ARC team. I couldn't do it without you.

Bloggers:
Thank you, doesn't seem like enough. You don't get paid to do what you do. It's from the kindness of your heart and your love of reading that fuels you. Without you, without your pages, your voice, your reviews, spreading the word it would be so much harder if not impossible to get my words in reader's hands. I can't tell you how much your never-ending support means to me. Thank you for being you, thank you for all that you do.

To my Kick Ass Crew:

The name of the group speaks for itself. You ladies truly do KICK ASS! I'm honored to have you on this journey with me. Thank you for reading, sharing, commenting, suggesting, the teasers, the messages all of it. Thank you from the bottom of my heart for all that you do. Your support is everything!

With Love,

Manufactured by Amazon.ca
Bolton, ON